MISSED
CONNECTIONS

WITHDRAWN

TAMARA
MATAYA

sourcebooks
casablanca

For Amber Tuscan-Clites and Heather Griffin.
I love you both more than you know.
Thanks for never giving up on me.

Published by Sourcebooks Casablanca, an imprint of Sourcebooks, Inc.
P.O. Box 4410, Naperville, Illinois 60567-4410
(630) 961-3900
Fax: (630) 961-2168
www.sourcebooks.com

Printed and bound in Canada.
MBP 10 9 8 7 6 5 4 3 2 1

Chapter 1

I BLOT MY SWEATY PALMS ON MY BLACK A-LINE SKIRT, feeling horrifically overdressed. The scent of sage and sandalwood hits the back of my throat as I inhale deeply and sneak a glance at the clock on the wall. Fifteen minutes down.

Fern crosses her jegging-clad legs and leans back in the seat. Her dark-chocolate eyes narrow thoughtfully. "Where do you see yourself in five years, Sarah?"

Damn. This is my least favorite question, second only to "What are your weaknesses?" Like anyone truthfully answers either of them. My typical answers would send me shooting up the corporate ladder, but I'm in unfamiliar territory dealing with New Age hippies and the patchouli highway.

I have to answer carefully. "I don't like planning that far in advance because it's too rigid. I think it's better to take things as they come and to stay as flexible in regard to the future as I can. There really isn't a future; there's only now. You know?" *Please buy my babbling.*

She smiles. "Great answer."

Ziggy nods. "*Great* answer."

Nailed it! I duck my head and try to look modest but maintain eye contact. New Age hippies are all about meaningful gazes. Should I add a *namaste*? No, that would be too much. God, I need this job. Even if I didn't have tens of thousands of dollars of student debt to repay, New York's cost of living would cripple me.

Ziggy holds his paper out to Fern and points at something. She nods. He swivels back and forth in his chair, and I try not to stare at his bony knees peeking out from his jean shorts. I also try not to stare at his hair. His salt-and-pepper ponytail wings out above his ears, giving him a sort of wild vibe, like Jack Nicholson in *The Witches of Eastwick*. "What made you want to work here at Inner Space?"

The fact that I got laid off from the law firm six weeks ago and my standards are rapidly plummeting in the city's employer-friendly job market? "There was just something about the ad. I couldn't not reply, if that makes sense."

Fern and Ziggy share a smile, and Fern leans forward. "I'm going to say something, and I want you to tell us the first words that come into your mind."

"Word association?"

"Yes! You're sharp." Fern's voice has grown steadily warmer through the interview. She brings her long, blond braid over her shoulder. "Okay. The law of attraction." She spreads her fingers like a slow-motion explosion.

Not this *Secret* "Law of Attraction" crap again. This is the third interview that's mentioned it. "You attract what you expect."

Ziggy squints. "And what does that mean to you?"

Nothing, because I put so much good out there and life keeps crapping on me but rewarding assholes left, right, and center! "Well." Can I answer this being mostly truthful? "If you go around treating people badly and putting bad energy out there, chances are that's what you're going to draw to yourself."

"Great answer."

Ziggy claps once. "Great answer. Do you have any questions for us?"

How much would you be paying me? "Why did the last receptionist leave?"

"Ah. We're sort of about looking forward, not backward." Fern frowns.

Damn it, I'm losing them. "I totally get that. I just sort of got a weird vibe around the desk when we walked in." In the dark, on a Sunday, in an empty spa.

"Very astute of you." Fern's smile returns. "She wasn't a good fit for us here at Inner Space. Between us, she was putting all kinds of negativity into the place that really messed with the whole business. But she's leaving just as soon as we find her replacement."

Suddenly, the Sunday interview makes sense. "She doesn't know yet?"

Ziggy shakes his head. "We had a talk with her spirit. A real etheric heart-to-heart about where she wanted to be. It wasn't here."

They talked to her spirit? What does that even mean? My mind scrabbles around in the rubble of a few New Age things I've read about and discarded as BS. "Like, astral traveling?"

"Yes!" Fern looks at Ziggy. "She gets it. You know, I'd be happy not looking at any other applicants."

"Are you guys typically closed on the weekends? Isn't that a lot of revenue you're missing out on? Some people can't make it in during the workweek."

Ziggy frowns. "The people who truly need us will find a way to make it happen."

Fern nods. "We pick up so much energy during the week, we need the weekends off to de-stress and clear our fields of any karmic weight that's not ours. Money isn't everything—and we do have a part-time therapist, Blake, who comes in on the weekends for anyone who absolutely can't get in during the week."

"I completely agree," I say, trying to erase the frowns from their faces. "I think it's a brave, admirable choice on your part to eschew the...rat race." Damn it, I need to learn more New Age terms if I'm going to make it work here. *If* I get the job.

Fern smiles again. "I think you'll fit in perfectly."

Relief that this might work out actually brings tears to my eyes. In the six weeks I've been unemployed, I've sent out hundreds of résumés and been to thirty unsuccessful interviews. This is my first glimmer of hope. "Really? I would so love to work here. It's such a beautiful place, and it's so peaceful."

"You're so open." Ziggy puts his hands out about three feet from me, palms up. "I get a good vibe from you. You have such a vibrant energy. We wanted someone who *wanted* to be here, who would be a good fit spiritually. We have a couple more applicants, but we'll give you a call tonight and let you know our decision."

"Thank you. I look forward to hearing from you." I stand and shake their hands before they show me to the door.

···············—————···········

The apartment feels empty when I return from my interview with the hippies.

"Pete?" Silence greets my call, so I relock the door behind me and step inside. Going to the duffel bag in the living room, I find a pair of shorts and a tank top and take them to the bathroom to change, thankful Pete's window-unit air conditioner is strong enough to cut through the sweltering heat. I've been crashing on my best friend Pete's couch since I lost my apartment. While I'd heard that we're all supposed to have a safety net of three months of salary in a savings account, with my student loan payments coming out of my bank account with alarming alacrity every month, I didn't have the chance to create that safety net while I was gainfully employed.

Then I was fired. It was just over six weeks ago, and the way they let me go still makes my face burn with resentment and shame. I'd made it to twenty-five years old without being fired. Technically, I wasn't fired, but whatever the wording, I was still marched from the building, clutching my small box of personal items as though it were a life raft as I sank further and further into my shock.

I savagely pull my dark hair back into a ponytail and scrub the makeup from my face. The worst part was that I was unable to stop the tears. Those bastards saw me cry. The dismissal clause in the contract had been ambiguously worded in their favor, but I'd been so eager to start work for one of the biggest law firms in the city that I'd foolishly signed anyway. I'd been so flattered, thought myself so lucky to find a salary that covered my bills—barely—without having any experience in my field. Fresh from graduation, they snapped me up…and spat me out six months later.

And I'd gotten such a good feeling from Brenda, the partner who'd hired me—and then fired me. She was sincere when she'd told me that if it were up to her, I'd be staying. She even assured me it had nothing to do with my job performance, as if that would have made me feel better. It hadn't. For whatever reason, the senior partner in the firm had decided he didn't like me, and since his name was above the door, his was the only opinion that mattered. He didn't even fire me himself, just slunk out early that day, trusting that he'd never have to look at my face again. Coward.

But he was right. I'm still unemployed, and he's still rich and powerful and a domineering misogynist with rancid breath. The last of the hopeful buzz from my interview at Inner Space fades away, and I head for the kitchen. The clock on the stove says it's 1:08 p.m. I could eat something for a late lunch, but my stomach is too tense for me to think about food, so I pad over to Pete's desk and turn on his laptop.

My desktop is still packed in a blue plastic tub in a ridiculously overpriced storage facility with the rest of my furniture. Pete's all about aesthetics, and even though mine's a shiny new PC, he wasn't about to let me clutter up his desk with it. I couldn't argue—he's let me stay here for free when I could have been kicked out on the street or, slightly better, been forced to move back in with my parents.

But that would have involved admitting that I'd been fired, which feels like admitting I'm a failure who can't hack it in the corporate world because I'm not ruthless enough—like my dad said—and I can't deal with that right now.

Because an ever-growing part of me suspects it's true.

I type in Pete's password to unlock the laptop and wait while it signs me in. The want ads have been pretty sparse lately, especially now that it's July and students are out of school, sucking up jobs from people like me who need them to pay the bills. The bottom of the Employment Opportunity barrel has become my new stomping ground, but I head for Craigslist, excited to see some new postings have popped up.

My excitement dims considerably as I read the first ad.

Sexy Executive Administrator Wanted
Candidate should be intelligent, organized, efficient, playfully sexy, positive, fun, flirty, and, of course, highly effective in all business tasks required.

Playfully sexy? What the hell?

Interested parties should reply with résumé and a recent photo.

Because looks are crucial in your ability to type eighty words per minute.

Our client is a successful businessman who—

Probably wants to spank the executive assistant over his desk. Yeah, this ad has *escort* written all over it. No thanks.

The next ad is a more standard one for a switchboard operator/receptionist for a busy company in the energy sector. With each passing week of unemployment, the jobs I'm willing to do have branched out considerably from my field. This posting doesn't list salary, but the company usually pays fairly well, so I quickly send a résumé to the email address they've provided, hoping I'm not the 273rd person to apply. Not my dream job, but at least it doesn't ask for a recent pic and a safe word.

I'm woefully underqualified for the next seven ads, and the following six don't pay enough to sustain me, even though I've lowered the bottom of my pay range a few times in the last three weeks. The next two ads aren't seeking employees—they're advertising a medical office assistant school, which I don't want and can't afford, even if I was interested.

The last new posting is one I replied to and interviewed for three weeks ago. The guy interviewing me stared at my tits the whole time and called me the wrong name while he had my résumé in his hand. They called me for a second interview, but I never replied. I needed a scalding shower after being in his presence for half an hour; I couldn't bear the thought of working as his PA forty hours a week.

For now, my desperation has limits.

Though I should go to another site to look at more job postings, I click back to the main page, needing a pick-me-up. Personals. My heart begins to pound a little, and I throw a look over my shoulder, even though I'm alone. I click on Missed Connections, click forward again, acknowledging I'm over eighteen and blah, blah, blah. Then I'm in, and a rush of anticipation streams through me. Maybe today is the day I'll read a post about myself.

This became a habit of mine shortly after I lost my job. After a particularly long day of poring through postings, I got curious about the Personals section—a place I'd never checked out, assuming they were all generic romance ads. Women seeking men for long walks in the park. Older guys looking for sweet young things to inject a little energy into their lives. If you love piña coladas and hate cats… But it was nothing like that.

These were things people had written about other people they'd seen in real life! A note to the stranger they'd shared a look or a moment with and wanted to find. God, it was so romantic, I was gripped from the first post I read. I'd had moments with guys. Maybe one of them was my soul mate, and he'd noticed me in the crowd of faceless commuters. Some of the entries were full of poetry and admiration and a hope so raw it took my breath away.

Some were crude, looking for hookups and nothing more, but if my true love is out there, he wouldn't post something like that. Maybe I'm naive to still believe in romance. Maybe love won't find me this way.

But maybe it will.

That hope makes me read through the ads nearly every day, looking for applicable experiences. In my darkest moments, when I'm licking my wounds after another failed day looking for someone who wants me as an employee, I can read these listings and hope to find someone who wants me as their Missed Connection.

When the apartment is empty, of course. Pete would never let me live this down if he knew what I was up to.

Yet another reason I need my own apartment again. Gorging on guilty pleasures isn't as satisfying when you have to keep one ear alert for the sound of your room-mate's key in the lock. I scroll down the page to the next ad.

Train Girl

I take trains to interviews sometimes.

I see you every day on the 8th Street platform wearing those killer heels.

Not me, then, since my schedule is all over the place lately and I don't wear heels every day.

I'd love for you to walk all over me with those—

Aaand I'm glad that one's not about me. Next.

The One Who Got Away

That could be me. I've loved and lost.

I regret not going with you every day of my life. You had to leave, but I didn't realize that I didn't have to stay. I tore us apart, not you. I've missed you every day for twelve years. I hope you found happiness. xo Cara

Not about me, but that's so sad, to pine for someone for twelve years. I wonder why she never went after him, or her. Of course, twelve years ago, the Internet wasn't what it is today. It would have been harder to find someone if they moved away and you didn't have their contact information.

The doorknob rattles, and I jump in my chair and fumble for the mouse, barely getting back to the main page of Craigslist before the door is unlocked and opened.

My heart pounds harder when I realize it isn't Pete.

Chapter 2

IT'S HIS IDENTICAL TWIN BROTHER. PERFECT TEETH, perfectly tousled light-brown hair, eyebrows that have a devilish arch to them. I always want to nibble the smile from his lips. "Hey, Sarah." Jack's blue eyes light up with the warm smile he shines at me. The tiny mole under the bottom outside corner of his left eye shouldn't be sexy, but it is. "How are you?"

This face is familiar, but Jack affects me so very differently than Pete. Not just because Pete's gay and Jack isn't. How am I? *Tingly now that you're here.* "I'm good. You?"

"Pretty good." He closes the door behind him, treating me to a nice peek at his tight ass and the strong lines of his back beneath the thin fabric of his T-shirt. God, he has nice shoulders. He pulls the bottom of his T-shirt away from his body and waves it, allowing cool air beneath—and giving me flashes of abs. "Hot out there."

Hot in here now too. "Yeah."

"Pete around?"

Want but can't touch. I wrestle my hormones into submission. "Nope."

"He still at the salon?"

"I'm not sure. He was sleeping when I got up and

then gone when I got back from my interview a few minutes ago."

He strides into the galley kitchen and rests a trim hip against the counter. "Had to have been a hair emergency to get him out of bed before noon on a Sunday."

"True."

"How did your interview go?"

I smooth my ponytail in what I hope is a casual manner, feeling self-conscious about my tiny shorts and tank top. "I think it went well, but they said they had a few more applicants to go through. And they're a little strange."

"Strange how?"

How much can I say without sounding judgmental? "They're hippies."

"As in cool stoners? That might be kind of sweet having them as your bosses."

"I don't know about that, but I suspect there's going to be a lot of talk of chi and auras."

"Ah, New Agers."

"Yes." Resting an elbow on the desk, I prop my chin in one hand. "And they haven't let the person whose job I'd be taking know she's fired yet."

He grimaces. "Harsh."

"But I'd work there in a heartbeat if they'd have me."

He crosses his arms, and I try not to ogle them. "They'd be stupid not to hire you."

"Thanks, Jack." His earnestness makes me smile.

"I know you said before you couldn't waitress, but they make awesome tips. I could—"

"I know you have all kinds of connections, but I couldn't work as a waitress at one of those clubs. I don't have the coordination. There's a reason you guys never let me carry the drinks back to the table. I'd end shifts owing more than I'd made."

"Fair enough. So—" he says, as my cell phone vibrates against the desktop.

"I've got to get this." I hold up my hand. "Sarah speaking."

"Hi, Sarah, this is Fern. From Inner Space?"

"Hi, Fern." *It's them*, I mouth at Jack. "How are you?"

"I'm fine. Listen, I just wanted to call to let you know that unfortunately"—damn it—"our old receptionist found out we were interviewing and came in for an ugly confrontation before she stormed out, so we're going to need you to come in tomorrow morning."

Wait. "You mean I got the job?"

"Oh yes, didn't I say?"

I punch the air. "No! Thank you, Fern. I will definitely be there. What time do you need me?"

"You'll be working Monday to Friday, leaving around six. Is ten too early?"

Too early? The firm had me start work at seven—and now I'll get weekends off. "Ten is perfect."

"Great. See you tomorrow."

"Bye." I end the call and spring to my feet. "I have a job."

"Congratulations!" Jack holds his hand up, but our high five turns into an enthusiastic hug.

And here, pressed up against his warm, muscular length, with my face to his chest, I remember why he's off-limits. Because I want him so very much, and he's so very wrong for me.

But for once, I don't care.

I tighten my embrace and breathe deeply, holding his

scent in my lungs because I want any part of him inside me right now. His hand splays across my lower back and presses me closer, but no lines are crossed except those in my mind…where we've already done everything. Twice. My skin's cooled from the air-conditioning, but he's still warm from the heat outside, making the difference even more interesting. How would those heated hands feel trailing up my thighs…

Pulling back, I slowly drag my gaze from his chest to his face. I've wanted Jack from the moment I saw him six years ago at a house party, spinning records in the basement. Ten minutes later, I'd learned his nickname. DJ Madhead. My gay best friend's identical twin.

He licks his lips.

Oh, Jack is sex personified and he knows it. The trouble is, a lot of other women know it too. A lot of women. Too many women.

And I refuse to be just another car on the train. Man whores are firmly off-limits; I've seen what cheating can do to people. My mom tore my dad's heart out again and again. The worst part is he always takes her back. His pride is the least of my worries. It's the stress that she puts on his heart that worries me and reminds me to never date a potential cheater—no matter how pretty they are, or how pretty their words are. I've heard variations on every justification in the book from my mother's lips.

But even if all that changed, Jack's rampant Peter Pan syndrome would still keep him from being an option. He's a DJ. His office is a dance floor covered with intoxicated people. Late nights, flashing lights. How could I live like that, never seeing him? Never getting to spend more than a few hours a week or a stolen moment on a noisy dance floor? How could I compete with all the women who throw themselves at him? I want more for myself—I *need* more. As lame as it may make me, I need someone who's serious about the future, about me—not just a hot guy who refuses to grow up.

So, despite the quickening of my pulse every time Jack comes near, nothing will ever happen between us. With a sigh, I step back, breaking contact, and head to the living room, hyperaware of him as he follows and sits on the opposite end of the couch, giving me the space I don't want but need.

He picks up the conversation as if he hadn't noticed the weirdness.

"They want you to start tomorrow? That's awesome."

"Definitely." Though it's weird that the old receptionist had to be the deciding factor in me getting hired. Maybe it just sped up the timeline and they had chosen me already.

The door swings open and bangs against the wall. "Honey, I'm homo!" Pete calls out.

"God, you're such a caricature," I call with a grin.

"I'm a campy delight." He and his shopping bags rustle into the kitchen.

"Your brother's here."

"Good. I could use a big, strong man to help me with these heavy bags while I freshen up. I'm sweating like a hooker in church."

Jack rolls his eyes at me but moves to help Pete. I follow, trying not to notice how great Jack's ass looks in those jeans. Pete's already deposited the grocery bags on the counters when we reach the kitchen, so I stay out of the way while Jack helps him put stuff away.

They move with a similar grace, but Pete's a little softer and flows more, while Jack's like a slinky jungle cat. There's something about the way he walks that has always hit me right in the nether regions. Other than style choices and Jack's adorable mole, they are shockingly identical. Jack's hair is still their natural light brown and lacks the dyed, lacquered finesse of Pete's. Pete's eyebrows are also more groomed, but they don't look overdone. He's a junior aesthetician and stylist at a trendy, upscale salon in Manhattan, and he does amazing work. I trust no one else with my hair.

"Guess who has news?" Jack asks Pete.

"What? Who? Spill!"

I laugh. "I have a job! Soon, you'll have your couch back."

"Thank God," he exclaims with relief.

I narrow my eyes. "You could sound a little less excited to spare my feelings."

"Honey." He smooths an eyebrow with the tip of his ring finger, managing to look long-suffering with that small action. "I love you, but if I had to see one more thong hanging over my towel rack, I was going to lose it."

"Pete!" My cheeks flame, and I look at Jack.

"Please. My little brother's seen more panties than you have."

Jack smirks. "You're only three minutes older."

I notice he doesn't deny the part about the panties.

Pete grabs me in a hug. "Sweetie, I'm so proud of you!" He pulls back. "Where is this fabulous new job? Will they be paying you meeellions of dollars?"

"I doubt it. I'll be doing reception."

"It may seem like a step down with your degree, but

it's a jungle out there. That you got hired right now just shows how great you are."

I raise my brows. "Reception at a New Age spa."

"Competition?" He rears back in mock outrage.

"No. Inner Space. They do massages and acupuncture and some crystal stuff. Yoga therapy. Nothing that makes anyone prettier. It's the spa Naomi told us about." Naomi was one of his client-turned-friends. She works at Inner Space and told him they were hiring, and he passed that news to me.

He smirks. "No one makes anyone prettier than me."

"You're the best." Jack humors Pete like a parent humors a child, then looks at me. "So you'll be moving soon?"

"As soon as I find a place." My happiness is tempered by something in his eyes I can't define.

"Let me know when you need help."

"I will, thanks. What did you want to do for supper, P?"

He rubs his hands together. "I was going to do spag bol instead of ordering in, but this calls for celebration! I heard about a new Thai fusion place in Williamsburg. Shall we go judge for ourselves?"

Pete's spag bol puts Del Posto's to shame. "Nothing's better than your pasta—please, let's do that instead. You won't get to cook for me much longer," I wheedle. "I'll even do all the dishes."

"I *should* try to fatten you up some before you go. Lord knows what things you'll be putting into your body while unsupervised."

I try and fail to keep my gaze off Jack. "Lord knows," I agree and move back to Pete's laptop. "Guess I should start looking for a place."

Plugging in my earbuds, I click on iTunes and hit Shuffle to give the boys a little privacy.

Privacy. I'll be in my own apartment again, with my own computer, in my own space. What a glorious concept.

Back to Craigslist. It's still open to the home page, and just a click takes me to the apartments for rent.

The past six weeks have been so stressful that I hadn't realized how much they've weighed on me until now. Laughter brews at the tip of my tongue, waiting to be released at the slightest nudge. The rich aroma of garlic and onions browning in the pan seasons the air. Pete's meat sauces need time to develop flavors, and though it will be a few hours until we eat, I feel hungry for the first time in ages, my stomach no longer in knots.

Fern emailed me with salary details. It's way below what I made at the firm, but enough that I can manage. I find and reply to a few brokers representing affordable apartments and see one that looks perfect. Tiny, over-priced, and way out in the ass end of Brooklyn, but it'll be a place I can call my own. It's all finally coming together. Soon, I'll have a job to go to and money to spend. No more scrounging and hoarding and denying myself deli-cious gourmet coffees and treats when I'm out and about. No more reading the magazines at the bodega and never buying them, feeling like a junkie seeking a free fix while the store clerk looks at me with judgmental eyes.

I've had my envious eyes on about seventeen new, hip restaurants that have opened since I got laid off. Soon I'll be able to actually go to them. My mouth waters.

I am not a failure. My old boss was wrong about me.

It's like I take my first real breath in nearly two months. Life couldn't get better.

Inbox (1)

A reply already?

My heart stops when I see the @. It's from some woman I don't know, but the @ is the law firm's name. Why would they email me? Is this like tantric karma—life saw I was happy and is now bending me over to creatively screw me because I wasn't depressed for a whole ten minutes?

It's from Brenda to reception@BladeLAW.com—and Sonya has accidentally forwarded it to me. I used to use my personal email when working from home, and people grew accustomed to contacting me via both. Apparently, they haven't removed me from the contact list. I shouldn't read it, but it's like creeping an evil ex on Facebook; I can't look away.

> **From: reception@BladeLAW.com**
> **Subject: Pest situation**
>
> ---
>
> Sonya,
> We have a pest situation. Droppings are appearing around the office, particularly the lunchroom. As you can guess, Bob isn't pleased. Call the exterminator and get them in here ASAP.
> Brenda

My ecstatic bark of laughter draws Pete's and Jack's attention, and I feel like doing a small dance. Hell, I'm so freaking happy I could twerk. "Jack, are you spinning anywhere this week?"

"I'm at Combined on Friday. Why?"

I motion for them to read the email, loving the way their faces light up. They're as happy as I am, having seen the way those bastards fired me like I was nothing. "Because suddenly, I feel like dancing."

My life couldn't get any better than it is right now.

Chapter 3

ONCE AGAIN, I'VE MADE A TACTICAL ERROR BY DRESSING in a black skirt, heels, and black cami/sweater combination. While perfect for the law firm and less formal than my interview clothes, the outfit makes me stick out like a sore thumb, blackened beneath the hammer of poor judgment.

Fern resembles a dull flower in an oatmeal-colored kaftan and green leggings. Her gaze starts at my tight chignon and wanders down to my four-inch heels. "I'm for expression in all its forms, Sarah, including through fashion choices, but we're really trying to go with a relaxed vibe here. We want the clients to feel welcomed, at home. People will come in for massages dressed in sweats and no makeup, seeking respite from the trappings of vanity."

"So you want me to dress in something less formal?"

"It wouldn't hurt to, I don't know, casual it up a bit. Just to blend with the rest of us. We're all about harmony. What you're in is very discordant."

"I'll be sure to dress more casually tomorrow."

She waves her hand. "Wear whatever you want."

Just not business attire. What if this is what I want to wear? "So, are jeans okay?"

"Just read the energy and flow with it."

Riiight.

She straightens a pile of papers on the desk. "Anyway, we figured we'd show you the booking and billing system while Ziggy's in with a client."

I glance around to be sure we're the only two in the reception area. No one else is in sight, so I have no idea why she keeps saying "we." "Sounds good."

"You're used to computers, right?"

"Yes."

"So, just play around with it. I've got to run to a meeting."

"Wait, you're leaving?" I've been here for exactly twenty-three minutes, and she's leaving me on my own?

"I'll be back at eleven thirty, and Ziggy will be done with his client at eleven. Plenty of time for you to get to know the booking system." She smiles and grabs my shoulders. "You're smart. I have every faith in your ability to do this." She disappears out the front door in a cloud of sandalwood and lemon verbena.

My gaze bounces from the Himalayan rock salt lamp on the wooden table to the large amethyst geode by the front door. A small stack of organic living magazines is nestled beside a pile of affirmation flip cards with finger labyrinths printed on the back. Apparently, they're soothing.

I could use a few cups of soothing right about now. What the hell am I supposed to do if someone phones or comes in or… No. I sit in the chair behind the computer and wiggle the mouse to take it out of sleep mode. Fern left because she thinks I'm capable and intelligent. Maybe it's a test, maybe it's an opportunity—either way, this is my chance to shine. This is nothing compared to the tasks the partners had me do.

The certainty in Fern's voice, the *trust*, is humbling and helps stave off the panic that I'll do something wrong. I can do this. It's just a piece of software, and I have a secret weapon: the Internet. I Google the name of the program and read the FAQs twice. There's a forum that discusses some common bugs and shortcuts.

By ten forty-five, I'm practicing scheduling fake appointments, shifting them to different days and times, and deleting them like a pro. As long as I stick to the basics and no one wants to get fancy, I'm functional.

Ziggy zooms out of a therapy room at eleven on the dot and speeds by me, a sky-blue blur. "Bathroom."

Oh.

"Hey." A fifty-something woman in capris and a peasant blouse steps up to the counter. There's no automatic bell to alert me when someone enters or exits Inner Space. I'll have to remember that when I leave the desk. "I have an appointment with Ziggy at eleven fifteen?"

I pull up Ziggy's day and hope she's in the schedule so I don't look like a dumbass. "What's your last name?"

"Tina."

"That's your last name?"

"No." She blinks at me a few times.

I so haven't had enough coffee to be dealing with this. "What's your last name?"

"Tina. Graham?"

Ziggy's schedule does show Tina in at eleven fifteen. Allowing myself a small breath of relief, I smile at her. "He's just finishing up with someone. Would you like to have a seat?" I motion to the row of sage-green pleather chairs.

"Sure." She wanders over to the cooler, where

packets of herbal tea and real cups are set up—
disposable cups were *not* an option, Fern informed
me. Tina pulls up on the red handle, then jiggles it.
"There's no hot water."

"You've got to sort of push it straight back before
pressing it down."

She jiggles it harder. "It's not working. I think
it's broken."

"No, you have to pinch it, not jiggle it." I use a
new word, hoping she understands this time, and
mime the motion, but she's not listening or looking.
When she starts twisting the handle around, I decide
to get up to help her before she breaks the handle off.
"Here, let me help." I take her cup and demonstrate
what I'd told her to do.

"Ah, I get it." She fills her mug with steaming
water. "You should have just said to pinch it."

I move back behind my desk for a little space and
focus on the soft music, but I need stimulants, not the
soothing tones of a pan flute. I wish I'd known the
only beverages here are decaffeinated.

Ziggy's previous client emerges from the treatment
room just as he returns from the bathroom, and he
preps his room while I deal with his client.

The billing software is one I've used before, so the
payment goes smoothly and the client says she'll phone
to rebook when she knows her schedule. Ziggy appears
as the last part of the transaction wraps up, and he
greets Tina with a smile. "So get undressed," he says,
leading her to the room, "and I'll be back in a couple
of minutes."

The door closes behind him, and he pads into

reception, grabs a cup, and fills it with water. Curiously, I peek at Naomi's schedule for the day, checking to see when she has a break so we can have a chat. She's booked back-to-back from eight in the morning until four. Eight full hours of massages? Ziggy's are spaced with fifteen minutes in between each client and an hour break for lunch, but he's the boss, and his schedule could be more lax because of that. I'm not an expert, but Naomi's schedule seems like a long time to be massaging people without taking lunch or even a fifteen-minute breather. And amazing stamina or not, she's going to need a pee break in there at some point.

"Ziggy? Why is Naomi booked so solidly?"

He swirls his water around in his cup. "She was concerned about not having enough clients to pay her bills. So we fixed that for her. Now she has all the clients she can handle."

That seems a little spiteful, but I say nothing. If it hadn't been for Naomi, I never would have heard of this job. She's how I got in, and I'm grateful to her, but I barely know her. Gratitude or not, I know which people need to be agreed with.

The ones signing my paychecks.

"The transaction went really well, Sarah. Good for you. Fern's doing a great job teaching you the ropes."

If giving me a quick tour, having me sign a contract, and then abandoning me is "teaching me the ropes," then yes. "Yes, she is."

"Where is she?"

Maybe she wasn't supposed to leave. Should I be honest about the fact that she left, or would that be ratting her out? Since she took off without telling him,

I think Fern's the one I need to keep happy. "I think she was talking with a client. I'm not sure. I was really in the zone going over the scheduling software she showed me."

He smiles proudly. "She's a fabulous teacher. She does workshops, you know. We do them together, but I'm really just her helper."

Fern's definitely the alpha hippie. "No, I didn't know you guys did workshops. What does she teach?"

He looks at the clock. "Oh, I've got to get in there with Tina." He leans over and grabs a flyer from a stack on the shelf that holds other flyers and business cards of people in his and Fern's network. He sets the glossy, rectangular slip on the desk and slides it toward me. "Check it out. You should come sometime." He fixes his watery blue eyes on me, walks back to the room Tina's in, and disappears behind the door.

A beautiful sapphire lotus flower covers the left side of the brochure, with Fern's and Ziggy's names printed in yellow across the center. The words *Passion, Fulfillment, Connection, Liberation* border the bottom in small, yellow script. The right side is the main message. Fern and Ziggy's course is called *Sex, Evolution, and You.*

The words *juicy*, *untamed*, and *admit two* sear my retinas, and I thrust the brochure away from me, suddenly feeling very conflicted about my bosses.

My married, hippie bosses, who just invited me to the sex workshop they teach. I'm not sure if I should be flattered or creeped out.

I'm still pondering that a few minutes later when Fern returns, clutching a small white box, and beckons for me to follow her to the kitchen.

The small kitchen would be a decent size, if it wasn't for the washer, dryer, and shelves for the massage table sheets that take up one of the walls and then some.

"Oh, you haven't done the laundry." She sounds surprised.

The laundry? Don't they have people for that or send it out to be done like they do at Pete's salon? "I didn't know I was supposed to do that as well."

"Yes. And the dishes." She points at the small stack of cups piling up in the sink, dirty and half-filled with the colorful herbal tea clients took and never finished.

"Sure, that's not a problem. Where's the dishwasher?" I open a panel and find another dirty laundry basket.

"Dishwashers are a horrible waste of water, Sarah." Fern's tone drips disapproval. "Not environmentally conscious at all." Her eyes narrow, and I feel caught out.

"I don't have one at home. My old work—they used one. I prefer washing things by hand."

"Good for you. Too many people are lazy nowadays and don't think about the Mother and what we're doing to Her. That's very environmentally conscious of you."

Dishwashergate avoided, I relax a bit and move the sheets from the washer into the dryer and scan the shelves. "Are there any dryer sheets for static?"

"Dryer sheets?" Her sharp voice is cut off by a commotion in the hallway.

"Screw you, Ziggy. I know what you're doing! You guys are trying to burn me out because I told you I didn't have enough clients."

"You wanted more work, and we gave it to you. Are you unhappy with your workload? Because we can—"

"No shit I'm unhappy with my workload. I don't have

time to take a piss with this schedule, never mind eat a proper lunch!"

I follow Fern into the hall and see Naomi: she's tall, athletic, and blond, with a light dusting of freckles across the bridge of her nose and tops of her shoulders—exposed in a tank top paired with light-blue cotton capri pants.

I'm definitely overdressed. Where the hell are they all buying these pastel clothes?

Naomi and Ziggy are squared off; she's tense, and he's slouched against the counter. Something about his posture screams "feigned casual," but I can't quite put my finger on what it is. Maybe the intensely gleeful glint in his eyes.

"What is going on here? There are clients in the rooms. Keep your voices down." Fern's lowered voice draws their gazes, and Naomi takes me in.

"You need to get out while you can. These people"— she motions at Fern and Ziggy—"are total whack jobs. Don't walk, *run* away. Especially from their workshop bullshit. It's a total cult."

"That's enough, Naomi," Fern snaps, her eyes filled with caustic heat. "We have let so much slide, but I will not have you insulting the good we do with our workshop. Hand over your key, and get out. You're fired."

"In case it missed your attention, *Fern*, I quit."

"You can't quit." Ziggy's eyes bulge in panic. "We need to calm down, achieve harmony. Naomi, your schedule is full today. I know you're angry, but breathe into it, feel the emotions, and then release them."

Naomi digs in her pocket and slams a key on the counter. "Fuck that. Breathe into this." She gives him the finger. "I'm out!"

Fern gasps, and Naomi leaves. I'm not sure where to look because…*awkward*.

"We're sorry you had to see that, Sarah." Ziggy's hand falls lightly onto my shoulder. "We've been having some issues with her for a while, but we never expected things to end like that. She handled it terribly, of course. If she'd just stopped and owned her part of the situation, breathed for a moment, she'd have calmed down, and we could have talked this out."

Fern rotates her shoulders as if working tension from them. "She was so irresponsible. Unprofessional. It already feels lighter in here now that she's gone. What a poisonous person. This is the type of person we don't want here, the type we've been weeding out one by one."

The type they've been weeding out, or who have been quitting? Naomi's schedule was insane, and I already have some concerns about my lack of training—and their lack of clarity about my job description. I had no idea I'd be doing dishes and the laundry as well as the administrative duties.

Not that I think I'm above doing them, but full disclosure and all that.

They both look at me. Shit. I was probably supposed to say something. "I like it here, and her quitting isn't changing my mind." Maybe it's different for the massage therapists than it is for me. We're employees in different ways.

"That's kind of you to say," Ziggy says.

Fern smiles. "So kind. And we won't hold her recommendation against you. In fact…" She wanders to the kitchen and comes back with the box. "Why don't you take the rest of the day off? We can handle things here."

"Really? I'd love to stay and work more, familiarize myself with the—"

"No, no. I think you've got it." Ziggy waves my concerns away.

Fern hands me the box. "Here's a little something from us."

"What is it?"

"Open it."

I slide the twine off and open the box. It's a small cake that says *Welcome to our Inner Space*. My face grows warm, and I feel something I never did at the law firm. Appreciated.

"Thank you, both of you. Would you like to join me and have a piece?"

Fern smiles. "You're welcome, but no, that's yours, and we've got work to do. See you tomorrow morning at ten?"

"That sounds perfect." I tie up the box and grab my purse.

I've decided to head for the bookstore off Union Square. I've got some studying to do.

....

I close the door behind me and tuck my newly purchased books against my hip.

"How was your first day?"

Pete sounds so excited and hopeful that I bite my cheek and kick off my heels instead of immediately launching into a description of the creepy/flattering workshop and the spectacular way Naomi quit. Despite some of the weirdness, I want to focus on the positive instead of bitching. I find a bright smile by the time I reach the kitchen. "Good. They got me a 'welcome to the team' cake we can eat for dessert."

"Aww, that's sweet of them! What are those?" He nods at my books.

I set them on the counter. "Research. My new bosses are into energy stuff, so I thought I'd bone up on it. Make a good impression with them." The bookstore had a huge section on New Age modalities, and I spent way too much time hemming and hawing over the selection, and then more time snuggling up in an overstuffed chair with an iced coffee while people watching. "How was your day?"

"My day was great. I did four Brazilians today."

"I hope you didn't smile that big while doing them."

He grates some carrots. "I tried to tone down my delight."

"You're such a sadist."

He sets aside the carrots and tosses croutons into the salad. "I know. Waxing people is my favorite part of the job."

"It's perfect for you," I agree.

"Except for all the vag."

"It is ironic that you see more in a week than most straight guys do in a year."

He sprinkles sea salt on the salmon frying in the pan. "It's wasted on me. I definitely don't see the appeal. They look like a rose that got its face trapped in a subway door."

I wrinkle my nose at his analogy. "No arguments from me there. I'm also a fan of the penis."

He smirks. "You used to be."

My thoughts rub themselves all over the mental image of Jack that comment brings up. "What, am I supposed to bring someone back and bang him on your couch?"

"You could always go back to his place." Pete's voice is mild, but his statement feels too much like a criticism.

"I've had a lot on my mind the past couple of months. Too much to think about hooking up with anyone."

"And that's all in your past. Time to live again. Put on some *short* skirts and let 'er breathe! Show off those killer legs I wax. For free," he adds, gesturing at my calf-length skirt with his spatula.

"Hey, I already said I'm in on Friday for dancing."

He grabs a couple of plates from the cupboard. "I know what you said. I've also witnessed a lot of flaking out lately."

He's right. I have been canceling on plans, but not because I've wanted to. The only money in my account has been earmarked for my new place—first month's rent, broker's fee, security deposit. It's not like I could just dip into that for a cocktail or a new top whenever I want to, and sponging off my friends has made me feel like a loser. Everything has been knocked away from me. My high-paying job. My awesome apartment. My independence has been eroded one accomplishment at a time, making me feel like a kid. I'm not even working in my field now. "I can actually afford to go out again, so that's not going to happen anymore."

He rolls his eyes. "You know I never cared—"

"I know you guys would have gladly paid for me, but I'm already putting you out by staying here for free." I hold my hands up at his glare. "I know you don't think it's an imposition. The good news is that I'll be out of here soon and things should get back to normal. But Friday night's dancing will have to tide us over until after the move."

"Come with us tomorrow as well, and I'll shut up."

"Fine, twist my rubber arm. But I'm paying for the cab there."

"Hmm. That's something, I guess. But you're not an imposition. You're my best friend. I love you."

"I love you too, Pete." I lay my head on his shoulder.

"Now grab a fork, bitch, and prepare to have your mind blown."

Chapter 4

I'VE LEARNED NOT TO WAIT FOR PETE OUTSIDE A CLUB, because he might (a) not show up or (b) show up early, head inside, and forget to come look outside if I'm late. Instead, I head straight into the bar, get a vodka slime—perfectly refreshing for a muggy night like tonight—and wait for Pete to find me.

Drink attained, I scan the room for an available table. It's pretty full, but not as bad as it'll get closer to midnight. I've never been to this club, Frisk, before. Rich blues and dark grays make up the color palette. Light hardwood floors and wooden trim make the decor look expensive but fresh. Roomy dance floors and my drink is perfectly mixed—I'll definitely be back.

I check my phone, but there are no texts from Pete yet, so I make a few passes around the perimeter, starting to get cranky from the crowd and the number of elbows I have to dodge. This club is the Next Big Thing, judging by the way it's filled up in the twenty minutes I've been here. With reckless disregard for the heat wave, I'm wearing a scandalously short—but long-sleeved—slinky red dress that makes me feel like Beyoncé but unfortunately doesn't give me the option of removing anything to cool off.

The sign to a rooftop patio is tempting, but it's doubtful Pete would be out there. He'll look for me in here.

The music is…different. I haven't heard hardly any of the artists they're playing, and I'm not sure I like the DJs. But I haven't been out much lately. Maybe it's just new music that takes some getting used to. But the next song is as bad as the first. No one's got time for bad aural—one more crappy song and I'm out of here.

Where's Jack when I need him? He knows all the songs I like, and I don't have to ask to hear them played. Guess he spoiled me for regular DJs; I'm getting too used to being a VIP.

Another crappy, overplayed song blares through the speakers, and I'm out, heading for the rooftop patio for a breather. The staircase is narrow and tall and sort of feels like it's a secret, or you're not really supposed to come up here.

But I push through the door at the top of the stairs and sigh in relief at the cooler temperature. The rooftop isn't huge, but bits of greenery make it feel intimate— like a private garden—and only about eight other people are up here. But everyone's paired up, rubbing it in that I'm here all alone. Now, I almost wish the DJs hadn't chased me here with their mediocre music. If Jack were here… I should just find Pete. Or go home.

"I'd hate to be the person who put that look in your eyes."

Startled, I turn toward the familiar voice coming from the shadows in the corner. "Jack?" *What a sexy coincidence; I was just wishing for you.* I head over to him. "What are you doing here?"

He smiles. "Drinking, dancing. You?" He's in a black

button-down and dark jeans—a more expensive look I'm not used to seeing on him, but one that my lady bits approve of.

I sip my drink. "Same, but the DJ is a raging poseur. I came to cool off. Why aren't you spinning tonight?"

He smiles. "Pete asked if I wanted to hang out, so here I am with the night off."

I bump him with my shoulder. "I love how close you guys are."

He leans closer. "Mostly I say yes to keep him out of trouble."

His cologne makes me want to press my face against his chest and stay there breathing deeply for an hour or so. I can still feel the place his arm touched my shoulder. I take another sip of my drink, savoring the sharpness of the lime and looking out at the New York skyline instead of staring at Jack. The stars wink out between the clouds, and with the patio's minimal lighting, the view is incredible. "This place is beautiful. I'm surprised more people aren't up here."

He sips his drink and nods, looking out across the city and clenching his jaw.

What's going on in his head? It's the question I always end up asking myself. Despite his easy charm, Jack is the quintessential cypher. The things I know about him aren't personal. I know all the facts and figures and can appreciate his appearance, but I don't know a thing about what's inside him. He's always been a mystery, despite how long I've known him. "Have you been here before?"

He nods. "Do you like it?"

I lean against the railing and peer down at the line

winding around the block. "Frisk is the new trendy place, I guess."

"You think so?"

I nod. "It's got all the right elements. I really wish you were playing though."

"Should I go talk to someone?"

I smile. "Nah."

"Why did you want me to play?"

"You know what I like without me having to say anything." Crap, that came out wrong. "What do you like about playing?" I try instead, even though I know he won't give much of an answer.

But he surprises me, angling toward me as he considers the question. "I love when I play the right song at the right time and get everyone dancing hard enough to forget everything except the music."

"There's a kind of power in that, I guess."

"I don't do it for power." He props his forearms on the ledge and leans on them. I could happily trace the lines of his back with my tongue.

Ugh, get a grip, Sarah. "Why do you do it?"

The seriousness in his eyes almost takes my breath away. It's like being given a glimpse of something fragile and important. I want it to be tangible so I can take it in my hands and cradle it, hide it from everyone else.

Keep it for my own.

He tips his face up to the sky. "In some ways it's like a disguise. I get to be a part of things but stay hidden in my booth. People hear what I want them to. They actually listen, and it's not about who I am. It's not about me at all."

I shiver. "It's nice to lose yourself sometimes. I need to dance off the past couple of days like nobody's business."

"Hippie shenanigans?"

I poke at the lime in my glass with my straw. "*Shenanigans* implies fun, but yeah, the hippies are proving to be less easygoing than I thought they'd be."

He flips a coaster end over end, one corner at a time, deliberately. God, he has nice hands, "You could come over after this. I've got everything set up at home. You and Pete, I mean." His tone is casual, but I swallow hard, imagining a private party with no Pete.

Jack would play all the songs I wanted while I danced. Maybe he'd dance with me until we were both writhing and sweaty, and then—

"Jack, there you are!"

I turn and take in the slinky brunette in a slinkier dress.

"Maxine, hey." Jack straightens, the easiness in his posture gone.

She glances at me, then back to him, placing her hand on his forearm. "Can I talk to you for a minute? In private?" she emphasizes.

I raise an eyebrow. We're friends. Whatever she has to say, she can say in front—

"Sure." He flashes me a smile. "I'll be right back." He heads out of earshot with her.

His easy dismissal of me burns. He's not my boyfriend, but we were having a moment before she came along and ruined it. I take a step to the side, trying to see the world from Jack's place in the shadows—and notice two glasses on the ledge.

One has lipstick on the straw.

Suddenly, I'm weighted by reality. Maxine isn't the

interloper—I am. She's probably the one whose lipstick was on the straw, and I interrupted their romantic evening of looking at the stars. And even if it wasn't her, another woman was here with Jack a minute ago. Alone in an incredibly romantic spot, probably deciding if they'd go back to his place or hers.

She grins and leaves, and Jack returns to my side. "Sorry about that."

"It's fine. You're in demand, as usual."

Jack frowns. "No, she's just—"

"There they are." Pete swoops in suddenly, offering a kiss on my cheek and a shoulder bump for Jack. "What's with the music? I've heard more authentic dubstep in Great-Aunt Ione's car!"

I smack Pete's arm. "Right? They chased me out of the room with Shaggy." I focus only on Pete. I've got to ignore Jack. Off-limits Jack. I could throw a stick into any bar and hit three chicks he's dated. *And given the best orgasms of their lives.*

Shut up, brain.

"How'd you find us?"

He grins at me. "I asked the girls downstairs. They knew exactly where Jack was."

Why am I not surprised?

Pete grabs my arm. "We've got to get back in there. You've got to shake some serious ass to celebrate the new job, darling."

I turn my back on him. "And I've got a serious ass to shake." I give a shimmy for good measure, looking at the boys over my shoulder.

I swear Jack's eyes turn black, but it's hard to tell from peripheral vision. I risk a full-on glance. Yeah, he's eye-fucking me hard, and my body reacts in all kinds of ways I have to trample down with unsexy thoughts.

"Jack!" A tall Indian woman strides up to us, leaning close to Jack like we're not even here. "I need you. Now."

Fortunately for me, Pete takes my hand and we head straight downstairs to the dance floor, leaving Jack on the patio with whomever this woman is.

Either the music gets better, or the second drink relaxes me enough that I don't notice how bad it is, but soon, I don't care about the heat, or the crowded floor, or Jack and stupid Maxine and stupid… I don't even know her name, but her hair was annoyingly shiny.

Pete and I shake and shimmy together before he sees someone else he knows and disappears, leaving me alone again. Jack has come back down at some point, but he stays at the bar and entertains his revolving door of admirers. Again, as usual. He buys one a drink, and they chat for a while before they part ways.

Another drink and more dancing later, I watch a seventh chick hit on Jack. For some reason—maybe I've had too much to drink, or maybe it's just the heat of so many bodies packed together on a sweltering summer night—I want to slap the foundation off her face when she looks him up and down like he's a slab of meat. When this chick leaves, I head to where he's standing by the wall with his arms crossed.

"You buy a lot of girls drinks, don't you?"

He bites his lip. "I wouldn't say a lot." His eyes stay focused somewhere across the bar, and I can just imagine some girl blushing and looking coyly away.

Yeah, he doesn't have to shell out money to strike up a conversation with anyone. Not with his looks and personality. He's funny and charming, someone you want to be around. I wonder how many of those girls realize that. "You don't need to do that to get a girl to talk to you. Why do you bother?"

Why am I making an issue out of this? I eyeball my empty glass and set it on the bar. When I drink, I can get a little…aggressive.

Jack doesn't seem to notice. Or maybe he's just willing to ignore how I'm acting because he's seen me at my worst. He runs his hand through his hair. "I guess it's a classic way to break the ice, but I'd rather everyone was just up-front about things. 'Hi, I like you. I think you're hot. Want to come home with me?' That sort of thing." He shrugs, then laughs. "I wish people were more like you, I guess. I always figured you'd take the direct approach."

He always figured? "What would happen if I came up to you and flirted? 'Hi, I like you' and all that?" The words are out of my mouth before I can let myself think better of it.

That's got his attention. Suddenly, the air between us feels thick. Tense. Like we're both holding our breaths. He licks his lips and I bite mine. His eyes narrow slightly. "Are you asking if I want to take you home?" he finally murmurs. His voice is deliciously husky.

I can't meet his eyes now. He knows I want to… just as much as he knows I won't. The truth lies heavily between us. Then a Wayne Wonder song comes on, providing the perfect distraction, and I flap a hand. "I love this song," I say, pulling back, both grateful for and disappointed by the distance between us. Another moment and I could have sworn he was going to ask—

"I know. You've only made me play it every week since it came out."

"It's a classic." I shake off the heaviness between us, determined to just let it be, and dance my way to the floor. I don't know what to make of our conversation, but I feel cute and have a nice buzz and am out with my bestie and his sexy twin. A goofy smile twists my lips, and I look back at Jack as I shimmy my hips.

The expression on his face nearly stills my feet.

There's *hunger* in his gaze.

I turn away and keep dancing, though less happily than before, more aware of every movement I make, knowing his eyes are on me. Breathless. Despite not wanting to take our relationship to the next level, I have to admit that I want his eyes on me. Seeing other women talk to him, look at him, annoys me more than it should. He's not mine, but they don't deserve him. So I make my movements a little sexier and imagine what it would be like if I *were* going home with him tonight, hating the reasons that can never happen.

I'm so wrapped up in a fantasy of tumbling into Jack's arms that it seems inevitable when his arms wrap around me from behind. He tugs me close to the curve of his body, and his heat is incredible—too incredible for the rational part of me to win. I smile and dance with him, allowing myself a moment of perfect, snatched happiness.

"Girl, you're making everyone on the dance floor jealous with those moves." Pete's voice in my ear shatters the fantasy, and my eyes open, gaze flying straight to Jack—who is still standing where I left him by the wall, an unreadable expression on his face as he watches me dance with his twin.

I wish it had been you, Jack.

But it's better for both of us that it wasn't.

Chapter 5

"SO YOU'RE THE NEW GIRL?"

Pete would gasp in horror if he saw her thick, shapeless eyebrows—like two mustaches have taken residence above her large brown eyes. She's pretty in an unkempt, granola way, but with some militant brushing and shine serum for her hair and a little grooming, she could be stunning. The shapeless top in shades of green—almost a kaftan—does nothing to hide her curves but doesn't accentuate them either. Her leggings end just below her knees.

She doesn't shave her legs. Power to her for being confident enough to walk around bare-legged and hairy. I'd never be able to do that, despite sometimes wishing I could. "Yes. I'm Sarah."

"Phyllis." She holds out her hand, and I shake it. My hand is shiny with massage oil when I pull it back. I try not to think about how this oil's been rubbed all over some stranger's naked body and now she's smeared it on *me*. "Oh, sorry about that." She doesn't sound sorry about it.

"It's fine." I grab a hand wipe and scrub. It's going to bug me until I can wash it off with soap, but I have to finish updating the schedule first.

"I just got back from vacation. We haven't really had a chance to chat."

"No, we haven't." I try to keep a mild smile, but I don't have time right now to get to know her.

Hands land on my shoulders and begin kneading the muscles. Hard. "Ouch." I flinch away. "What are you doing?"

"You're so tense." Phyllis reaches for me again. "You should book an appointment with me."

"I have no time. And I don't really like being touched." *Hint.*

"Your poor boyfriend." She stops the assault and steps back. "You're going to end up with a stress hump unless you see someone to work out that tension."

"My tension is what's holding me together." Ten bucks says I bruise from her ministrations. And now there are two dark patches on my shirt where she touched it.

"Phyllis, that was wonderful." Her client, Deanne, ambles into reception, and I step around them and slip into the room they just exited. It's been four days of trial and error, but I've found a rhythm for my job that works—if I move like a scalded rabbit.

It turned out that during my first few days, they had taken it easy on me. Now that I'm more comfortable on the desk, I'm expected to prep the rooms between sessions as well. If I'm fast, I can do it while the therapists talk to their clients, finishing just as they're done assigning stretches or chatting about the massage. Then I take payment as the next client goes in.

As long as no one phones, the rhythm works.

Even in the dim light, I can tell it's a bigger mess than any other masseuse has left all week. I hope it's a one-off and not Phyllis's usual style. Sliding the dimmer switch as bright as it will go, I cringe at the mess and spring into action, hoping the phone won't ring.

First stop: the massage table. I peel off the fuzzy blanket and fold it as fast as I can, despite the shocks assaulting my fingertips from the static buildup. Four days of this, and I don't even swear under my breath anymore. I use a towel to wipe up the puddle of massage oil leaking onto the shelf, then toss the towel to the table. I peel back the sheets and ball them up, trying not to let them touch my body, before tossing the self-contained ball to the floor. I don't want to leave a grease spot on my shirt like I did yesterday.

I wipe down the bed with the all-natural cleaning product Fern and Ziggy swear by. It's made with chrysanthemums and dries out my hands but still somehow manages to be greasy. Next, I take fresh bedding from the shelf, snapping the elastic of the fitted sheet around the edges of the table, then slinging the top sheet on, turning it down invitingly at the corner. Finally, I fold a face towel over the headrest. Grabbing the used bedding from the floor, I rush next door to the kitchen and fire it into the laundry hamper just as the phone starts ringing.

I hurry back to the desk where Phyllis is still discussing stretches with her last client. The phone is on its third ring when I step around Phyllis—who doesn't move despite my urgent body language and polite "excuse me"—barely managing to answer it before they hang up.

"Good morning, Inner Space. Sarah speaking."

"Hi, Tara. I have an appointment with Phyllis at eleven?"

I open Phyllis's schedule on the computer. "Is this Danni?"

"Yes. I'm going to be about half an hour late."

Damn. "Actually, Danni, I have you in here for ten thirty, not eleven."

"Oh. Can I still come at eleven thirty?"

Luckily Phyllis's schedule is clear until her break at one. "Yes, I'll change it to eleven thirty."

"Awesome! See you then!"

We hang up, I process Phyllis's last client, and she leaves.

Phyllis wanders over to grab an herbal tea. "So where did you work before this?"

"At a law firm."

"Really?"

"Yes. I'm actually a paralegal."

She grimaces and selects a tea bag. "Awkward."

"Why is that awkward?"

"I'm in a bit of legal trouble myself at the moment. Nothing I did, of course." She pours hot water into her cup. "Do you live alone? Or are you married?"

"I live alone."

"Ah. I should get going and prep my room for my next client."

"Oh, I've already done that."

"Really?" She sets the cup down as the phone rings again.

"Yes." I answer the phone and deal with booking a client while Phyllis walks past me to check out her room. I've hung up by the time she returns.

She purses her lips. "So, not to be confrontational about it, but I'd really like it if you'd put the leg pillow back under the sheets when you remake the bed."

"It wasn't in there when I cleaned the room, but sure."

She gives me a perfectly friendly dead-eyed smile. "I always use the leg pillows."

Except that she just did a massage without one, but I'm all about choosing my battles, so I smile. "No problem."

"Awesome." She stretches her fingers. "It's fine anyway. I have to fill in more receipts for insurance." The therapists print their names and registration numbers and then sign their receipts. I can fill in the rest of the information when a client asks for one. "You should get Blake to do some too while he's in. He only has one signed page left." She pats my forearm with her oily hand and riffles through my stack of papers, leaving greasy fingerprints all over them before finding the receipt book and grabbing a pen, then taking them back to one of the reception chairs.

Since Blake usually only works on the weekends, we haven't met. I am a bit curious about the masseuse who's capable of doing things by himself and never makes a mess for me to clean up on Monday. If Phyllis worked weekends alone, I'd come in on Monday to a spa that looked like someone was partway through a game of Jumanji.

Blake is in today, covering for Fern, who had some energy crisis to take care of. He was with his client before I got here and hasn't come out yet.

I wonder if he's like the other after-hours massage therapist I've met—a large, forty-something man with a mustache and booming voice. Now that I'm caught up with everything, I rush to the kitchen to wash the oil off my hand while Phyllis fills in her receipt book.

A guy with an olive complexion and a medium build folds a towel and sets it on a stack on the shelf. I blink hard. Since I started working here, no one else has done the laundry, except for Ziggy—and he screws it up so badly that I've forbidden him from doing it…not that he listens. The other therapists don't even restock the fresh towels in their rooms.

"Hello?"

He turns to me. "Hey."

I'd pictured him completely wrong, assuming he'd be another version of Ziggy—unkempt and blond, puka shell necklace maybe. He's Italian, or maybe Hispanic, late twenties, attractive with dark, sparkling eyes, a straight nose, and nice lips. Strong jaw. Hot. "I assume you're Blake, since the laundry fairy isn't real."

His smile reveals dimples and nice teeth. "Maybe I'm both."

"No. The laundry fairy would have brought us dryer sheets that don't hurt baby animals."

"That's true, but don't let Fern hear you say that." He holds out his hand. "I am Blake. And you must be Sarah."

"Yes. Hang on a second." I hit the sink and scrub like I'm going into surgery, literally shuddering with relief as the oil is washed away beneath the lather of the eco-friendly hand soap. When my hands are dry, I shake his hand. "So you normally only work on weekends here?"

"Yeah, I work full-time at another clinic. I pretty much only sneak in here when no one's looking."

"Can't blame you there."

"I had an opening today and was able to come cover for Fern."

"That's nice of you." I feel weird watching him do the laundry, so I grab a towel. "Do you have to get going? Don't feel like you have to finish the load."

"You sure? I hate to leave a mess, but I do really have to get back to the other clinic."

"It's fine." I'm not used to having help anyway.

"Okay, but I've already rebooked my client, and she paid before going in, so you don't have to worry about that."

"Thank you! You didn't have to do that."

He smiles and takes a pile of sheets. "Just the way I do things. Nice meeting you."

"You too, Blake." On the way back to reception, I see he's cleaned the room and remade the bed for the next therapist. He's considerate too. None of the other therapists give a crap about taking payments or rebooking their own clients—never mind doing a load of laundry or making a bed.

I wonder if he's single. I get back to reception with a smile.

"You met Blake, I take it?"

"Yup." I double-check to make sure he's really gone before I grin at Phyllis, expecting a moment of bonding over his cuteness.

Instead, she frowns. "You know we're not allowed to date other employees, right?"

"Oh. I didn't know that."

"Yeah. So don't even go there."

Well then. That moment was squashed like a Tokyo train commuter at rush hour. The receipt book is back on the desk, and I flip through to check if she's done the whole book, but she's only signed her name on each page. "Phyllis, you didn't put your name or RMT number on these."

"No. I figured you could do that when you're bored out here with nothing to do."

"Well..." This is a battle that seems worth fighting. "There really isn't much time for me to be doing things that you're supposed to be doing. Not with all my responsibilities and everything."

"What's this about?" Ziggy's voice behind me freezes me in my seat.

"Oh, it's nothing." Phyllis smiles easily. "I was giving Sarah something else to do because she's so productive and already caught up with everything else—including meeting Blake and spending some time getting to know him! She's so efficient. Thanks, Sarah. It really helps me out."

"We're all team players here." Ziggy moves to refill his water bottle. "Glad to see you helping out, Sarah. I wish our last receptionist had had the same giving attitude. Doing the bare minimum around here isn't acceptable."

Phyllis's smug expression radiates my way while I process Ziggy's client. I get away from Phyllis when I leave to set up Ziggy's room. When I come out, she's gone.

She's made me seem like the star of the show while railroading me into doing more of her work. Maybe she's not as stunned as she looks.

By the time I finish filling out her information in the receipt book, the load in the dryer is done, so I fold in between phone calls until my shoulders ache from more than just Phyllis's massage. I definitely need to watch out for that one.

Chapter 6

THE BASS LINE IS HARD AND FAST AND THRUMS through me, loud and welcome after the soothing spa music that saturated my eardrums all week. I want a large glass of wine and to dance. And another glass while dancing. After that, I'll wing it. Pulse by pulse, the minutes of the last few days fall from my shoulders. By the time I've reached the brushed chrome bar, I'm unable to stop shimmying my hips and bobbing my shoulders, despite sweating my makeup off.

I pull my hair up off my neck and fan myself.

"What can I get you?" Eighty-five degrees outside and not much better in here, and the bartender's wearing a black suit jacket over her black bikini top. Her neck is covered in tattoos—a welcome sight after all the organic earth-mother types I've been around at work.

"I'd like something scandalously red, please."

She grins. "I've got just the thing." She pours me a glass. "Try this Syrah."

Syrah for Sarah, yes please. The dark, intense liquid caresses my tongue, leaving an almost peppery after-taste. "Mmm, thank you." I open my purse.

She shakes her head. "You're on Jack's tab."

"Oh." I tuck the twenty into her tip jar anyway.

She grins and moves down the bar, and I head for our table in the VIP section, grinning when I see Kelly.

I set my glass on the table. "This seat taken?"

"Sarah!" The tiny woman jumps to her feet and wraps herself around me in a hug bigger than her platinum-blond Afro. I've missed this. Not being able to afford going out is bad for morale.

"How are you?"

She moves back, still holding my hand, and pulls me to sit beside her. "I'm great." She fans herself. "Taking a break from dancing—the music's hot tonight."

I sip my wine and grin as my song comes on—a Bowie remix that's totally blown up this summer. The DJ booth is slightly to my left, up the stairs overlooking the dance floor, and Jack points at me when we make eye contact. He's like having my very own jukebox with all the best, newest music and old favorites. "Jack's the best."

"Totally. Where have you been? It's been ages since I saw you out and about. I've missed your face."

"I know. I fell off the radar and have been crashing on Pete's couch, but I found a new job, and here I am. What about you?"

"Congrats. I'm still everything. Same, same, we know my name."

I smile. "How's Meeka?"

"Oh, she's around here somewhere. We just got a dog from the shelter, and that's exactly as disgustingly domestic as it sounds, so let's change the subject." Her smile is huge and satisfied. They've been together forever, and though she acts like it cramps her style, she's the one who put the ring on Meeka's finger. "You seeing anyone? What's the new job?"

I take another sip of wine. "Still single. The new job is working reception at a spa."

She tips her head to the side. "That must be so relaxing and quiet."

The only reason the phone was so quiet the first day was because Fern had turned the ringer off without telling me. We get about a hundred calls a day. Relaxing? No. Quiet? Hell no. "Yeah, it's nice."

"And you're still at Pete's?"

"For a week or so. Probably till next Saturday."

"Shame you won't be at Pete's much longer."

"Why?"

Her gaze flicks up to the DJ booth. "No reason."

"Kelly…" I don't rise to her bait and look up at Jack. Her smile grows. "Did I say anything?"

"Your eyes said plenty."

She shrugs. "He's a nice guy, Sarah."

"I know." It's the truth.

She leans closer. "And?"

"And what? I'm not interested. Are you forgetting his nickname?"

"A nickname doesn't negate the way you feel."

I regret that night six months ago when we drank too much and I overshared about my lust for Jack. I've been forced to overcompensate since. Kelly's a vicious matchmaker. "The way I feel? He's my best friend's hot brother. He's a total man whore. There are no feelings."

"So you don't like him?"

"He's sexy as hell, but even if I wanted to go there, he's not a long-term prospect. He's older than me, and he's still just a DJ. What part of that screams 'I take my future seriously and am ready to take you seriously too'?"

"Protesting too much."

"Yeah, because I'm secretly in love with Jack and have been pining away for him for years."

She nods and sips her drink. "And on the sarcasm front…"

"Bit much? But for real, I'm not into Jack."

"Then it won't bother you that Rhonda Lavee's all up in his shit right now?"

My head whips around so quickly that I crick my neck. Sure enough, Rhonda Fucking Lavee is standing by the door of the booth, leaning over the partition in a tackily low-cut shirt. She was our friend until we discovered her hobby: banging other people's boyfriends. Including mine, which is why we broke up. "Gross."

"She's hot for a chick with no shame. Too bad she's a liar as well as a cheating cow."

"She's dirtier than a truck-stop toilet. Why would anyone want to be with her?"

"Maybe she gives good bowl jobs." Kelly laughs at her own pun.

Jack's fraternizing with the enemy. "If Jack wants to lower his standards for her—"

"Oh, so now you think he has standards?"

"I am so over this conversation." And I can't look at Rhonda hitting on Jack for one more second.

"He's looking at you."

And when I look back up, he is. Seventeen completely inappropriate sex acts flash through my mind, and I want to do them all with him right now. But I keep it flirty, smiling and waving, enjoying Rhonda's pissed-off expression a bit too much—until the intensity in Jack's eyes reaches me even from here. Jack's so sexy up there, bobbing to the music and seamlessly transitioning to the next song without taking his eyes off me. I've danced with Jack, next to him, in group settings like any other friend, but we've never *danced* together. Bodies pressed together, hands brushing across skin, nothing between us but the beat. No room for thoughts at all, just rhythm and movement.

Kelly taps my shoulder. "When you're done eye-fucking the man you're not interested in, come dance."

I don't bother dignifying that with a response. "I need another drink first. You want?"

"Nah, I'm good." She grins and shimmies away.

A few minutes later, I have my drink in hand and am about to head to where Kelly and Meeka are dominating the dance floor when I realize who the tall blond standing beside me at the bar is. "Naomi?"

She turns with a haughty expression—probably expecting I'm another guy hitting on her—before recognition dawns in her eyes and they light up. She grabs me in a tight hug and squeezes me hard enough to crack my back. Massage therapists really should watch that around us mortals with normal upper-body strength. "You still working for those crazy assholes at Inner Space?"

"It was only my fifth day today."

"I'm so glad I got the hell out of there. Worst seven months of my life." She slurs her *s*'s, and her eyelids look heavy. "I swear, the stories I could tell you would make you puke in your mouth just the tiiiniest bit." She takes a large swig of her martini.

I frown. "If you hated them so much, why did you tell me they were hiring?"

"I'm so sorry about that, Sarah. I guess I wanted one coworker who wasn't a crazy fucking hippie, and he said you really needed the job." Her expression brightens. "Maybe it will be different for you being a receptionist rather than a therapist. But you need to know how nuts they are so you don't get blindsided like I was."

"I guess," I say without much conviction. They're a bit much at times, but they don't seem like bad people.

"Just get out of there as fast as you possibly can, okay? There's a reason they've gone through six receptionists in nine months."

That's a huge turnover rate, but maybe the other receptionists were incompetent. I know I'm a hard worker and can keep up with whatever they throw at me. I'm used to swimming with sharks. These hippies will be a piece of cake compared to the ruthless partners at the law firm. "Thanks for the advice. I'll keep looking." I've already started whipping them into shape though. Sure, the job is different than I thought it would be, but I can handle it. I can handle them.

Naomi smiles and waves at someone across the bar. "I'll catch you later, Sarah—and if I hear about another job somewhere else, I'll let you know. But remember my advice. They act like they're all about love and understanding and honesty, but they'll turn on you. And watch out for Crackie."

"Crackie?"

"Phyllis."

"Why? What's she gonna do?"

But Naomi has already faded into the crowd.

Yikes. Maybe one more drink won't be enough. Not wanting to spare one more thought for my job, I dance until my drink is gone, set the empty glass on a nearby table, then dance until my throat screams for water.

"There she is. How's my tiny dancer?"

"Hey, Pete." I lean back into the warmth of his arms as he wraps them around me. "I'm good."

"I worried you'd flaked out."

"Flaking is for fish."

He peers around my shoulder without letting go of me. "My, we have been having a good time, haven't we?"

"I may have had a drink or two. Guess my tolerance has gone down a bit."

"Just a bit. See anyone bang-worthy?"

My gaze flits back to Jack. "Nope."

"Me neither." He leads me deeper onto the dance floor, and the music seamlessly switches to Pete's favorite song. He grins up at the DJ booth, thankfully now Rhonda-free, and waves at his brother. From profile, their faces are identical; I could be dancing with Jack. Parts of me that have no business tingling start to tingle at the thought. Then Pete turns back, and he's so undeniably my best friend that the attraction fizzles out.

I'm twenty-five years old. The layoff showed me I need to get my life together. I've got to get serious about my future. Inner Space is a job, but it isn't a career. The next man I'm with could be for keeps, and a sexy-as-hell DJ who can't keep it in his pants isn't going to cut it. He's the perfect fantasy, but not a real option for my future.

Pete—and shockingly, Jack—didn't find any romantic prospects tonight either. We'll all be going home together tonight…not that I'd be bringing anyone back to Pete's if I *had* found someone I wanted to get physical with. There's tacky and there's *tacky*—and banging someone on your best friend's couch is definitely crossing the line. Even if it's his insanely sexy brother. Maybe *especially* if it's his insanely hot brother.

Another reason I'll be glad to get back into my own place.

Not that *we'll* be… Damn it.

Chapter 7

MOVING IS THE WORST. MY ONE CONSOLATION IS THAT I'm almost in my own place again. That, and the sight of Jack's muscular arms exposed in a sleeveless T-shirt.

Thou shalt not look.

"Hey, princess. Grab another box." Pete jams a box into my front, and my breath leaves me in an *oof*.

"Thanks, Pete." I walk the box down the hall to my apartment, number nineteen. The landlord gave us the key, so we loaded the ancient elevator with my stuff, then locked it on my floor to unload. So far, it seems to be going quicker this way than other moves. Then again, my last apartment didn't have an elevator, so carrying everything up three flights of stairs was brutal.

We've made great time, but my shoulders are still burning—more from all the laundry I did at work on Friday than from the actual moving, I think. Pete and Jack have done the heavy lifting, sparing me the worst, but I've done as much as I can.

A tinny, poor-quality version of a dance mix stains the air. Pete sets down the two garbage bags he's carrying and answers his cell, obliviously blocking the narrow hall. "Ahoy-hoy."

Unfortunately, he's in front, so Jack and I also have to set our stuff down and wait while Pete gabs.

"No way. No way! Ugh, total nightmare. Uh-huh. Ten minutes. Bye."

"Who was that?" I wait for Pete to grab his bags.

He turns to me. "Don't hate me forever, but we've got a situation at the salon. It's a pubic hair emergency, and they've specifically asked for me. It's a high-profile client, and this could totally make my career."

"Oh. Well, we've gotten everything into the elevator. I guess Jack and I could handle the rest of it. Right, Jack?" I glance over my shoulder at him.

"Yup. Shouldn't take too long. If you're really going to the salon."

Pete rolls his eyes. "Of course I am."

Jack continues. "I know all about those prescheduled scams for getting out of dates. You have a friend schedule a phone call so you can bail out of a crappy date."

I laugh. "I think there's an app for that."

"I'm not skipping out on this. But they're paying me double, and it's a very sensitive situation. I can't even tell you the client's name, but trust me—you'd squeal if you knew!" He grabs my shoulders. "You're sure?"

So dramatic. "Yes, go."

"I owe you a dinner." He air-kisses my cheeks.

I'll take it. "Later this week?"

"Done."

Jack sighs. "I'll ride the elevator down with you with the key. Let's get these boxes out of the elevator before we go, so Sarah can keep working."

I point at him. "No dawdling on the way back!"

"Wouldn't dream of it." He winks.

I grab a tub and carry it inside my apartment so he won't see my blush.

In the five minutes Jack's gone, I manage to drag the remaining boxes and bags from the hallway into my apartment. Moving in the summer is particularly awful. A thin sheen of sweat has formed on my body, and I peel off my T-shirt, tossing it away, and pull the bottom of my tank top up and down, fanning my torso.

"No air-conditioning?" Jack's voice startles me, and I jump, dropping my shirt.

"No. I'll have to look at getting a unit in."

"Do you like big units?"

"Well, a tiny one wouldn't do it…"

"Big ones are better for doing it."

My apartment's dinky but will need more than a small air conditioner. "For sure. I mean, mine's pretty tiny, but it would still need…"

He bites the inside of his cheek and raises his eyebrows.

When he said *unit*, he was referring to… "Oh my God, so not what I meant!"

"Sure. And this?" He nods at the bag in his hands.

"I want it on the bed." For crying out loud, am I capable of speaking without everything sounding like a "that's what she said" joke? "In the bedroom is fine." A giant, throbbing innuendo…

What is wrong with me? This is Jack, my friend. *Only* my friend for reasons. Shaking my head, I shift a blue tub with my kitchen stuff into the tiny kitchen and move one from there into the equally tiny bathroom. On the way back, I trip over a bag and slam my leg into the corner of a box.

"Nice one, Grace."

"Shut up." I hiss through my teeth while rubbing my shin. "Ouch."

"Are you bleeding?" He squats in front of me, cradling my calf to pull my leg closer. It's tight quarters, and I can smell him—something fresh but mixed with his sweat. My mouth waters. Would I be able to taste it on his skin?

His fingertips graze the sensitive skin behind my knee.

Jesus. He's never touched my bare skin there before. It's just my calf. How can that make me feel…restless and unfulfilled?

He traces the skin around the injury with a fingertip. "The skin's broken, but it's just the first layer. Nothing serious."

Tell that to my pulse, which is doing a splendid imitation of a jackhammer.

"Yeah." My voice is raspy. "Nothing serious."

His gaze crawls up my shin to my thigh, my torso, my eyes.

Oh, he knows what this is doing to me.

Deliberately, he slides his hand up my thigh before letting go. Then he stands and licks his lips, eyes locked on mine.

Now I'm covered with goose bumps, suddenly feverish with wanting his hands on my body again—and not wanting to let him leave my apartment until we're sweaty for another reason. The intensity of the attraction I feel for him spreads through me from cell to cell like a virus. Liking him is deadly because I can't feel this for him, can't want him this much.

His fingers tangle in my hair and lift my face.

I shouldn't be taking a step toward him, grabbing the front of his shirt, and pulling him closer like this.

He crushes his body to me as his lips gently meet mine as if this means something. His tongue teases my lips open and eases inside my mouth, and when it touches my tongue, I shudder and clutch at him, desperate to pull him closer when I should be pushing him away.

But his hands are gentle, his lips are firm, and his tongue strokes mine in ways that dissolve rational thought and all the bones in my body. He tastes like peppermint and the last lover I can imagine ever wanting again because no one has kissed me like this—and I want more. I want it all.

He wraps me in his arms and squeezes. I stretch up, allowing more of my body to press against his, then wrap my arms around his neck and gently grind my hips against his. One of his hands slips down my side and around to palm my breast, lifting and gently kneading it through my shirt and bra. He's already hard.

He breaks the kiss, and I'm left breathless, but then he pushes me against the wall and pins my hands above my head—and who the hell needs air anyway?

I arch against him, pressing my breasts against his chest, trying to ease the ache as he nibbles my earlobe and kisses his way down my collarbone, releasing my hands to palm my breasts.

I trail my hands under his shirt and over the cut ridges of his abs. He pulls one of my thighs up, pressing against my core, making me moan in his mouth when his lips find mine again. His mouth is everything.

God, I can't wait. This is going to be so damn good. We'll have amazing sex, and then…what? Live happily ever after? I tip my head back to give him better access to the tender flesh of my neck.

Shut up, brain.

He'll be going out a few nights a week to work, where he'll be surrounded by chicks like Rhonda Lavee, who have no compunctions about sleeping with guys in relationships. He'll be surrounded by women only too happy to jump his bones in the coatroom—last names not necessary. Jack's sexy as hell, and his track record doesn't vouch for his ability to say no to temptation. The longest relationship he's had was three months, if that.

But with his hands on me, I don't care if he can't be trusted. I just want more and more. And that's the part that scares me into sanity.

I tear myself away from him and stumble a little. He reaches out to steady me, but I right myself.

"What's wrong?"

I push my shaking hands through my hair and try to think unsexy thoughts. "We can't do this."

"What, kiss?"

I want nothing more than for him to press me against the wall and kiss away my protests. "No. Yes. We can't do anything."

He drags his lower lip through his teeth. "Why? The attraction between us is insane. And based on that kiss, I'd say we feel the same way about each other."

"It's not as simple as that!"

"Then what is it?"

"It's…" Best to just forge ahead with the truth so he knows where we stand. "I'm not looking for a random hookup."

"Neither am I."

"Please. Does the nickname DJ Madhead mean anything to you?"

He frowns. "That was years ago."

"Either way." No need to get into my cheating mother, my dad's heart attacks, and my refusal to be broken the same way. "We're friends."

"And that fucking hot kiss changes nothing?"

"No." Even though I keep my voice gentle, he flinches like I've slapped him. "I'm so sorry. I shouldn't have let it happen. I never meant to lead you on."

"So because I have a bit of a past, we can't date at all?"

"A bit of a past? Your nickname is DJ Madhead because eight girls lined up to give you blow jobs in the DJ booth at a gig!"

"It wasn't eight. It was more like four."

"That *so* doesn't make it better, Jack."

"I was twenty-one when that happened. We hadn't even met yet. I've been tested, and I'm clean, if that's what you're worried about."

My heart sinks. Because no matter what he says, it's still not over. To this day he has a group of fangirls who stalk him from gig to gig—including a girl who slept with my ex while we were dating. The fact that it's all these years later and he's still happy to be the life of the party says it all. "I can't just be another of your girls."

"If I could take that back, I would, but I can't."

I didn't want to tell him the whole truth. "It's not just that. You've been doing the same thing since we met."

"So?"

"You play other people's music for a living, and you're really good at it. I do like you, but I need a grown-up—not one of the Lost Boys who refuses to put his toys away."

"Is that how you see me?" He leans against the wall with a dazed expression.

My rationalizations are harsh, but I lay them all out there. "You're not the relationship guy. You're the fun guy, the wild ride. It's better for us both if we skip a relationship that ultimately will go nowhere. I want more than a good time." Mom was always chasing what she thought was a more exciting man than Dad. I had a front-row seat and had to watch as she wrecked our family and literally broke my dad's heart. I refuse to go through it myself. "I'm too old for roller coasters. I need stability."

"That's bullshit. If I'd known that your only objection was money—"

"I'm not looking for a sugar daddy. The kind of stability I'm talking about has nothing to do with money. I need to know I can trust someone. I need a man who takes things seriously."

"And I don't?" He crosses his arms.

"You party for a living."

"Is that all that's standing in the way? Because you think I don't take life seriously?" He raises his chin. "What would you say if I told you I bought the brownstone I live in three years ago?"

"What? But what about your neighbor downstairs?" Jack has the upstairs of a modernized brownstone. The downstairs is a separate suite with an elderly man for a renter—perfect for Jack because the man is hard of hearing and doesn't complain when Jack spins records at home.

Jack shrugs. "I let him stay because his rent nearly covers the mortgage payments and because he's eighty-three with nowhere to go. His useless son barely visits him. There's no way I'd kick him out."

That's surprisingly sweet, but I'm stuck on the fact that Jack owns his brownstone. Those things are worth millions. I had assumed he'd lucked out with rent control when Pete had helped him move. (I hadn't been able to get the day off to help.) "Why didn't Pete ever say anything?"

Jack shrugs. "It wasn't important. My assets are nobody else's business. And that club we were at the other week? Frisk? I'm a co-owner."

With the rooftop patio? Jack actually owns his place *and* a business? Maybe *I'm* the Lost Boy here. "As of when?"

"Six months ago."

"Wait. You're a business owner?" The staff had been deferential to Jack, but I'd thought it was because they were friends and liked him because he DJs there a lot. "Why didn't I know that? You haven't changed anything about your life."

"Why would I? That's not who I am."

"So those women who kept coming up to you on the rooftop patio?"

"Employees."

He has employees. What the sparkling fuck? When did Jack, the man-whore DJ, become a responsible adult with more going for him than I do?

Whatever. I'm letting myself get distracted from the point. He may own a business, but he hasn't *really* changed a thing about his life. The girls are still there. He's still the life of every party. And the fact that I didn't know about all of this just proves that he's about as open as a Chinese puzzle box. "I'm happy for you, but it doesn't change anything."

He shakes his head. "There's no arguing with you, is there? You've made up your mind about me."

I don't say anything. Jack sets the elevator key on my counter. "I'll take the stairs."

Too many emotions buzz beneath my skin, but I don't want him to leave, not like this. "Jack, I just can't. You're—"

"I'm not your fucking mom. Grow up."

I get a nice view of his back and then the inside of my door as he leaves me in my lonely, new apartment.

I would flop morosely to the floor, but there's no room with all the boxes. Not enough room to pace either. Frustrated, I kick a box, but that only hurts my toe.

I'm all keyed up, but he's gone, and I don't really know what happened—except that he's not quite what I thought he was.

Maybe I'm not either. I'm an asshole, but I can't be completely wrong about him. Maybe he's doing better than I thought he was, but he's still partying for a living. Surrounded by flashing lights and women sipping drinks while shaking their tits at him. That's not work. That's a commercial selling a fantasy—and I'm not buying it. Sooner or later the lights come on, and you have to wake up and see the harsh light of day.

And if he can't trust me enough to tell me *anything* about himself, how I can trust him not to stray?

I focus on unpacking, but two hours later, my body's still humming with tension and my throat aches from thirst.

Needing to take my mind off things, I unpack my computer and sponge off the neighbor's Wi-Fi, signing on to Missed Connections as quickly as I can to take

my mind off Jack. By the time I open my browser, my
hands shake on the mouse.

Where Are You?

I double-click.

I'm looking for you. Blond hair, blue eyes—

Not me then—I'm a brunette with hazel eyes. I close
them now, regret washing over me at the look on Jack's
face when he left. I came off like a judgmental bitch.
Pushing away the shame, I focus on the next ad.

The tattoos on your legs were amazing, but the one
on your pinky finger drove me wild.

The places where Jack touched my body suddenly
tingle. Wild? His hands drove me three blocks past teen-
age fangirl insane.

I hate how all I want is more.

You can't have more. He left for a reason.

I shake my head and click on the next Missed Connection.

It's a vain attempt to distract me from how shitty I feel
about the things I said to Jack.

And the discomforting fact that maybe I really don't
know him at all. The worst part is that now I may have
ruined our friendship as well.

Chapter 8

OUR MAIN CLIENT BASE IS MADE UP OF HIPSTER-yuppies—a fairly new breed of people who are a mixture of crunchy granola and corporate successes. A perfect blend of both worlds, becoming more common as the world turns more corporate and greener at the same time. You can find them riding their bikes to work in their suits and getting baristas to pour seven-dollar coffees into fancy eco-friendly thermoses. They're about the environment, not spirituality like Ziggy and Fern, and boy, do they care about money… as I learned when Ziggy overrode my scheduling and double-booked two of them this morning. They took turns bitching about the egregious waste of their time and money for ten minutes.

The days that suck the worst are when Ziggy decides to try his hand at reception. Without supervision, he'll check the messages—and he always screws them up. Unless I want to spend hours trying to decipher Ziggy's messages or search the schedule and hope I stumble upon the change, I'm forced to wait for Ziggy to reappear and tell me what his hippie shorthand means. But before that, he'll come out and wonder why I haven't dealt with the messages yet, as though I should just know what he meant by a misspelled name and nine digits of a phone number.

Unfortunately, last week when I responded that one of the scheduling conflicts was not my doing, I got a lecture about being defensive. Judging by Ziggy's and Fern's reactions, being defensive is one of the worst things you can be. I thought being a shitty secretary was worse. Apparently not.

At the law firm, I was responsible for drafting and filing contracts that were worth millions of dollars. It was stressful, but the work I did was important. That, and the partners I worked with didn't screw up my efforts and then treat me like an idiot when things went wrong. If you caused a problem, you copped to it, simple as that.

The fact that Fern and Ziggy care more about an agitated tone than the truth is highly aggravating. Tiny bubbles of annoyance float through me, but there's nothing I can do. Even if I know better and my way is more efficient, Ziggy is the boss, and it's his place. At the end of the day, what he says goes.

Though sometimes, I'd like to punch him right in the aura.

The laundry leaves too much time with my mind unoccupied. I haven't been able to get Jack's kiss out of my head. He has no idea how close I came to shoving him into my bedroom and then breaking in the apartment one room at a time. He's definitely better off financially than I imagined, but he's found a way to party for a living. He's still not a safe dating prospect, but even if he were, I'm pretty sure he's never going to talk to me again. I should have softened my words.

Morosely, I toss the last towel onto the shelf and head back to my desk to fill out Ziggy's next client's receipt so it's ready to go when they're done. I fucked up. Even though I have my reasons, I owe Jack a huge apology.

Phyllis is curled up in a chair in the corner. She clears her throat as soon as I sit down. "Um…" I can feel that she wants me to ask what's up, but I hate people trying to pique my interest that way. Besides, the other day, she started talking about her sex life in way too much detail and didn't even stop when clients started coming in. It was super awkward.

I was only nodding and not actively encouraging the conversation, but it still looked like we were both discussing inappropriate things at work—something Fern lectured me about later at length. She practically snarled at me when I told her the conversation had been one-sided.

More of me being defensive.

I sucked it up and apologized, and she promptly brought up her workshop again as a better place to "explore and learn."

"Uh, Sarah?" Phyllis finally gets tired of waiting for me to ask what's up.

"Yes?" I keep typing the promotional poster Fern asked me to create.

"My name is spelled wrong in the receipt book."

That's odd; I don't usually make mistakes like that. "I'm sorry to hear that. Tear that page out and start a fresh one." I change the font on the poster, aiming for something more whimsical.

"It's on every page."

"What?" Insurance companies look for any excuse not to pay out, and I'm always super careful about forms. But mistakes happen; maybe I did screw it up. I finally give her my full attention.

She moves to the desk and thrusts the book in my face. "See?"

I take it and hold it at a more comfortable distance. Sure enough, when I flip through, I see that the name I printed on each page is spelled the same. I double-check it against the spelling on her schedule on the computer, and it's the same. That means it's incorrect there as well. "Spell your last name for me."

"*H-e-n-d-e-r-s-e-n.*"

That's what I wrote, and what's on the computer. "Phyllis, that's what's printed on every page in the receipt book."

She rolls her eyes. "Not the printed name. The signature. It's spelled wrong."

Is she fucking with me, pranking the new girl? "Uh, you're the one who signed them." I wait for her to laugh and tell me she "got me."

Her glare is glassy and condescending. "Why would I sign my own name wrong?"

"I have no idea."

"I wouldn't do that. No one would."

Does she seriously not remember signing her own name on every page? It was only a few days ago. "I don't sign the sheets. I don't normally even fill in the therapist's name and RMT number. If you remember, you're the one who had me do that for you, but I never signed your name." I stop talking as she rips the book from my hands and stalks back to her chair.

"Well, you did it this time and did it wrong." She flips through. "It's every page, Sarah."

What is her problem? Maybe if I prompt her, she'll laugh and realize her mistake. "I know. But that's not my writing."

"Well, it certainly isn't mine!" she snaps. "What's your agenda?"

"My what?"

Her eyes narrow. "Are you trying to get me fired or something?"

"Why would I do that?"

"Why would you sign my name wrong in the book?"

"I didn't! You did!"

She laughs and shakes her head. "I'm onto you. If you're trying to intimidate me, it's not going to work." She steps up to the counter and looms over me. "I'm telling you right now, I'm here to stay. Better bitches than you have tried and failed to get rid of me, because you know what? Ziggy and Fern love me. I've got them wrapped around my little finger."

"Phyllis, you were the one who signed your name wrong. You signed your name on each page and left the rest for me to do."

She sneers. "Everyone knows the massage therapists are the ones who are supposed to fill out the receipt books. You just enter the amounts and the clients' names. And the date. And yet *you* filled it out and messed it up."

"But you made me. Are you serious right now?" My hands shake from frustration.

She opens her mouth to speak, but the phone rings and cuts her off. "You'd better get that. Be a shame for you to lose your job like the last receptionist." With a wink, she sashays into one of the massage rooms.

I take a deep breath, hoping my voice won't shake when I answer. "Inner Space, Sarah speaking."

"How's my little girl?"

"Dad?" He never calls me at work. "What's wrong? Are you okay?"

"I'm fine, sweetheart. Sorry to call you at your job. I know employers hate that."

"It's fine. I can talk for a minute. What's up?"

"Well…" He hesitates for a long moment. "I hate to put you out, but there's been a bit of a mix-up. I need my prescription and can't get it."

"Why can't Mom get it for you?"

"Uh… She's pretty busy right now." I know that tone of voice. He's covering for her.

My parents downsized and moved to Jersey to pay for the hospital bills after Dad's last heart attack, but they have their own transportation. "Can't you take the car?"

"Your mother's got it."

I sag in my chair, suddenly feeling tired. "She left you and took the car?"

"No, no. She was just going to your aunt's for a while. I thought I had more pills than I do. It's my fault, really."

Tears sting my eyes and I can only shake my head, hating that this is his life. "Which pharmacy and when do you need them?"

He gives me the address. "Is Tuesday okay?"

That means he probably only has enough for Monday but doesn't want to put me out.

"I'll get them and stop by Monday."

"Thank you. I really appreciate it, honey."

I hate the gratitude in his voice. My mom should be doing this for him, being his safe place to fall, taking care of him so he's not so stressed out. He needs a real partner instead of my irresponsible mother who's more concerned with finding a good time than being his wife—and my mother. This is why I can't let myself fall for someone like Jack. "Love you, Dad."

"I love you too."

Chapter 9

Starbucks Beauty

I'VE STARTED GOING TO STARBUCKS AGAIN — AFTER work or on days off only, because I took a cup into work once and got a lecture about the evils of big corporations and the consumer's responsibility of only purchasing fair-trade coffee beans.

> Long blond hair. You were checking your Facebook on your Mac.

Not me then. Can't a brunette catch a break?

> You are unbelievable, but I saw the guy in the orange jacket pick you up. I'm not into splitting up couples so I kept to myself. Hope to see you there again.

Interesting how he wants to see her again, if only from a distance. I can't decide if that's stalker-ish or romantic.

Sexy Neighbor

I just moved—what if someone saw me and fell in

love? I may have seen him in the elevator or in the lobby where we get our mail. It could be so romantic if we've been eyeing each other for a while. But if he's a creeper, he could be pressing his ear to our shared wall right now. For once I'm hoping it's not me in the post.

To the sexy woman next door. I've wanted you for over nine months now.

It's not me. Relieved, I read on, now curious.

But we're both married, so I must admire you from afar. We're both home during the day. You are on oxygen. You saw me recycling a lot of "special magazines." Reply with your dog's name if you want to see what could happen between us.

What the flaming fuck? My fingers take me back to the menu, and I scroll down, trying to find one that doesn't sound so strange.

Then, stepping from the computer, I head to my kitchen and pour a glass of ice-cold milk so I can dunk a white chocolate macadamia nut cookie. There's a fancy grocery store on the same block as Inner Space, and while I can't afford most of their prices, their bakery is worth it. Since moving out of Pete's, my diet has been pretty lackluster. I miss his cooking almost as much as I miss him.

It's sad how eager I've been for Saturday all week. The hippies are doing one of Fern's courses, so I get Monday off as well—a much-needed mental break from Inner Space. Realizing how tense my shoulders are, I

decide to head to the bathroom for a hot shower before
my second cup of tea.

Dad's prescription can't be filled until Monday
morning, so I'll pick his pills up and take them to him
Monday afternoon, just in case. It wouldn't be the first
time he didn't have enough and went without for a day
or two, worried about inconveniencing me—which is
ridiculous. I would do anything for him.

The water gently pounds the knots from my shoulders
and back, but it's way too hot, so I turn it down to tepid
after a few minutes. Being a paralegal had me chained
to a desk, which is hard on the body, but I wasn't doing
load after load of laundry all day like I am now. It's the
folding that sucks more than anything, but I'm faster at
it than when I started. Not only that, but I'm constantly
navigating unfamiliar territory, worried about what mis-
step I'm going to make.

My wardrobe, my opinions on feminism, dryer
sheets, and dishwashers… More often than not, I have to
be on full alert for potential land mines with my bosses.
Despite my research into energy work, I don't know the
rules yet, and Ziggy and Fern are so different from me.
They've noticed my tension and encouraged me to get
massages from them, but the thought of either of my
bosses or my coworkers getting me naked and rubbing
away my tension weirds me out. Some lines can't be
crossed, and I'd like to keep it professional.

Maybe not with yummy Blake…but he's still a
coworker and off-limits. Why are all the guys I could be
into off-limits to me?

I dry off before wrapping the towel around my hair
and walking to my bedroom naked. Another perk of

living alone. Not that Pete would have cared, but I'm not an exhibitionist. Besides, just because you're besties doesn't mean you need to parade around naked in front of each other. There's such a thing as *oversharing*.

I have three glorious, hippie-free days before me, and I'm going to yoga-pant my way through them like a boss. I pad back to my computer, now dressed, and look through the job postings for something a little better suited to me, but there's still nothing.

Might as well head back to my favorite place.

Eye Contact Extraordinaire

A hot guy in a business suit totally eye-fucked me at the bodega last night.

I was caught in your gaze as we left the movie theater last night.

Not me. Damn.

Maybe we can share popcorn and our own matinee sometime. Tell me what movie we saw and what I was drinking.

I like how people leave instructions like this, but sometimes they're so vague I doubt the person involved would remember, even if they were interested. "We met at the Summit bar. You had a brunette friend; I had a friend with a green hat. Would have loved to get to know you better. Tell me what my friend was drinking." Like, what the hell is that? I pay attention to what people *say*, not what they drink. Especially strangers. And if I like you, I'm not paying attention to your friends in minute detail—though, if two people were really into each other, I'm sure there'd be other ways of establishing identity.

I move on to the next ad.

Not too late for us. It's been way too long since I've gotten to use your nickname. We keep going around and around, breaking up and reuniting.

Not me then; I don't recycle exes—they're exes for a reason.

So many amazing memories. There could be so many more if you'd let me back in. You'd be proud to know I haven't crashed my way into any cabbies this year. Every day, I wake up hoping to find you on my doorstep, knocking to get back into my life.

Next!

If Only You Knew

There are a lot of ads like this, from someone the person knows. A lot are from strangers, but the ones where the admirer is someone in their life really make me sad. To go through life wanting someone you know to the point that you'd write a Missed Connection makes my heart hurt a little for them. They have different reasons for not declaring their love, but at the end of the day, the longing is what gets to me. Sort of like with me and Jack.

I push him from my mind and read on.

Hopefully you find a piece of happiness. I hope that
lying to me was worth it. You took advantage of
me, Jill.

Oh, *so* not what I thought this was going to be. What
did Jill lie about?

You are everything they said you are, and I hate that
they were right, and I hate that it took me this long to
see that about you. Good-bye, bitch.

Wow. I doubt Jill will ever see this, but ouch.

I reach for my drink, then realize I finished my milk
before my shower. Someone knocks on my front door
just as I grab the milk and bite into another cookie. Damn
it. The relaxation my hot shower bought me evaporates,
and my shoulders tense up again.

The worst thing about working reception is that when
the phone rings, I have to get it. When someone comes
in, *I'm* the one who has to rush back and deal with them.
I have to jump at the whims of other people even when
someone else is standing right there and could grab that
phone themselves.

But that's my job. I'm away from the office now.

Can I just not answer? Pretend no one's home? I'm
not expecting anyone, so technically, I don't have to
open my door. Ever. Or answer the phone. That's it!
I'll stand here quietly eating cookies until whoever it
is gets tired of waiting and goes the hell away. Relief
fills me.

Being a receptionist is giving me social anxiety.

More knocking. "Sarah, open up."

Jack? I take a step in one direction, then another, and another, smoothing my hair and brushing crumbs from my mouth before I remember I'm not supposed to care what Jack thinks I look like. Why is he here? Curiosity wins out and I open the door.

Why does he have to be so sexy? Why? *Damn you, summer!* Jack is wearing a pair of worn jeans and a bright-white tank top that shows off his tanned, muscular arms. *He* is my type. The way his physique is muscular but lean so his muscles seem casual and dangerous, instead of the result of spending hours at the gym. And then there are his stupid cheekbones and dark-blue eyes and his silky brown hair that I want to use to pull his mouth toward mine… "Jack."

"Hey."

I nod at the box in his arms, using the opportunity to ogle his biceps. "What's that?"

"A few things you left at Pete's. He asked me to bring it over." He hands me the box.

"Come in." I hold the door for him with my foot. I still remember the way his lips felt on mine, the way he seemed to focus every cell in his body on me, on joining together in that kiss like it was the only thing he was meant to be doing for the rest of his life.

Then the words I said to him crash over me, and I feel awful all over again. "Jack, I'm sorry for the things I said to you." I don't mean to blurt it out, but every syllable is sincere. "I was an asshole." I clutch the box. "It's all my shit, you know? Issues because of my parents and their fucked-up relationship, but that's no excuse. I wanted to tell you I'm sorry. For everything. No qualifiers or buts. I just want us to be okay."

He gives me a small nod. "We're okay."

Relief makes my legs shake. "I was just having milk and cookies. You want?"

The look in his eyes burns my skin, but it disappears beneath a friendly smile. "Sure, I could stay for a cookie."

For a cookie—meaning there's somewhere he needs to be, or he's making it clear that there's an expiration date on this visit. Maybe I'm not completely forgiven, but he's giving me a chance to be friends again. Whatever it means, I'll take it.

"Pete says hi."

I step past him into the kitchen. "Yeah, I'll text him later. We're hanging out on Monday. I get the day off because the hippies are doing a course."

"Ah, yeah. So."

"So."

Neither of us says anything for a moment. He bites the corner of his mouth, and I'm filled with the urge to feel his teeth on my lip. My manners show up then. "Thanks for bringing me my stuff."

"Sure. I was in the neighborhood anyway."

"Help yourself to a cookie. Glasses are in the left cupboard. Or there's juice in the fridge if you'd rather." While Jack grabs a glass, I fold back a flap to see what I left at Pete's—I was sure I'd brought everything—and grin at the Tupperware container of his killer taco salad that he's placed on the top. "Awesome."

"Food?"

"Yeah. Taco salad."

"Nice."

I move the container to the fridge and look in the box again. Next, I pull out a half-used bottle of shampoo. Pete's hypercritical of my brand, saying it's not up to his high standards and salon quality, but I love the black cherries and vanilla smell of the cheaper brand. Perfect and not sickly sweet. Beneath the shampoo is a plastic grocery bag tied with three knots. I can't undo them, so I tear the bag.

A couple pairs of panties fall to the floor. Thankfully they are pretty ones, but my face heats in a slow burn as I bend to retrieve them before Jack does and stuff them back into the box.

He says nothing, only grabs a cookie and takes a bite. "What are you up to today?"

"Not a lot. Just hanging out."

"Job hunting online?" He points to my computer, and I blush harder, but luckily the writing is tiny and he can't see that it's not an ad for a job.

"Yeah, I need to see what else is out there."

"Things not working out at Inner Space?"

"It feels like a waste of my degree, and there's no real opportunity for advancement." I grab another cookie. "I mean, it's okay for now. Other than them being slightly crazy hippies."

"There's that. Pete was telling me about Phyllis."

Of course I'd told Pete about Phyllis and the receipt book. It was too crazy not to. "Yeah, it's nuts. That one's not playing with a full deck. But a job's a job."

"True." He nods and sips.

Nothing was casual about us the last time he stood here. I've apologized and he's forgiven me, but I can't stop thinking about that kiss. Maybe it means more to me than him. Maybe it was better for me than it was for him.

Do I even measure up to the other women he's been with? He's a sexy club owner with impeccable taste in music and rock-hard abs. Women swarm all over him. Irrationally, I want to prove that I'm just as good as they are.

But mostly I'm horny as hell and he's my sexual kryptonite, but neither of those reasons justifies ruining our friendship for a quick roll in the sack. Unable to think of anything else to talk about, I grab my glass, and we stand a couple of feet apart, sipping milk and drowning in all the words we're not saying.

My phone rings, and I jump to answer it, thankful for the break from the silence. "Hello?"

"Sarah." Fern's voice is flatter than usual.

"Hey, Fern. How are you?" *My boss*, I mouth to Jack.

"We have a little issue."

My heart falls. "What's happening?"

"There's a problem with the receipt book."

Oh, that. "Ah, yes. Phyllis's right?"

"Oh good, you're aware of it. Though I'd have preferred you come to me with it, instead of waiting for me to discover the problem."

"I didn't know about it right away either, but—"

"So would you rather pay us for the book when you come in next, or just have us deduct the cost from your next check?"

My face stiffens from shock. "What?"

Jack sets his glass down with a concerned expression.

Fern sighs. "For the receipt book."

I don't want Jack to hear this, so I slip into my bedroom and close the door. "Why would I have to pay for the receipt book?"

A heavy sigh. "Sarah, I'm getting a lot of tension and defensiveness from you right now."

My nails cut into my palm. "I'm sorry, Fern, but I don't understand why I have to pay to replace a receipt book that Phyllis wrecked."

"Sarah, the writing in the book is yours."

"The writing is, but the signature isn't." My voice rises despite my efforts to keep it calm.

"Why would you write in Phyllis' book?"

"She had me do it after she signed it."

"I doubt that she'd make you do anything. Besides, I find it hard to believe that Phyllis would spell her name wrong on every single page."

Not hard to believe if your head isn't lodged up your...root chakra. "You can even ask Ziggy. He knows about it. I'm not denying I filled in the rest of the information. But I did not sign her name, and I certainly didn't sign it wrong."

"I've just got a horrible feeling about the whole situation. Maybe we made a mistake with you. I don't want to deal with another employee who is just out for herself and filled with defensive energy. It's very prickly and hard to be around."

"You'd seriously fire me over a receipt book I didn't even ruin? But I—"

"If you're going to continue to be so defensive, there isn't going to be a place at Inner Space for you."

My legs feel hollow, and I sit on the bed. I can't lose this job when I haven't found anything else out there.

So I swallow back the outrage, burning with righteous indignation. "No, you're right. I'm sorry, Fern. Just deduct it from my check." It can't be more than, like, twelve bucks for one of those receipt books. It's the principle of the thing that makes me want to scream, but Phyllis was right about one thing—she knows how to work Fern and Ziggy.

And I can't get even with her if I'm fired.

"Good girl. I'm so glad we cleared the air about this. And I'm all for taking initiative, but you shouldn't have filled out the rest of her information either. That's the responsibility of the therapists so that things like this don't happen."

My teeth are gritted so hard my jaw aches. "I hear you. I won't overstep my bounds again."

"Great. Oh, and I'm going to need you to come in tomorrow."

"On a Sunday?" I swear I can feel her disapproval radiating through the phone, so I ask brightly, "What time?"

"Four o'clock—but just for a few minutes to talk to Blake. Ziggy booked a new client with him, but he can't remember if he put it in the schedule. Or told Blake about it."

Damn it. Blake goes by the online employee schedule alone, so if he wasn't told and it's not in the system, then he won't show up. And there's no guarantee he'd see a note left out for him. "You can't phone him?"

"We're not at the office anymore."

And you can't mosey back there? "And you don't have an employee contact information list at home?" Silence. "Ah, I see. What was the new patient's name?"

"Ziggy can't remember the last name." Of course not.

"But he remembers her first name. Janine. Or Jolene. Maybe Jennifer."

"And the appointment is tomorrow?"

"Either for tomorrow or next Sunday. He can't recall."

"I'll take care of it." At least it's only for a few minutes.

"And we'll need you to go in from nine until five on Monday as well. Actually, nine until six."

My three-day holiday is swiftly evaporating. "I thought you gave me the day off."

"Right, but if clients call to book, it would be best to have a real, live person answering the phones even if we're gone. It shows them we're always available to them. And you don't normally get three-day weekends, so you're not really missing out on anything."

Disregarding that since I have to go fix Ziggy's screw-up, I'm not even getting a two-day weekend—and I have to take Dad's pills to him. He called in the prescription, but I couldn't get there before they closed on Friday. I won't be able to pick his pills up if I'm working nine to six since his tiny pharmacy closes at six on Mondays. "Fern, I can't. I have to pick up my dad's pills and get them to him."

"We don't support big pharmaceuticals. He should really find a homeopathic tincture or something holistic instead."

"They're for his *heart*," I snap. "Aromatherapy or a soothing chant isn't going to cut it!"

"We prefer if you keep your home issues at home to avoid clouding your work energy."

"But—"

"Sarah."

I blow out a breath. "It's fine. I'll take a cab there during my lunch break."

"Oh, you can't leave during your break. Since you

won't really be taking care of clients, you may have lunch at your desk, but we want you there the whole day."

"But his pills—"

"Be there Monday at 9:00 a.m. and stay until 6:00, or don't bother coming in again."

She hangs up without bothering to hear my reply.

I turn my phone off. What am I going to do? They'll be able to check the electronic records for the security system, so they'll know when I disarm and arm it. I can't leave the place open and go to get the pills. Especially since an hour is optimistic for traveling to the pharmacy at that time of day.

Bitter tears of frustration slip down my cheeks. I'm barely breathing, not wanting to make a sound and cry in front of Jack. I just got things back on track; I can't let anyone know how perilously close everything is to going off the rails now. I have no choice but to make this job work.

Like that saying goes, would you rather be right or happy? Only in my case, it's would I rather be right or employed. I'm going to renew my efforts to find a new job though. I've been a bit complacent about finding something else these past few weeks, but if this call was anything to go on, I'm not as "in" as I thought I was— and Fern and Ziggy are not as good as I thought they were. Naomi was right. I scrub my face. Jack won't be here more than a few minutes. I only have to hold it together until he leaves. Then I'll be pathetic for a few minutes and sort this out. If that's possible.

One more deep breath and I stride into the kitchen like nothing's bothering me. "Sorry about that." I busy myself turning on the water in the sink and fussing with the two dishes that are in there like they need to be washed *now*.

He sets his glass down. "What's wrong?"

"Nothing, I just have a lot to do this weekend. Thanks for bringing the box."

"Sarah."

My face heats up, and I let out the breath I'm holding. "If you could show yourself out, that would be—"

"Stop it." His hands stroke my upper arms, and his body heat warms my back. "Tell me what happened."

Tears of frustration leak from my eyes despite my efforts to hold them back. "I hate them so much, Jack." My voice cracks on his name and he turns me around, pulling me close.

His arms wrap around me, blocking out the frustration and shading everything except his warmth and scent. "What happened?"

I summarize the phone call while sniveling into his chest.

He gives me a squeeze. "No problem. You quit working for those soulless pricks, and I'll give you a job at my club."

My heart soars for a moment before crashing back to reality. "No, that feels like running away. Besides, what am I going to do at your club? I can't bartend or serve. Dishwashers don't make enough money to sustain me, and I haven't got the upper-body strength to be a bouncer."

"You'll be my new all-star DJ."

"Jack."

"You're so fucking stubborn."

"You know I'm right." I pull back. "And I can't let Phucking Phyllis beat me."

He sighs. "Then you go to work Monday, and I'll pick up your dad's pills and take them to him in Bambi."

Bambi is the old Civic Jack has had forever and parks in a private lot that charges more than the car is worth. He and Pete christened it Bambi after an unfortunate road trip upstate in high school when they discovered the car was a deer magnet. The deer were fine, but Bambi still has dents. "I can't ask you to do that."

"You're not. I'm offering." He strokes my hair. "No, I'm *telling* you. You go to work for those assholes, and I'll sort out the rest for your dad. And you will come home and look for a new job where the bosses aren't evil assholes."

Sinking back into his hug, I wallow in the comfort for a few seconds. I've missed this. I've missed having someone to give me a hug when I've had a shitty day— someone to talk to who isn't a phone call away. But it's not just missing a warm body. It's Jack.

This feels really domestic for the guy I normally see across a crowded dance floor—and I like it. The fact that his biceps are on display doesn't hurt either.

Kiss me, Jack. Just do it. "You're a great friend, Jack. Thank you."

He rubs my back and steps away. "No thanks needed."

"Hang on." I text him the address of the pharmacy. "It's all paid for, ready for pickup. Thank you so much. For the job offer too."

"Let me know if you change your mind. We'll figure something out. See you later."

I walk him to the door. "Bye."

Feelings other than gratitude bump against themselves, knocking around inside my heart as Jack walks away.

I close the door and lock it.

Chapter 10

THE LIGHTS ARE ON AND THE SECURITY SYSTEM IS disarmed when I step into the clinic at three fifty on Sunday afternoon, cranky from the heat and the annoying number of assholes on Citi Bikes who I had to dodge on the way over. It's Sunday—I should be lounging around without a bra on, but instead…

An attractive redhead is filling out paperwork. My computer is on as well, and I open Blake's schedule and see the name of the new patient.

"Dannica?"

She looks up. "Yes?"

"You're here to see Blake today?"

"Yes. He gave me the forms."

"Perfect. Just checking." I blot my upper lip with the back of my hand.

She smiles and goes back to the clipboard.

Ziggy was way off with her name. More annoyingly, I came here for nothing. Blake obviously has things under control, but I might as well stay and catch up on the last load of laundry from Friday night. I'm not eager to hop right back on the sweltering train either. At least it's reliably air-conditioned in here. Funny, dishwashers are the machinery of the devil, but Fern and Ziggy are fine with air-conditioning.

Maybe chakras spin better in colder climates.

The first thing that catches my eye when I enter the kitchen is Blake, bent over and pulling the last towel from the depths of the basket. Damn, that's a tight butt. "You're doing the laundry *again*? I think I might keep you."

He throws the towel into the washer and smiles at me over his shoulder. "Promises, promises. How are you?"

"I'm fine. You?"

"Pretty good. Not to seem rude, but why are you in today? I normally never see anyone."

I lean against the door frame. "Ah. Ziggy and Fern weren't sure if you knew about Dannica, so they asked me to come in and check."

"Why didn't they come in themselves?"

"Holiday. They went on a weekend retreat somewhere."

"Nice." His lips tweak into a wry smile.

"Yeah." I notice the load in the dryer is almost done. "Have you been here awhile?"

"Long enough to do some laundry."

"My shoulders thank you."

"Hey, if they're in bad shape…"

While the thought of him rubbing my tension out is actually appealing, it's appealing for the wrong reasons and would end up being an awkward situation. "Maybe another time."

"Let me know. I should get out there, see if Dannica's finished the intake."

"Yeah." I move to the sink to do some dishes that were

left after I cleaned on Friday, and Blake leaves. I hear the door to his room close as I dry the last cup and head back to the front desk. Blake is looking for something in the top left drawer and perks up when he sees me.

"Have you seen the label maker?"

"Yes." I pull it from the bottom desk drawer and hand it over.

"Thanks." He takes it with a wink and heads to the kitchen. I want a reason to follow to see what he's doing with the label maker, but I can't think of an excuse, so I sit and admire his butt as he walks away.

A moment later, the dryer's buzzer goes off, and I scurry to the kitchen. In Blake's hand is the special sugar for the teas. We keep it in a glass jar labeled "Fair-Trade Raw Sugar" so everyone knows how green and eco-friendly we are. I arch an eyebrow at him as I open the dryer door and pull out a towel. He turns the jar, and I immediately see no difference.

Then I realize that instead of saying "Fair-Trade Raw Sugar," the little red label says "Forced-Labor Raw Sugar."

"Forced-labor raw sugar?"

He scrunches up his face. "God, that label's been bugging me for months. Yeah, fair-trade sugar is such bullshit. Fair pay would be worth promoting. Frigging hippies."

I ugly-laugh at this unexpectedly delightful turn of events. Finally, an ally in this place. "And Gandhi forbid you bring in chocolate that isn't certified organic." I tap the jar. "You have no idea how much I love this. Why can't you work here full-time?"

He grins. "Too much of a good thing? Don't tell on me." He nods at the jar.

"No way. It's more fun this way."

He disappears into his client's room to get to work. I wonder how long it will take for the hippies to notice. But their anticipated reaction isn't even the coolest part—it's the inside joke, and also Blake changing the label in the first place. He didn't do it for a reaction; he just did it for the sake of doing it. He knows the label is there, and that is all that matters to him. That the label bugged him enough to bother creating a new one for his own peace of mind is one of the funniest things I've seen.

Oh, I could like Blake a lot.

I decide to wait until the load of towels is finished in the washer. I'll put them in the dryer and make a quick getaway to salvage the rest of the evening.

Might as well check out the Missed Connections while I'm here waiting. I normally wouldn't surf the Internet at work, but since the hippies called me in on my day off for no reason, I feel a certain degree of latitude is warranted.

It was that look in your eyes.

I look at lots of people.

It's uncommonly rare to find a woman in passing who will give you direct eye contact. Most avert their gazes, denying the smallest, yet most important connection two people can share.

Okay so far.

You walked in the north entrance of Fairway, and our eyes met.

Not me.

I guess it's true though. I don't look strangers in the eye for long, not wanting to encourage an unwanted interaction. Some guys skip being assertive and land in aggressive, and I'd rather avoid the awkward moment when I have to convince a guy I'm really not interested. The catcalling is especially out of hand now that it's hot out. If one more strange man tells me to smile, I swear to God...

You, Polka Dots

I wore polka dots last week.

So just a few minutes ago at the deli at 3rd and 34th, you, polka-dot miniskirt, and I shared a long look. Wanted to get closer to you in line, but it didn't happen. I left with another long look to see what would happen. Polka Dots, if you read this, we should do something about it.

Kind of cute how he calls her Polka Dots, but definitely not me.

Daniel. Barber. Nose Ring.

This one's just someone looking for their old barber because they went to the shop and got a "mediocre haircut from someone else." Guess I'm spoiled to have Pete at my beck and call when it comes to my hair.

For the Third Week in a Row

Could be about my transit habits.

For the third time in three weeks, the shower in the gym was crowded and my penis was the smallest. Needed to get that off my chest.

I snort, laughing.

"What's so funny?"

Blake's voice from behind me makes me jump, but the hands that begin rubbing my shoulders make me melt into a puddle on the desk. "Oh. I, uh… There was this thing; it was funny." I close the browser and my eyes, sinking into the warmth of his strong hands. "Oh my God, you're so hired."

His thumbs stroke up the back of my neck. "Wow. Your levator scapulae are some of the tightest I've ever felt."

His hands feel so amazing that I'm pretty sure I'm drooling. "I bet you say that to all the ladies."

He chuckles. "That's not a good thing, Sarah. And your right trapezius is awful."

"Your pillow talk needs work, but your hands can stay."

"Whether it's with me or not, you really need to book an appointment with someone." His magic hands stop, and my sad groan brings me back to myself, allowing embarrassment to heat my cheeks as I turn back to him. "Done already? Your real client, I mean."

"She just wanted half an hour."

"Ah." I pull up the billing system and begin filling in her name, marveling at how relaxed my shoulders are. I'd forgotten what having no neck pain was like. Guess I really should book a massage. I hadn't realized how tense I've gotten.

Blake grabs a pen and scribbles something in Dannica's file. "I can take care of that if you want to head out. No sense us both hanging out here."

"I have to wait for the towels in the washer to finish."

"I've got that too. You should go do some stretching—yoga, maybe—for that back."

"Are you sure?" I'd love to get out of here, but I feel bad about leaving him. Then again, he does this by himself all the time.

"Definitely. I have one more client to take care of after this, but thanks. It was nice seeing you again, Sarah."

"You too." I like the way my name sounds when he says it. I grab my purse from beneath the desk and pass him.

"Maybe I'll see you again sometime." He shows me those dimples again.

Maybe naked under a sheet on a massage table with his hands all over me. "Maybe." I return his smile and walk out of the office.

Weirdly, for a few minutes there, I didn't think about Jack once.

Chapter 11

His strong hands gently cradle my head, long fingers dancing across my scalp and winding through my hair. Tingles swirl across my skin, and I moan. "That feels amazing."

"I know."

"No one likes a cocky—" But my words are cut off by the way his thumb hits my temple and works back to land behind my ear. "Wow."

"You were saying?"

"Can I rent your hands for an hour or four?" I gaze up into his deep-blue eyes. "I promise I'll wash them when I'm done."

Pete laughs. "No way. You'd abuse the privilege."

"Damn right I would." I sigh and enjoy the warmth of the water as he rinses the conditioner from my hair. "Ever thought of becoming a masseuse?"

"Yeah, but then I wouldn't get to make people pretty."

"True. But massages make people happy."

"But they don't improve the scenery. And I'm all about the packaging."

"Yes, you are."

He wraps a huge, white towel around my hair. "I'll put you in with Lenora while I set up the color."

He leads me to the pedicure station and sticks my feet into the peppermint-scented water. Pete had called last night as I was leaving Inner Space, still chuckling about the label maker, and asked if I wanted a spa night and haircut. Since he doesn't trust anyone else with my hair, he's forgoing his pedi to take care of me, leaving me in Lenora's capable hands. "You spoil me."

"Someone's got to."

I wiggle my toes and send a cheeky look his way, smiling at Lenora. I close my eyes and think of Blake for a moment before wiggling my eyebrows at him. "I'm working on that."

"Oh?" He pours some cream and powders into a container, mixing colors.

"Not actively, but one of the massage therapists is pretty cute. Really cute."

Pete wrinkles his nose. "A hippie?" He's not a fan of their chemical-free lifestyle choices.

"No, he seems pretty normal." I smile, thinking of the forced-labor sugar yesterday.

"Hmm. What does he look like?"

I try not to flinch as Lenora exfoliates my heels. My feet are way too ticklish. "Who's that guy you like from *Magic Mike*?"

"Adam Rodriguez?" His voice raises an octave. "Are we talking Tito?"

I know it's Tito, but I couldn't resist. "Yes, but with less chin and a tighter ass."

"And you aren't naked in his bed because…?"

"Because I've only met him twice. And we were at work yesterday—not the best place for a torrid affair, though his hands made sweet, sweet love to my shoulders for a couple of minutes."

"And you weren't naked on his massage table because…?"

"Oh, to live the way you do."

He mixes more powder into the cream. "If I were one of the Golden Girls, I'd be Blanche Devereaux."

"That's for sure."

"I *am* double-jointed," he says with a Southern accent.

"Yes, but shoulder pads aren't your thing."

"Maybe not. But I was thinking of working more sequins into my wardrobe."

"You were not." I snort. "Though the lack of flash in men's clothing is a little unfair."

"It's getting better, what with the hipsters." He mixes things while Lenora blazes through the rest of my pedi. "You done over there?"

"Yup, we're finished," Lenora answers him.

Blue polish and small pink-and-white flowers improve the nails. "Wow, nice work!"

Lenora smiles. "Thanks."

I walk carefully over to Pete and sit in the chair.

He clips a smock over me. "Your coworkers sound terrible. They made you work all day today, extending both of our days—"

"I'm sorry and I so appreciate you opening the salon after hours just for our spa day."

"—and they turned Jack into your errand boy." He tactfully doesn't bring up the specifics of my dad's situation in front of Lenora. "And why?"

"In case anyone phoned." Annoyance washes over me.

He raises an eyebrow. "And how many people called?"

"One. And it was a wrong number."

"Yeah. Be careful with the hot masseuse. Even if he's not one of them, that kind of behavior may be contagious. Now." He flips my hair. "What did we have in mind?"

I take a breath and decide to go for it. "I'm going to make your wish come true. You get to do whatever you want." His eyes get big, and I feel the need to add a qualifier. "No Chelsea shave—nothing that involves shaving my head."

He nods, steepling his fingers beneath his chin. "I'm going to add some color. And we're going to go a bit shorter. And more dramatic."

"No spoilers. Just do it before common sense sinks in."

Pete flaps his hands. "Honey, I'm going to make you fabulous."

"Are you saying I'm not already?"

He scrunches his face. "You've always been adorable. Now, I am going to make you irresistible. Mr. Massage won't be able to keep his hands off you."

Jack's hands flash through my mind, but I suppress the image. He's even more off-limits than Blake, despite the "no dating coworkers" rule. Jack texted me earlier to let me know he'd picked up Dad's prescription and delivered it. I definitely owe him one. "Sounds great."

Pete stirs the batch of color and begins applying foils. I close my eyes and wait blind, not wanting to see anything except for the reveal.

We rinse and blow-dry and let things set, and nearly an hour later, he spins me around to check myself out in the mirror.

He's only taken a few inches off, but I look so different.

The way my hair frames my face makes my eyes look huge and my cheekbones stand out. I look like someone with style. I'm a bit surprised to realize that is something I've let slip during these past few months. My hair feels ultra-silky when I run my hands through it. It just hits the tops of my shoulders, and some razored layers give body and take it into sexily tousled territory instead of fussiness.

"Pete."

"I know." His smile is smug and so deserved.

He's darkened my hair a couple of shades—which makes my skin seem luminous, instead of pale and pasty—and added a few deep-red highlights that bring out the green in my hazel eyes.

His gaze meets mine in the mirror, and he snaps a picture with his phone. "He won't be able to tear his eyes off you."

The only reason I think of Jack now is because Pete's face is so similar.

·························

My apartment feels emptier when I get home from seeing Pete. He fills up a room like nobody's business, a crowd of one. I turn on my computer and switch on the fan, pouring a glass of lemonade before I change into my pajamas.

Pete was really excited about Blake, but I don't know if anything will come of that—or if I even want something to come of it.

True, it wouldn't be like I'd have to see him every day at work, which I think could really burn a couple out. Me time is healthy and so necessary in relationships. I can't imagine living together, working together, and hanging out together. Where's the breathing space in that?

But Blake might already be dating someone, so even thinking he's available is jumping the gun. Massage therapists don't typically wear rings—at least not at work—so the fact that there was no wedding ring means nothing. He's attractive and obviously has a good sense of humor and a job, but beyond that, I know nothing about him and have no idea how to find out more.

I'd want another couple of interactions to gauge if he's interested in more than flirting, and with the way our schedules are set up, we never cross paths. Asking him out implies I'm more interested than I am at this point. Really, I want to get to know him a little better to see if I even want to date him.

I grab my glass and an apple before settling at my computer. My first stop on the Internet is Craigslist Jobs. The mouse hovers over Missed Connections, but I resist. If things get worse with Phyllis and Inner Space, I could be out on my ass again. I'd rather find something else first. Not that any job is one hundred percent secure, but Inner Space barely pays me enough. At least, in another place, I'd have the opportunity to stash a little away in savings again.

The ads are slim. Only seven new listings in the past two weeks, and a couple of them are ones I've already seen and rejected or replied to and gotten no answer. I resend résumés to the latter listings anyway and scour the usual job sites, including a few newspapers. Naomi has replied to my email, but there's nothing at her new clinic, and she hasn't heard of anything else.

I dig around in different law firms' websites, seeing

if they're hiring, and even send a few résumés out just in case, but a fruitless hour later, it looks like I'm stuck at Inner Space for the time being. Who knows? Maybe things will get better. The longer I'm there, the more Ziggy and Fern will get to know me. And I'm a hell of a lot better employee than Phyllis is. I actually do my work, and do it correctly.

The two emails I get make my pulse pick up until I read them. Two spam messages: one trying to sell me Viagra, the other from a Nigerian prince needing to send me all his money. If only that were true. How can these scams still survive this many years after their inception? Are new scammers discovering the Internet and thinking, "OMG, if I tell people I want to *give* them money, they will fall all over themselves giving me their bank information! Maybe I can get some money out of them if I tell them they need to send me some money first. Yes! It's genius!"

Or they're just lazy and uncreative, which is more likely.

Another email hits my inbox from an unfamiliar address. I open it.

From: bwilde@mail.com
Subject: Label maker

I think the label maker got you a treat. Check the drawer when you come into work. Nice seeing you again. Blake.

Blake's last name is Wilde? I grin, mark him as a safe contact, and hit Reply.

I get another email before I can send my reply to Blake. It could be another email from him, so I save my response as a draft and go back to my inbox.

It's another email from my old boss.

How have they not noticed I'm cc'd on these? Lawyers should pay attention to details, no? I hit Reply, intent on asking them to remove me from their contacts, but then I read what's in the email.

> **From: reception@BladeLAW.com**
> **Subject: River Inn Chinese**
>
> ---
>
> Do not order from River Inn Chinese again. We all got significant food poisoning. Won't be in the office for a couple of days. Reschedule all appointments for today, tomorrow, and Wednesday.

My heart sings with schadenfreude, and I delete my reply unsent. Maybe I won't bring their attention to the situation just yet. To celebrate, I head back to Missed Connections.

This Weekend

I click on it.

> I can't describe what you were wearing, as it was your eyes that caught my attention. Such a fascinating shade between green and hazel.

My eyes are that color.

> Gorgeous, but not as gorgeous as your sweet smile. Your initials are S. J.

My heart pounds a little faster, but my nerves rise too. My initials *are* S. J.!

This is the closest one I've seen to being about me!

What if it is about me?

I don't know what to think about that. I've read about these interactions, these Missed Connections, for so long, and now that one might be me, I'm left a little... conflicted. The only person I encountered was Blake. Could it be him?

The memory of his hands roaming over my shoulders morphs into thoughts of him taking it further. Those fingers, maybe this time covered with oil, dipping under the fabric of my shirt, sliding down to cup my breasts. I'd tip my head back, and he'd lean over and kiss me while his fingers teased my nipples, sliding warmly over them.

Excitement rises to the surface again, drowning out the nerves. I'd actually really like it to be him. Maybe this is his way of getting to know me better before anything happens. I go back to Blake's email. What should I write? Something cute and fun, but not presumptuous. I won't bring up the Missed Connection. Yet. I settle on:

From: sarah@mail.com
Subject: RE: Label maker

Is the label maker trying to pay for my silence?

Then I add a winky face and hit Send.

Chapter 12

I DON'T WALK SO MUCH AS STRUT FROM THE TRAIN station to work on Tuesday morning. If I'd known how amazing the makeover would make me feel, I'd have given Pete free rein ages ago.

Fern is standing at my desk when I cross the reception area. "Morning, Fern."

"Hello, Sarah." She stares at me for a second, and I wait for her to say something about my hair. "I have a bunch of old files for you to archive today." She looks at me—my hair, my shoes, and back to my face.

"Sure." I slide past her and put my purse in the lower drawer of the desk. If Fern noticed, she doesn't seem to care about the change in my appearance. Oh well, I didn't do it for her anyway. The tall stack of manila folders is dusty and some of them are stained, stacked in a pile about two feet high. "I'm surprised I never came across these. Where have they been?"

"These were some we kept at home."

I'm pretty sure that's illegal. "I'll get to it then."

She hesitates, as if wanting to say something, but leaves silently.

An hour later, I've made a decent dent in the pile of

folders when the craniosacral therapist, Ginny, emerges from a room and comes to the front. "Hey, Sarah."

"Hi. How are you?"

"Fairly well." She writes something in her client's file and puts it in my tray. We're not that chummy, but her smile is always warm. I think she's just an aloof person, but her clients float out of the office feeling amazing, so I've got nothing but respect for her. And since her clients don't undress, she just changes the top sheet and pillowcase herself, saving me time and energy. "Love your new haircut."

"Thanks." I grin and show her next client into a room before checking the laundry, but it's not finished. Ginny is just closing the door to her room when I pass by on the way back to reception. Phyllis, Ziggy, and Fern are hanging out there with herbal tea when I get back.

Phyllis catches my eye, then refocuses on Fern. So annoying, but at least I can go to lunch soon. Phyllis continues, "I just find the whole thing incredibly unhealthy. I mean, what kind of energy does that put out into the world?"

I settle behind my desk and begin checking the messages, half listening to their conversation.

Ziggy clears his throat. "And that's the thing. It's all about balance, but it shouldn't all be external."

"It shouldn't be about the external at all," Fern admonishes. "Appearances aren't important in the least."

Surely, they're not talking about me?

Phyllis continues. "I mean, I cut my hair myself at home because I don't agree with the trappings of the antiwoman fashion industry. It's so inorganic."

"Completely. All the chemicals are terrible for a

person's body, but the treadmill of insecurity is terrible for their soul. For their energy. And for what, to attract a mate?" Fern's voice burns with passion.

Ziggy nods. "Unfortunately, they end up attracting someone who is only interested in their wrappers and not who they are as a person."

My fingers fumble my pen. They are literally talking about me in front of my face.

Fern sighs. "It's just sad that people will go to such lengths to capture love. It really says something about them that they will stop at no cost—to their bodies, health, or energy systems. I mean, if they only knew what such dramatic changes do to their root chakras."

"Never mind their root chakras—think of their hara lines." Ziggy sets his tea down.

"If only they'd be in my class. I could teach them so much in such a short time!"

"Of course you could, Fern. But some people will resist progress no matter what," Phyllis says, simpering.

"It's the way they cling to the things harming them that scares me. But I can't force someone to evolve beyond the physical and focus more on the spiritual. Nourishing the soul." Fern sets her cup down as well. "Shall we?"

Ziggy nods and looks over at me as though I've appeared from thin air. "Oh, Sarah! You're back."

I don't know what to say. "Yes."

"Fern, Phyllis, and I are leaving early for a course. We've cleared our schedules."

"Oh. Okay. Will you be back today?"

"No."

"Too bad you can't come with us." Phyllis smiles.

"Well, I'm working. So…"

She purses her lips and makes eye contact with Fern. The "see" look isn't lost on me. "Maybe another time."

"Maybe." My throat burns and I don't dare say another word. A couple seconds later, they've gone, and I take the phone off the hook, needing a moment to gather myself. For people who are all about building others up and helping people connect to the lightness within, they sure know how to tear a heart out.

It's a makeover. No bunnies were drained of their blood for the red highlights in my hair. It isn't in an outrageous Mohawk with swear words shaved into the sides of my head. I didn't take a day off work to get it done and lie about it. It's not like I've come in dressed unprofessionally and then sat here gazing lovingly at my appearance in a tiny mirror. Not liking someone's decision is one thing, but talking shit about it in front of them is another.

If I didn't have a few hours left before I could leave, I'd cry. But I won't.

And yet, a small tear gathers at the corner of my eye.

The law firm wasn't a great place, but at least there was one paralegal who wasn't a total ass and we used to have lunch together. Even Brenda, who fired me, was friendly. It's so lonely in this place without anyone to chat to or do lunch with. Ginny's nice but obviously uninterested in engaging, and Blake's never here when I am.

Screw this place. I need an early lunch.

I buy a turkey panino with extra, extra bacon—the better to eat my feelings with—from the bodega next door and take it to eat on a bench in the shade in the dinky park nearby. At least it's not a dog park—in this heat, the smell wouldn't be conducive to lunch. I flop down and stretch my legs out, wishing I'd brought something to drink. Fresh air that doesn't reek of sage oil and judgmental hippies helps a little, but distance doesn't give me much relief. I need to download some of this embarrassment to someone who will make me feel better about the situation and myself.

A lady walks by with a Yorkie who sniffs at me—probably smelling my sandwich—before its owner pulls it away.

Two guys about my age play Ultimate Frisbee, throwing harder and puffing out their chests when they notice me, but I don't even care about their abs.

Pete answers on the fourth ring. "Hey."

"Oh my fucking God, Pete, this has been the worst day ever. They were talking about me right in front of my face. They didn't care that I could hear. They just went on and on about how bad it is for your energy to only care about appearances. I was feeling so good about your makeover, and now I feel really crappy and alone and I need a hug and a reminder that I'm fabulous." I stuff a bite of my panino in my mouth to soothe myself with bacon.

"You what? This was your boss and coworkers making you feel bad about yourself? Give me names."

This isn't Pete. I swallow my bite of sandwich and close my eyes. "Jack?"

"Yeah. And for the record? You are drop-dead gorgeous."

Mortification overtakes my purring ego. "Where's Pete? I called his phone and not yours, right?"

"He sprang a sushi date on me and then abandoned me to flirt with the host. His phone rang, I saw it was you and answered…and fuck those hippies."

Could this day get any more embarrassing? Gratitude seeps through the murky mortification. "Thank you for getting my dad's pills to him, Jack. I owe you one."

"No, you don't. But I want to hear more about these assholes who were mean to you."

Screw it, he already knows too much for me to salvage any dignity from this story. "I can't believe it actually happened. They weren't even pretending to talk about someone else. They didn't say my name, but it was obvious and makes me feel like I'm shallow and want meaningless things from life because I got a haircut."

"No way. Are you supposed to never change the way you look? Never want to try something different? Pete would starve if women believed that. You're helping keep businesses afloat!"

I laugh.

"You strut back in there and show them how a confident modern woman doesn't let people keep her down. I mean, shit, are you supposed to walk around with a bag over your head? Pete showed me a picture of your new haircut. You look fucking hot."

The slight growl in his voice makes me feel a lot better.

"They're clearly jealous," he continues. "Go back in there and tell them to fuck their own faces. Flip 'em off."

Laughter bubbles through me. What would it be like to come home to him every night? He'd make me laugh and then make love to me, making it all better. I could call him anytime through the day when something happened. But no. Being with Jack would be like having a panther ranging around at home. "That might get in the way of my chakra chi or whatever."

"Your chakra chi is fine. Don't let those hippies get you down. It's Sarah." Jack's voice is muffled before sounding normal again. "Pete's back. Want a word?"

I glance at my phone. I've already been gone twenty-three minutes. I only get half an hour for lunch. "No, I should be getting back."

"All right. I'll talk to you later?"

"Yes. Thanks, Jack."

"Anytime."

I let myself roll around in the softness of his voice for a minute before walking back to Inner Space. He really is a nice guy—despite the shitty things I said to him. Also, he's right. The glass doors reflect my new and improved appearance. Finger-combing the ends of my hair, I remember how great my makeover made me feel when I first saw it, and I let that thought buoy me across reception to my desk after pausing to chug a cup of water.

Screw my judgmental coworkers.

I open the lower drawer to put my purse in and find the label maker, reminding me of Blake's present. With the business of the morning and then the shit-talking about me in reception earlier, I completely forgot about it. Moving the label maker aside, my fingers brush against the small chocolate truffle bar.

I could kiss Blake right now for this perfectly timed pick-me-up.

I slowly unwrap it, a brand I'm not familiar with, and take a bite while reading the package. It's glorious.

Silky smooth, semi-dark with raspberry cream, and delicious. It's organic, so even if the hippies saw me eating it, I wouldn't get a lecture, but it doesn't taste like cardboard. And there's no carob in it—the chocolate of hippies.

I sit with a small piece of Blake's chocolate melting on my tongue, letting it sweeten up my bitter day.

··········—··········

The next night, I settle in front of the computer with some wine to unwind.

Anniversary of Sorts

Well, that could be anything. I click it open.

Bumping into you again gave me butterflies even after all these years.

I haven't been estranged from anyone long enough to warrant "all these years." Oh, and it's from a woman to a man.

On to the next one.

Girl Pissing in the Men's Room at the Grilled

What the hell?

Your piercings were hot. Wish I'd gotten your number, but my hands were full and you left the bar right after you left the bathroom. I'd love to watch you piss again. Maybe more.

I feel my eyes become two different sizes. Whatever happened to romance? Taking another slug from my glass of wine, I click open the next post.

> Saw you outside work yesterday. You were wearing a light green top and huge sunglasses in your dark hair.

I gasp. I wore my favorite green cami yesterday.

> Love the new sassy haircut.

My heart pounds. This has got to be me, right? And he said work, not "your" work. It's totally Blake. Unless it isn't. What if it's a total stranger? Some creeper who wants to romance me, love me, and chop me up to keep in his freezer—or watch me pee like that other ad?

But what if it's someone sweet who reads these posts like I do? I'm not a freak, so not everyone into these is weird. Odds are that a lot of normal people check Missed Connections as well. I have to know if it's about me, so I hit Reply and begin typing.

> Tell me the color of the jeans I was wearing, and the new shade of highlights in my hair...

This should be interesting. I wore a black skirt today, not jeans. We'll see if he tries to bluff and guesses a color, or if this one is actually about me.

Let the games begin.

Blake has left me an email too.

From: bwilde@mail.com
Subject: RE: Label maker

No one likes a label maker that stoops to extortion.

Short and sweet. This email was sent within half an hour of the ad being posted. I open my email and send a message to him.

From: sarah@mail.com
Subject: RE: Label maker

Tell your label maker (more like troublemaker!) friend that it has fabulous taste in chocolate.

I read the ad again. Do I want Blake to be my secret admirer? Do I want to take my mind off an impossible attraction to Jack by taking up with someone I barely know?

I grin. The ad might not even be about me.

But maybe it is.

And maybe I do.

Chapter 13

IT'S 10:43 A.M., AND MY HEART IS RACING, THOUGH unfortunately not from the pot of coffee I inhaled at home in the hopes of at least appearing awake this morning. The UPS guy walks in with five big boxes on a dolly and drops them in front of my desk, blocking the doorway, and thrusts his electronic board in my face to sign.

"First name?"

"Sarah."

"First initial of your last name?"

"J."

"Have a good one." He walks out whistling obnoxiously, leaving the boxes.

Now, not only do I have to call back six clients about various things, catch up on the laundry, and prep four rooms, but I have to deal with these boxes. I've also had to pee for the last forty-five minutes.

"Gee, it sure must be nice to have your job." Ziggy's client vacantly smiles at me. "It would be so relaxing to work here."

She has no idea. My smile must be manic, but I play along, wanting to scream. As soon as she's gone, I focus on my tele-nemesis. It's been ringing nonstop today, as if some people have "I'm busy. Please, no one call now!" radar that signals them to phone at the worst times.

And the fact that I'm a teensy bit hungover isn't helping.

But ten minutes later, the messages are sorted out, the phone is quiet, and I dash to the back and fold laundry like an origami artist on speed. The load fresh from the dryer burns my hands a bit, but I forge ahead. Fifteen minutes later, the shelves are stocked, the last load is in the dryer, my hair sticks up all over from static electricity, and my throat burns for a drink.

And I still *really* have to go to the bathroom.

My thirst can wait; my bladder cannot. I rush into the washroom and pee like a racehorse, sagging with relief.

And then notice someone's used all the toilet paper and not replaced it. I can't bear drip-drying on top of everything else this morning. *Please*, I hope, reaching into my cardigan pocket. Yes! I'd tucked a couple of tissues away, and thank God for that. The bathroom is filled with my annoyed swears, muttered quietly so no one hears them, as I finish up and head for a drink of water.

Instead, I find Fern. "Hello, Sarah. Have a seat."

I become aware of the fact I'm sweating, frizzy, and annoyed from the laundry. I must look red and deranged, so I surreptitiously smooth my hair and blot the tiny beads of sweat from my upper lip as I sit at my desk.

Fern hands me a cup of spicy herbal tea and rolls a chair over by my desk. She settles into it and sips her own tea. "Is there anything you want to tell me?" Her intense gaze isn't quite a glare, but I still feel uncomfortably scrutinized. Does she know I'm hungover? But why should that matter? I was here on time and have been working steadily since I walked in the door.

Is this about Blake? Surely flirting doesn't violate the "no dating coworkers" policy. Best to play dumb.

"About what?" I blow on and sip my tea, wishing it was cold water instead of a steaming beverage. Honestly, even with the air-conditioning, how can they drink so much hot tea in the summer?

"Anything at all. I'd never judge you; you know that. And even if something was wrong, you could come to me. I'd never be anything but fair."

"I appreciate the offer, but I don't have anything to confide."

It's clear she really wants me to tell her a secret, but there's nothing I want to tell her. Is this the way she makes friends with people? Does she do this as one of the steps in her energy programs? People confess weird secrets, and they laugh and bond over herbal teas?

"Okay. But my offer stands."

"Thanks."

She stands and takes my cup, even though I'm not done, and disappears into the kitchen before heading into her appointment with her client. I pour a cup of cold water from the cooler, finally soothing my parched throat. I really should have tried harder to come up with something to share, but what?

People like her grab on to your personal things and think it's fine to talk to other people about them. I don't trust her not to chat about my life to Ziggy or anyone else in the office—including Phyllis, since they're such besties. And I sure as hell don't need Phyllis latching on to any of my problems. She'd exploit anything she could.

No, I made the right decision to keep silent. If I learned anything at the law firm, it's that people don't actually give a shit about how you are. One time I was honest when a coworker asked how I was feeling the week after my dad had his third heart attack. My mother had told Dad she'd been having another affair. They'd fought and he'd had another heart attack. Mom told me when I got to the hospital. And he still took her back that time. Not wanting to upset him, I'd contented myself with glaring at her over his body when he fell asleep.

I'd come back to work from lunch a few minutes late—having bitched my mom out on an extra-long phone call. I'd been honest with my bosses when I apologized for being late, but all they wanted to know was if I was emotionally compromised and unable to do my job. They told me if I wasn't able to keep home issues at home, then I should seek employment elsewhere.

Real charming.

I've kept my feelings to myself since then while at work.

With a sigh, I move Fern's chair back to the wall opposite the door, chug three cups of cold water from the cooler, and get back to typing up the files. I catch Fern giving me strange looks all day when our paths cross, but I pretend I don't notice. What's her deal?

....

Weariness from worrying about Fern's motivations evaporates when I get home and open my email after pouring a glass of wine. New message from unknown sender. Subject, *Missed Connection*.

My fingers tremble above the mouse's buttons. He has my email address. Not that a hundred people or so don't have it, but this is proof I know the person—or rather, that they definitely know me.

If I open this email, there's no going back.

My finger double-clicks the mouse, opening the email with a little help from my nosy nature.

From: anon@mail.com
Subject: Missed Connection

Trick question. There were no pants. Your hair has new red streaks that complement the paleness of your skin. Care to continue this on Skype? Chat, not video, unless you're open to it. Add me—Missed.Connection.

It *is* about me! I bounce in my chair, hop up, and brew a cup of coffee, though the last thing I probably need right now is more stimulation. I need my wits about me. Of course I'm going to reply, but I need a moment to stop the buzzing beneath my skin. Cup of french vanilla attained, I open Skype, making sure to shutter my camera before adding him as a contact. Just in case. No way am I going to see him for the first time with unwashed hair, bad lighting, and no makeup.

Adding him to my contacts only takes a second, and I start a text conversation. The first question is mine.

Me: Do I know you?

Him: Not as well as you think.

Someone I know but have the wrong idea about? Or is it just an acquaintance? I lick my dry lips.

Me: How well do you know me?

Him: Not as well as I'd like.

He's quick at typing too. Excitement and unease war for dominance in my stomach. If it's not Blake, it's still someone I know, maybe someone from work. I nearly shudder myself inside out imagining Ziggy on the other end of this conversation. After working at Inner Space, there's no way in hell I'd date a hippie or a married person—though at this point, I think dating a hippie would be worse. Maybe that's what Blake means about not knowing him. Does he think I think he's one of them?

But maybe it isn't Blake at all. So who else could it be?

A cute guy manages the wine shop next to the grocery store by work. We had a long chat about the uplifting qualities of champagne the other day. Since then, when we catch each other's eye as I walk past, he waves. But he doesn't have my email address.

Okay, maybe it's a tad creepy that this person knows me and I have no idea who he is. I guess as long as he doesn't ask for my bank details or any weird personal information that could lead to him scamming me, I'm safe. I mean, if he meant me harm, he could have grabbed me off the street when I was strutting around in my little black skirt.

A shiver rolls across my skin as I realize how vulnerable I am. How vulnerable we all are to people who might mean us harm. Anyone at any time could pull us into a car, or hit us across the head with something and drag us into an alley. But we can't live in fear. The locks on our apartment doors don't keep the bad guys out. They just lock us inside the illusion of security. If someone really wants to get in, a lock or door won't stop them.

And this feeling is closer to excitement than fear.

This is crazy, I type.

Him: I know.

Me: Have you ever done anything like this before?

His reply comes immediately. *Missed connections or online relationships?*

Both. Not like I'd know if he's lying, but if this is going to work, I need to trust a little.

Him: Never done online dating. And Missed Connections is a new thing to me. A friend showed it to me, and she was really into reading them, which piqued my interest. But I just got this feeling when I started cruising through them. So many ads, so many people. Filled with such…hope. All these people are reaching out, putting themselves out there, hoping against hope that the person they felt a momentary connection with—no matter how tenuous—will see it and maybe even be reaching back for them.

And then they'll make contact. Like we did.

Him: If they're lucky.

A blush heats me from within. He feels lucky to have connected with me? Sudden boldness possesses my fingers. *What's your name?*

This time his reply takes longer, almost as if he's typing, deleting it, and typing again. *Are you sure you want to know?*

Is there a reason you don't want to tell me? Mild unease seeps into my chest. What's he got to hide?

Him: I'd love it if you'd get to know me first.

Me: But you already know me.

Him: If it's okay with you, I'd prefer no names until a little later.

I bite my lip. *But you already know my name.*

Him: I know. It's not fair, and yet, I'm asking. But it's ultimately your decision.

Me: You're not a hippie, are you?

Him: I promise I'm not a hippie. In real life you know I'm not. We've ranted about them together.

It's totally Blake. Well, if he wants me to not pry

until we've talked a bit more, that's okay. Maybe most women get caught up on the fact he's a massage therapist and somehow think it's weird, or that he's a cheater, since he's always around naked people.

I'd wanted to get to know Blake before actually dating him. Maybe this is the universe's way of providing me with that opportunity. *All right. Let's get to know each other.*

Chapter 14

> We've got things covered here today. Feel free
> to take the day off. See you Monday.

I READ FERN'S TEXT FOUR TIMES, BUT THIS IMPROMPTU
Friday off still doesn't feel like a good thing. Does
this have anything to do with Fern's sudden need to
bond? Is Phyllis trying to set me up? But with what?
She's already flogged the receipt book fiasco into
the ground.

Is it something to do with Blake? We've only
exchanged a couple of emails, and the ones we sent
were pretty innocent, so even if Phyllis knew about
them, there's no way Fern would care. Is there? Has
she found out through her etheric minions that Blake
and I spent four hours talking online last night and it
was totally amazing and I have a major crush on him
now? I call Inner Space.

"Inner Space, Fern speaking."

"Hey, Fern. It's Sarah."

A pause. "Oh, hello." She sounds neither friendly
nor hostile.

"Um, so I feel weird about having today off. Is
something up?"

"Why would there be? We just felt you could use a bonus day off. You've been working hard lately. You're entitled."

She's saying the right things, but Fern and Ziggy are brutally cheap. They aren't into giving something for nothing. For crying out loud, they buy one-ply toilet paper, which practically evaporates before making contact, and they're going to give me a day off out of the blue? But what can I say without seeming confrontational or, worse, defensive?

"Okay, well, thanks. If you're sure?"

"Yes, we're sure. Take care, have a good weekend. Balance and recharge, and we'll see you on Monday."

"Okay." I hang up feeling no better than I did before I called, but she didn't sound mad or like they're interviewing someone to replace me. Not that I'd be able to tell from a phone call.

I hate this.

On the plus side, I now have a three-day hippie-free weekend, which is music to my shoulders. I never knew stripping beds, remaking them, and doing laundry could be so tough. Since it's only nine, I crawl back into bed and sleep until eleven, feeling even better when I wake up.

Starbucks should deliver. They're seriously missing out on opportunities to wow me by enabling my laziness. Deciding not to leave the apartment all day, I brew a cup of Irish cream in my single-cup coffee machine—a late housewarming gift from Pete, which I still need to thank him for—and head to my computer.

Creamy goodness warms my tongue, and I dial Pete's number.

"Shouldn't you be at work?"

"Hello to you too." I take another sip. "We don't make with the niceties of small talk anymore?"

"Hello, my darling. I do so hope you're well. Shouldn't you be at work?"

"I've got the day off today." My feet bounce happily.

"Are you throwing a sickie?"

"No, they just gave me a day off," I say smugly.

"Paid?" I can hear his eyebrow rise in doubt.

Bugger. I never thought to ask if this was a paid day off. I'll just wait until I get my check—no point bringing it up to Fern and Ziggy unless they actually short me. Wouldn't want to be accused of not being a team player. "So what are your plans for the weekend?" I ask in lieu of an answer and open my browser.

"We're going to that new club, Gated Way, Sunday night. You're coming, right?"

"Who all's going?" I try to keep my tone casual, wondering if Jack will be there.

"The usual."

It's like he knows what I'm asking but trying to be obstinate. "What time?"

"We'll pick you up at ten thirty?"

We. Definitely Jack then. I try to drown the butterflies in my stomach with more coffee. "Sounds good. I'm breaking in the amazing coffee machine you gave me."

"How is it? Do you love it?"

"I do. I wasn't sure at first that they get a good balance of flavor and strength. You know I'm particular about my caffeine."

"Yes. But they're fabulous—and you don't even have to commit to a whole pot of something."

I sign into my email. "You're such a commitment-phobe."

"The caged bird doesn't sing because it's happy, dear. It sings because it wants to get the fuck out and stretch its little wings."

"One day you'll meet someone, Pete, and you'll want nothing more than for him to tie you down."

"As will you."

Maybe I already have. "Well, I should get going. See you tomorrow night."

"Ten thirty. Wear something slutty."

"Just for that, I'm going to wear pants."

"No!"

I laugh and hang up and sign into Skype.

He's there, and he's sent me a message already. But when I open it, it's just *'?.>;'*

With a grin, I reply. *? ?! !!!*

He replies a moment later. *What? Oh crap. Sorry about that.*

Me: Your random punctuation startled me.

Him: So cute. I read a poem once that was just punctuation.

What? *Like ^(&^(&%? Because I hate to break it to you, but that probably wasn't a poem. It was someone saying bad words.*

Him: I don't know what they were going for, but it was too highbrow for me. Do you like poetry?

Me: Do dirty limericks count?

Him: Of course!

I laugh. *I like some poems but haven't really read many. Do you have a favorite poem?*

His reply is immediate. *Yes.*

He sits around contemplating poetry in his spare time? That's so different from anyone I've ever dated. But I like it. *What's your favorite?*

Him: Okay, I do love the classics, and some of the Beat poets. But...you can't laugh. But there's this book, "Plague Dogs."

My mouth drops open. *Are you talking about Snitter's poem?!*

Him: You know it?

Me: When I was little, I saw the cartoon of "Watership Down," and I came across the book when I was in high school. I loved it, so I read "Plague Dogs" as well. It was so different, and depressing and haunting. Gorgeous. Snitter broke my heart.

Him: Mine too. Confession time—I donate part of my income every year to fighting against animal testing because of that book.

This does nothing to shatter the sensitive, intelligent image of him forming in my mind. Even now, thinking of that poor little dog with the messed-up mind, wanting nothing more than to find his "stolen" master, brings poignant sadness into my heart. *It's really a great book that sticks with you like that years later.*

Him: Definitely. It's one I read and was like, "Wow that was beautiful. I'll never read it again." It was beautiful but too much.

He's too perfect. *Do you have any flaws?*

Him: I hog the blankets.

If he were here right now, *I'd* be all over him like a blanket.

....

Saturday morning, I'm in the bathtub wallowing in the decadence of three types of oils and sweet almond bubble bath as a way of continuing the feelings that our online talk last night gave me. I don't know his age or birthday, but I do know he's smart and witty—and I want to know more about him. I could have talked to him all night, but I thought it best to tear myself away. No sense appearing too available.

My phone buzzes. Unknown number. Is it him? How did he get my number? Why is he calling? Should I not get it? Third ring. I'm getting it.

I clear my throat and answer. "Hello?"

"Sarah?" The deep voice is vaguely familiar.

"Yes?"

"It's Blake."

Oh my God, I was right. "Hey. Not to sound as though I'm unhappy about it, but how did you get this number?"

"Employee contact list. I'm sleuthy like that."

I smile. "Should we pick up where we left off?"

"You want to make it a three-way with that naughty label maker?"

It's a good thing I'm lying in the bathtub because my blush would have set me on fire. It's strange he's referring to the label maker when we've spoken online since then, but he did say he wanted me to get to know him first. Maybe I'm not quite ready to jump into something that forward either, but I do like him, so I keep it flirty. "I barely know the label maker. I don't want it to think I'm easy."

He chuckles. "You weren't at work yesterday."

"No. Fern gave me the day off." He'd have been at his other clinic and assumed I was talking to him from my phone.

"I heard." He sighs.

"Was the label maker pining for me? Tell it there's no one else for my labeling needs, I swear!"

"I'll pass that on. But no. I just wanted to give you a heads-up."

Damn it, what has Phucking Phyllis done now? "About what?"

"I was in to pick up my check and heard an interesting conversation between Fern and Zig."

"About me?"

"Indirectly, but it explained something she asked me about a week ago. Do you know why Fern gave you the day off yesterday?"

My stomach sinks. Was she interviewing someone for my position like she and Ziggy did to my predecessor? "No. She said it was because I'd earned it. It felt a bit hinky, but I didn't push it. Why?"

"I almost don't want to say anything in case it makes it worse."

"Please, Blake, you have to tell me. If I'm about to be fired, I want to know about it and not go into work blindly. Just tell me what it is." My mouth feels like it's stuffed with cotton.

"No, she's not firing you. But have you noticed her treating you any differently in the past week or so?"

I let his words roll around my mind for a minute. "I guess she's been a little off. Not as friendly and she hasn't stayed to chat, but I assumed she was just busy or preoccupied. Why?"

"Has she asked you about the float?"

We keep about seventy-five dollars in float for change, but I don't have to balance it or anything. Fern does that. "No."

"About a week ago, she started asking around work because money was missing from the float. She asked everyone."

"She never asked me."

"Because she thought you were the one taking it."

My face grows hot with shame I shouldn't feel because *I didn't do it*. I don't steal from people. My silence stretches on too long.

"Sarah?"

"I'm here. I just can't believe it. I didn't take anything. I'm not a thief. If I needed money that much, I'd have asked. I—"

"I know you didn't take it. And now Fern knows too."

I sit up with a splash. If it was Phyllis, then two of my problems would be solved in one fell swoop. "Did the person who took it confess?"

"Fern caught them in the act. She thought it was you, so she gave you the day off to confirm that no money went missing when you were gone. Then she saw Ziggy going into it at lunch and confronted him. Other than you, he was the one person she hadn't thought to ask. He told her he's been raiding it for a few bucks here and there to buy his lunches from the deli in the grocery store."

I shake my head. "So it was Ziggy all along."

"Yup. They were arguing about it pretty loudly in the back room when I stopped by. But either way, your innocence was proven today, so I imagine things will get a little better for you."

"Maybe." But the fact that Fern didn't even ask me is very telling. She must think I'm a liar as well as a thief. And what if Ziggy hadn't needed the cash for his lunch? Would I have lost my job out of circumstance? "Thanks for telling me."

"Of course. We're in this together, right?" His tone thaws the icy fear lodged in my gut.

"Yeah, we are."

"Have a good weekend. I'll talk to you later."

"You too."

It doesn't matter that the issue has resolved itself. Fern still thought I was taking money, and she may have even fired me without confronting me about the cash. She doesn't know me at all, which is an unsettling realization. With Phucking Phyllis fueling their insecurities to try to get me out of there, my job is even less secure than I thought.

I feel the urge to phone Fern and confront her myself to clear the air, but what would that serve? I'd seem confrontational and defensive, and I'm not supposed to know about this, so Blake might get in trouble. And if Phyllis was there, damned right she'd bring up Blake. I could raise a stink, but would it really help me? Fern believes she's always right, so she's bound to feel a bit prickly that she couldn't, I don't know, read the energy and magically tell who the culprit was. If I bring the subject up, even in the interest of making things right, she's not going to take it well.

I've got to let it go and hope that the truth is enough for Fern to realize I'm a good person. With a sigh, I pull the plug on the tub and climb out.

Chapter 15

By the next day, the sense of betrayal has faded and I'm looking forward to going out with Pete and dancing. The bar we're going to is new, which is always either great or a horror show—never a happy medium—but Jack is DJ'ing, so at least the music will be good. My outfit for the night is a pair of jeans so inky purple they're almost black and a silvery-gray T-shirt. I slide on a pair of buckled, red, high-heeled boots and a belt the same color to go with my highlights. Maybe it's too matchy, but it makes me feel good.

I must have done all right, because Pete had no criticisms when he picked me up, other than "You should have worn a skirt to show off your legs." We get the cab driver to switch the radio to an indie station we love, so when we pull up to the bar, we're already bouncing.

"How was your week?"

How much should I tell him? It's way early days to talk about Blake and me. Besides, I don't know where that's going yet. I could tell Pete about the stealing debacle, but I'm tired of feeling bogged down with negativity. "It's a whole lot better now."

"Awww." He squeezes my arm. "I feel like I never see you anymore."

"I know." I climb out of the cab. "But I bet your couch is happy to have seen the last of me."

"Yes. I do love you, but I'm glad to have my man cave back."

"You mean the cave of masculinity where you dance around in your thong?"

"Yup."

We've always been honest with each other, but reality presses close to me for a second. Pete would let me come back to his place in a second if I lost this job, but if the situation with Inner Space goes pear-shaped, I don't want to have to go back to Pete's. I'm going to have to try harder to fit in at work and gain a little security. And I've been letting Phyllis get to me too much. I refuse to let her chase me away from what's actually a decent-paying job. She's not a criminal mastermind, and I can out-Zen her every day of the week.

My resolve makes me strut a little harder, and Pete and I enter the club with flare, flash our IDs, and get stamped.

Specific parts of my body register Jack's presence before my eyes do. The T-shirt and low-slung jean combination was invented so he could own it. It says a lot about him that he hasn't changed much despite finding obvious financial success. He doesn't go around flashing cash to impress people.

"Pete, Sarah, hey. I got us drinks." Jack hugs Pete and then me, and my hands itch to wander south instead of keeping in the friend zone. Why is it getting harder to keep my hands to myself around him? *Because he's fuck hot and a great guy.*

But Pete is family. A part of me knows that if Jack and I dated and then broke up, I'd lose Pete too. That's a scenario that can never happen. Pete means too much to lose because of casual sex. Trouble is, the more I hang out with Jack, the more I want.

Looking everywhere but Jack's face is easier tonight since the club is one we've never been to before. Honestly, I can't see us coming back very often. The club has a calculated roughness that screams "bar fight." Not to judge the clientele by their covers, but the body language is tense for an opening night when we're all supposed to be having a good time celebrating the owner's success. Or maybe I'm just projecting my tension onto everyone else.

Fortunately Jack leaves to play his set a few minutes later. Right away the music improves.

"I love this song." I tap Pete's arm. "Dance?"

"You go ahead. I'll watch the table and get a head start on the drinking."

"Do a shot for me."

"I will." He puffs out his stomach and pats it. "I'm drinking for two!"

I grin and ease through the crowd to the dance floor with the martini Jack bought me. This early in the night it's a bit sparsely populated, which is perfect. More room for me. The music combines with my drink and loosens my movements with each song that passes. Man, it's sweltering in here. Pete was right—I should have worn a skirt.

Still, the music is amazing, and I don't care if I sweat my face off. I'm not here to impress anyone. I'm here to cut loose. Pete joins me for a while with a fresh drink just as I get thirsty. Jack plays the best music. I love these guys.

Jack points at me from the booth, and I realize I've been dancing while staring directly at him for a few minutes.

I wave, then turn away. I'm the one who said we couldn't be a thing, and here I am violating that boundary—well, maybe not violating it, but definitely sticking my toe over the line.

Pete is talking to some guy whose pants are too tight. He touches the guy's arm—asking him to dance—but the guy shakes his head and walks away. He sits at a table full of guys—none as cute as Jack or Pete. One of them is even wearing a trucker hat.

Pete notices me and weaves his way over. "He was only a seven anyway."

"What, he didn't want to dance with you? Does he know who we pretend we are?"

"Nope. Denied. Looks like I'm going home alone." He's slurring his *s*'s.

"How many have you had? You should get some water."

"I need some air." Pete is really sweaty, and his limbs are clumsier than normal. He clearly drank too much too soon and is feeling it in this heat.

"You okay?"

He doesn't answer, just heads toward one of the exits, but if he goes out that door, he won't get back in without having to go through the line again. I sigh and shake my head, walking over to the exit with my purse. I'll pour Pete into a cab, and if the line's too long, I'll grab a cab home too.

A familiar-looking guy in a green-and-black trucker cap pushes past me.

"Rude much?" I snap.

He glares at me over his shoulder and hurries toward the exit.

Maybe he has to puke or get some air…but uneasiness slithers around in my gut, and I hurry to follow.

The door swings shut behind me as I hear him demand, "Are you a fucking fag?"

I can't have heard that right. This is New York, not some backwoods, redneck watering hole. Disbelief turns to rage and a blatant disregard for my own safety when I realize he's addressing *Pete*. I step in front of Trucker Hat, stopping him with my body as he keeps striding toward Pete. "What does it matter if he is?"

He tries to get by me, but I block him. Luckily he's not as cool with beating up women as he is with gay men. He doesn't push me out of his way or manhandle me at all, just tries to get around my body. "Because I'm going to kick his ass, that's why," Trucker Hat yells over my shoulder.

Is this really happening? A strange wooden sensation invades my legs, but I stand my ground, fear of what will happen if he catches up to Pete keeping me light on my toes. "And what's that going to prove? How does that make you cool or strong?" I throw a glance over my shoulder, but Pete's still walking. He's so drunk he doesn't even realize this asshole has targeted him. If this guy gets past me, Pete's screwed. There's no way he can defend himself in his condition.

"He's been cruising or what-the-fuck-ever all night. He asked one of my *friends* to dance." Trucker Hat's eyes are swimming in the liquor he must have drank earlier, but that's no excuse for this.

I need to get his attention on me so Pete can get

away. Where are the fucking bouncers? *Run, Pete.
God—anyone up there—please let him get away
safely!* I smirk up at the drunken bigot, even though
my heart is pounding so hard it's making my neck
throb. "Jealous? What, did he hand your ass to you on
the dance floor and impress whatever chick you were
trying to roofie?"

"That little fag's getting his ass kicked. He asked one
of my friends to dance."

I'd laugh if I wasn't so livid. "What, and you were
jealous?"

His hands ball into fists and he takes a step toward me.

"You looking for a fight?" The voice behind me isn't
familiar, and I turn to see who's joining me to protect
Pete, insanely grateful to not be alone anymore. It's
three guys in their late twenties who look like they live
at the gym eight days a week. The tallest looks like he
should be a cast member on *Jersey Shore*, built and
groomed, and right now he looks livid. But I think it
was the bearded redhead who spoke. He stands slightly
in front of the others, hands on his hips.

The dark-haired one smiles at me and jerks his head.
"Go to your friend."

Four more guys come spilling out the door and take
positions by Trucker Hat's side. "What's up, Trent?"

Oh God. Is there about to be a brawl in the alley? The
door opens again. *Not more bigots, please.* But it's Jack.

"Sarah?"

"I have to check on Pete." I turn and sprint down the
alley on shaky legs. By the time I turn the corner and
find him, he's opening a taxi door. "Pete!"

He turns. "Hey, Sarey. How's it hanging?"

He doesn't know. He has no idea what happened, and I hope he never does. "Pretty good."

He squints at me. "How often do you wash your hair?"

What does that have to do with anything? "Every couple of days?"

"What do you do the rest of the time, pee through a straw?" He cackles at his own joke. "Come on, that was funny. Why aren't you laughing?"

Because someone just wanted to hurt you for being who you are, and that makes me want to vomit with fear and rage. "Just, um… You left without saying goodbye. I wanted to make sure you were okay."

"You're the sweetest." He flails forward and hugs me before flopping into the backseat. "You wanna share a cab?"

"No. I'm going to hang for a little while longer." *And make sure Jack's okay.* I shut the door, and the cab pulls away. I jump as a warm hand gently touches my shoulder.

"It's me."

I turn to Jack, who's shaking his hand. The knuckles are red, like he's hit something. "Oh God, did you—"

"Everything's fine. Security came and stopped it before anything really happened. Was that Pete in the cab?"

I nod. "He's safe and fine, making jokes. Oh God, Jack." Horror at what could have happened to Pete tonight ricochets through my hollow stomach and bounces around my legs, making my knees weak. Those bastards could have—they *would* have—hurt him, maybe worse.

Jack throws his arm around me in a half hug and pulls me close. His warmth makes me shake harder. He wraps his other arm around me too. "I saw you leave the bar after Pete but didn't get there in time to see what happened."

"That one guy followed him from the bar and was going to beat him up because Pete was gay. I didn't know, but I had a bad feeling and followed them outside in time to hear the bullshit he was saying. Pete didn't even know."

My stiletto heels rattle against the pavement. Jack's hard body tightens around me, as though every muscle has flexed at once.

"What happened when I left to put Pete in a cab?"

He rubs my back with long, calming strokes. "The group from the bar was going to beat on the other three guys—or try. I jumped in to help, and then the security guards came."

With a sigh, I lean into him and clasp my arms behind his back, drawing strength from his warmth and steadiness.

"Are we in the fifties? What the hell is even happening right now?" My heart hurts for Pete, for the ugliness he never saw directed his way. Was this the first time something like this has happened to him, or the thirtieth? The three hundredth? "Has anything like this ever happened to him before?"

Jack sighs. "Not since high school."

I squeeze my eyes so tightly to hold back the hot tears that they hurt. How would I feel, knowing a stranger wanted to literally hurt me because he thought I *might* be gay? I want to hug Pete and hold him and apologize for every asshole who ever hurt him or made him feel bad about himself just for being who he is.

Instead, I cling to Jack, trying not to let the bitterness and anger eat me alive, anchoring myself with someone who understands this angry, bewildered feeling surging through my stomach. I hold someone who probably got into a lot of fights protecting his brother in high school. Jack is an amazing person. An amazing friend. His hands coax calm from me one lazy stroke at a time.

And then when my nerves settle, I enjoy the way his body molds to mine a little more than a friend should. I want to be even closer. I want Jack.

"Will you see me home?"

"There's no way I'll leave you if those assholes are still around. Of course I'll get you home." His hand tangles in my hair, brushing errant strands away from my face. "I'll grab us a cab." A reckless heat flares inside me at his kindness.

Maybe my heart is off-limits. But tonight, he can have the rest of me.

Chapter 16

NOT THAT HE KNOWS IT YET. I COULDN'T GET THE words out before the cab came and now...I choke on silence for fear of talking myself out of this. The drive seems to take forever.

I haven't drunk enough to pretend it's the liquor talking. While I could blame the situation or the music or my loneliness, really I just want him so badly it hurts. Not so badly I can't think straight, because all I have are straight lines—Jack and me heading straight upstairs, straight to my bedroom, and getting him naked straight away. No, my mind is very clear about what I want.

What I need.

What I've been waiting to happen for years but have danced around because I cared too much about measuring up to the other girls he's been with. Because I didn't want to lose him as a friend and have that screw up my friendship with Pete. Because he surrounds himself with temptation just like my mom does. Because instead of caring about all the fun we could be having together, I looked at it as something that had to be "forever" when it could just be "for now."

He sits with his arm around me, stroking my hair as

the cab stops at the curb by my apartment, unaware of my decision.

Tonight, I find I don't give a flying fuck. I just want him hard, and fast, and… "Come upstairs."

His inhale is audible, and his eyes widen before he leans closer to me and pauses. "What?"

"I said a lot of shitty things to you, and I'm sorry for them all. But I really need you tonight, and if you're still interested—"

My sentence is cut off beneath the urgency of his lips pressing against mine, teasing a sigh from me. His hand brushes my forearm, my shoulder, my jaw, and traces the contour of my cheek before slipping to the nape of my neck and pulling me closer, deepening the kiss.

His tongue darts into my mouth and slides across mine gently, then more aggressively when I move mine around his in a quick spiral. My fists ball his shirt at his chest, pulling the fabric, trying to bring him closer. But we're still in the freaking cab, and why isn't teleportation a thing, so I don't have to break this contact to get him to my bedroom—because if this is what his kiss does to me, what's sex with him going to be like?

I've got to find out. I break away from him with a gasp. "Upstairs."

The cabbie clears his throat, and Jack throws some bills out of his wallet at him and opens his door. By the time I've fumbled mine open, Jack is already there. Stepping closer, he takes my hand and slams the door shut behind me.

Has an elevator ride ever taken so long? The slow circles he traces on the back of my hand with his thumb have me debating about stopping the elevator and dragging him into a stairwell to get him naked *now*, but then the elevator stops on my floor and we're so close to my bed.

Door open, door closed, shoes were on, kick them off. No stopping to ask if he'd like something to drink. I pull him straight to the bedroom and turn to face him. His momentum crushes us together, and I press harder against him, wrap my arms around him, and grab that tight ass I've wanted to squeeze for years, grinding against him. This time, when my lips meet his, they're curled into a satisfied smile because now there's nothing stopping us but clothes and common sense.

One down.

His skin is smooth and warm beneath my hands, which I slide under the hem of his T-shirt before coaxing it over his head. Kissing down his throat and chest, lightly grazing it with my teeth, I'm rewarded with his intake of breath and his hands finding their way to my shoulders. He pulls me upright and kisses me hungrily. One hand wraps around, bending me back like a cobra, and he tangles his other hand in my hair, squeezing my body in his arms like he can't get enough.

I want him on top of me. Now.

We're riding the same lusty wavelength because he straightens and pulls back. "Take your shirt off. I need to see you."

"Take your pants off," I counter. "I need to feel you."

His jeans hitting my floor is the most glorious sound I've ever heard.

"Now you." His order is paired with hungry eyes.

I pull my shirt over my head slowly to make him wait. When I get it off and can see again, he's moved closer and stands only inches away from me.

"Hi." His voice is a smoldering bed of hot coals I want to roll around in.

"Hi." I smile. "Want to help me with my pants?"

His long, well-formed fingers curl into the belt loops of my jeans and tug me closer. "You sure you need help, beautiful girl?"

I trail my hands over the chiseled contours of his abs and up his well-defined chest. "My hands are busy."

The pull of the button and the slide of the zipper, and then the kiss of the cool night air greets my thighs and calves. He's bent closer to coax my jeans down, and his hair smells woodsy and fresh, like a forest after a storm. I stop him on his way up, my mouth on his again. How will I ever get enough of these lips, this tongue, now that I've tasted this forbidden fruit?

The bed hits my legs as he walks us backward, one more step closer to the point of no return. Maybe we passed that point the moment I asked him to take me home. He pulls my knee up and wraps my thigh around his hip, the tip of his cock nudging against me through my panties. I wrap both legs around him, hooking my ankles together behind his back, allowing full access, and he moves us up my bed and rubs his hands down my back in one long sweep that ends at my ass.

Unlocking my legs from around his waist, he pulls my boy-short panties off, and I hook my big toe into the waistband of his boxers, returning the favor by pulling them down. Arching forward, I undo my bra and throw it across the room, suddenly impatient to be naked. He straddles me and runs his hands up my ribs to cup my breasts, gently kneading them and palming my nipples until they harden further.

"God, Sarah."

I reach up and take his thick, hard length in my hand. "I could say the same thing, Jack."

He lets me slowly stroke him from root to tip a few times, then pushes my hand away and moves up my body. Lips land on my neck and burn a trail of shivers across my skin and down my collarbone and chest before he takes one of my nipples between his teeth and rakes the sensitive tip with his tongue. A jolt of hot pleasure leadens my limbs and bucks my hips when he sucks harder, using his fingers on my other nipple to mimic the movements of his mouth, even as his free hand slowly meanders lower.

My thigh muscles tense as his fingers get closer, then relax when he grazes my clit with a fingertip. I tap at his shoulder and he looks up at me.

"Kiss me." The pleading in my voice annoys me, but I regret nothing when he takes my lower lip firmly between his teeth and slowly runs the tip of his tongue from one side to the other. He releases my lip and once again claims my mouth in a kiss as he plunges a finger inside me. I cry out into his mouth, and he gently sucks the tip of my tongue while lightly rubbing my G-spot with a finger too talented to be legal.

Wars would be fought over his hands if people knew what he was capable of.

His tongue plunges deep inside my mouth, but it's not what I need as the pressure builds. A second finger joins his first, and when he angles his thumb against my clit, I'm gone, pleasure flowing over me and drowning me in its silken depth as I come silently, deeply, intensely.

When I can form words again, I whisper, "There are condoms in the nightstand."

He opens the drawer and pulls out the box, cocking an eyebrow at me. "New box?"

"It's been a while," I admit.

Then he puts on a condom and repositions himself over me. He rubs the tip up and down my wetness a couple of times, not penetrating, driving me crazy. "How do you want me?" He brushes my forehead with his lips.

My heart thrills at being asked, at him caring. He's a considerate lover. "Hard and slow."

"Perfect."

Then he's pushing, slowly sliding inside inch by inch, and I can't exhale until he's all the way in and filling me so completely it almost hurts.

"Relax, baby." He nibbles my earlobe. "I'm going to make you feel so good." His lips and tongue dance over my throat, sending a drunken pleasure haze into my brain.

I run my hands down his biceps and forearms, loving the hardness of them—loving the hardness inside me more when he rubs the base of his cock against my clit. Propped on his elbows, he uses one hand to caress my face. The other meanders down my side, brushing my breast and belly and hip, gripping my thigh, pulling my knee up to spread me more, to expose more flesh.

Then he pulls out and thrusts in again, and now I wish he would never stop moving like *this*. Hard and slow. Pushing into me with all he's got, but in no hurry. Making it feel like he could do this forever.

The things he's doing with his hips... I underestimated how good he can make me feel, and I've never been happier to be so wrong. I clutch him tighter and try to absorb the pleasure he radiates into my every pore. Jack's hard to get to know when his clothes are on. Right now, he's expressing himself very clearly, really well.

So goddamn well.

He kisses my cheeks and forehead and jaw, and then my mouth, sweetly, lightly, while rocking his hips against mine and fucking me so thoroughly that another orgasm builds—but that's impossible because I never come twice.

Maybe I never came twice because no one's ever fucked me like Jack is.

"You feel so fucking good, Sarah." He claims my mouth with his, devouring any response I would have come up with, as if I'd be able to form words with the things he's doing to me.

I rotate my hips more severely and, despite what I said about slow, urge him to go faster, deeper.

He laces our fingers together, pins my hands above my head, and drives into me harder than I'd thought possible, unleashing sounds of pure pleasure I didn't know I could make. I want to wrap my arms around him again and hold him close, but the way he's physically dominating me gives me shivers. Pressure builds, pleasure swelling deep from my core. He lets my hands go to grab my knees, spreading them farther apart, and then I do clutch at him, scratching at his back and begging him not to stop.

He *doesn't* stop, and after a moment, I shake for a good twenty seconds, coming harder than I ever have, with him twitching his own release while still buried deep inside me.

After a moment, he carefully pulls out and rolls off, pulling me into his arms, both of us breathing heavily.

I swallow. "That was—"

"Fucking amazing."

I smile. "Mmm. For real."

"I've seen you move on the dance floor, but I had no idea you could move your hips like *that*."

"There's lots you don't know about me. And God, Jack, those *fingers*."

"All this time we could have been doing this."

I hope he's not thinking about a relationship. I know that would never work. That's not what tonight was about. "I have an idea of something we can do to get to know each other better."

"What?"

"This time"—I roll over and face him—"I'll be on top."

Chapter 17

I SLICK ON ONE LAST COAT OF WATERPROOF mascara—to combat the humidity—and toss it back into my makeup bag. Jack didn't give me much information about our date, but he said other people would be there, so I've slithered into a strapless little black dress that's never let me down, pairing it with peacock feather earrings, cobalt heels, and a matching clutch. I give my hair another squirt of shine serum, but the humidity is winning the battle against my straightener.

Really, I shouldn't be going to this much trouble. It's just Jack. We were supposed to be a one-night thing, but he asked me out while I was still floating in a haze of postorgasmic pleasure, and I said yes.

Besides, it's one date. One.

I bite my lip. If this goes well… A knock sounds from the door.

No point getting ahead of myself.

When I pull the door open, Jack's face makes my ego flutter its eyelashes. His gaze does a slow crawl up my body, and by the time it reaches my eyes, his are hungry. "You look amazing."

I lock the door behind us. "Thanks." He's in dark jeans and a black button-down with the sleeves rolled up his forearms. That shouldn't do things to my belly, but it does.

I check him out in the elevator mirror.

His hair is brushed back but still damp from a recent shower. I want to run my fingers through it, but I keep my hands to myself. "Where are we going tonight?"

"Some fancy cocktail thing."

"Don't sell it too hard." I quirk an eyebrow.

He grins and guides me out the front door of the building with a hand at my lower back. "Sorry. It's schmoozing with some old rich guys."

"And you thought I'd be into that? Where's Bambi?" I frown at the sleek black Mercedes he's leading me to. It's crouched at the curb like a panther.

"At home. I decided I should upgrade. Look the part a little."

He opens my door, and I slide onto the expensive leather seat.

We drive over in silence, my mind boggling the whole way to SoHo. How the hell much money does Jack have? It doesn't matter, but you think you know someone, and then this comes out of left field.

When we pull up to the brick Puck Building, with its huge, white columns and golden statue above the arch, I glare at him.

"This is where we're going?"

He nods.

Suddenly I feel grubby. "You could have told me. I'd have bought a new dress, worn something different."

Jack cups my jaw and leans in. "I fucking love what you've got on, and so will everyone else. They're all going to be jealous that you're here with me." He growls the last word and crushes his lips to mine, causing heat to flare in my body and radiate out, melting away any feelings but sexy ones.

At least until we get inside.

Now I know how Eliza Doolittle felt.

I'm so busy feeling self-conscious about my appearance and gawking at the penthouse itself that I miss the names of the hosts, smiling and nodding my way through the introductions like a mannequin.

"I'm going to steal Jack for a moment." The older gentleman smiles at me and I nod, though he's already taking Jack away, leading him over to a group of men smoking cigars in the corner.

I sip from a glass of perfectly chilled champagne, unable to remember how it got in my hand, and wander over to the spectacular view of Soho from the floor-to-ceiling windows in the great room.

This is someone's house. They see one of the most expensive neighborhoods lit up like this every night. It feels like an expensively decorated dream.

Gleaming hardwood, base moldings—and *two* chandeliers over the table in the dining area. You know, because one isn't enough.

Surreptitiously, I glance around the room, eyeing the other people. There are about twenty-five other guests, milling about in clothes that probably cost more than what I make in a year. A woman in next year's hottest Chanel dress is talking to a twentysomething whose engagement ring is blinding me from thirty feet away.

Every article of clothing is a must-have. A Brazilian supermodel is in the corner talking to an actor from one of those cop shows.

And I'm here in feather earrings and three-year-old Louboutins.

I don't know whether to kiss Jack for bringing me here or kill him for bringing me here without a week to prepare my wardrobe and accessories.

An hour later, I'm leaning more toward the latter. He's maybe talked to me twice since we've been here, for a grand total of ten minutes. People keep "stealing him away" and taking him to talk shop, and while I'm happy he's in demand, it also really sucks to be left alone feeling like a designer impostor in a room full of the genuine things.

The only time people look directly at me is when they're taking Jack away. No one even talks to me, despite my friendly smiles and attempts at conversation. I'd pull out my phone, but it would probably self-destruct in embarrassment at not being next year's upgraded model that's not available in stores yet.

I head toward the powder room to kill some time.

It's so ostentatious. I mean, whose private residence has fancy rooms within the powder room?

People who throw major parties, I guess. There's no way to pretend I'm not impressed and way out of my league.

I'm squinting critically at the mirror in my little stall, dabbing at the smudge beneath my eyes, when the outer door opens and I hear the water in the sink running.

"Have you *seen* him? What's his story?"

"He's a DJ, but apparently he bought a club recently, and let me tell you, I wouldn't mind taking him for a spin. Pun intended."

My ears perk as my stomach sinks. Are they talking about my Jack?

"What's his name?"

"Jack, or John. Jacob, maybe? Who cares? Did you see his tight ass in those pants?"

"I was too busy checking out his abs—you can see them through his shirt. And my gaze strayed a little lower and stayed there. Those jeans do him *huge* favors."

I bite my lip hard.

The first woman giggles and continues. "And he's got to be loaded as well or he wouldn't be here."

"I don't even care about that. You remember Anita? Apparently she hooked up with him last year. The jeans aren't doing him favors. He's hung like a horse and knows exactly how to use it. She had to upgrade her vibrator after being with him."

I feel like I might puke up the expensive hors d'oeuvres I ate.

"I wish Gerry wasn't here. I only said yes to his invitation for the free champagne, but he's definitely lacking in the girth department."

"Maybe you can get J's number. Unless I get it first."

"Isn't he here with someone? Who's she?"

"She's nobody. Did you see her purse?"

The door swishes shut behind them, and I wait a minute so I'm not leaving right after them. I don't even know which two women they are. Models? Trust-fund babies who belong in this world and who slum it for kicks?

This sucks. This is Jack's world now, and I don't belong here. To people like this, I'm a nobody and Jack's a mover and shaker. And even among the people who don't care about his money, sex-hungry she-wolves will be lurking, devouring him with their eyes. No matter where we go, this is going to happen. It's not Jack's fault he's sexy as hell, but could I deal with this on a daily basis?

I let cool water flow over my wrists and blot my face after drying my hands. I've never been the jealous type, but… Wait a minute. I don't have to be jealous at all.

We're not dating. We're fucking.

I shouldn't feel bad that other women want my date. I should be proud that I'm the one he's going home with. Me. The only one here whose family never summered in the Hamptons, whose name will never be on the list for a crocodile Birkin.

Me.

Little nobody me is here with one of the hottest new up-and-comers.

Head up, I stride out of the powder room and head for the terrace. Jack's shaking the hand of a fiftysomething guy in a suit and catches my eye. I jerk my head toward the door and walk outside.

The door opens and closes behind me, giving a flash of voices and crystal glasses tinkling in toasts and casual cheers.

I head around the corner of the wall of the great room and into a little alcove. Leaning on the railing, I take in the sight of SoHo at night—a rare, gorgeous view. I didn't know there were views like this in real life. My hands are bracketed with his a second before he presses against me. "The party's inside, Sarah."

I arch my back, pressing my ass more firmly into his crotch. "Have you seen the stars, Jack? They're so pretty tonight." I don't give a rat's ass about the stars.

His hands dig into my hips as he pulls me closer and nibbles my earlobe. Jealousy over what those women said—at seeing him charming everyone in the room—is stupid, but I still feel it like a rock in my shoe. I can pretend it's not there all I want, but nothing will take that feeling away.

Nothing but his mouth on mine. I tip my head back and he kisses me deeply, firmly. Jack kisses like in the movies. It's intense and makes me feel like I'm the only one in his world and he's claiming me in case we're torn away from each other. He pulls back and I'm breathless, dizzy for more.

What we have is physical. It's amazing and the best sex I've ever had, but that's as far as it will go. He doesn't let me in, and I'm tired of trying to dig deeper.

I'll appreciate this for the intense physical connection it is. He pulls me into the shadows of the terrace and kisses the smile off my lips.

Chapter 18

ZIGGY HAS SCREWED UP FOUR MESSAGES TODAY AND dropped a full cup in reception, shattering it and sending Madagascar spice herbal tea everywhere, but nothing can kill the smile Jack put on my face last night.

And again this morning.

I hum happily as I pick up the shattered remains of the cup and mop up the tea. Screw meditation and yoga—all it took to unwind the past couple of months of stress was a little naked time with Jack. He was so cute on the way out the door. I asked him if he had everything. He started patting himself and called it his ready-to-go grope. He keeps his phone and keys in the same pocket every time, so he pats himself while running out the door. It saves time and he knows right away if he's missing something.

I offered to do it for him, which led to another round of sexy shenanigans that almost made me late to work. God, it was even better than I'd imagined. The memory alone is enough to bring a smile to my face again.

Phyllis strides in with a razor-thin blond with sharp features, mean eyes, and three children. "This is the office, Marjorie. Would you like a tea before we start?"

"You don't have coffee, do you?" She turns her nose up at the selection of teas.

"Of course. Sarah."

"Yes?" I squat to sweep the bits of Ziggy's shattered cup into the dustpan.

"Coffee." She says it like I'm simple and do this every day but have mysteriously forgotten that it's an expected duty. But I don't have time to be running to buy drinks for people when the phone is ringing and there are people in the lobby.

"We don't have any, but the bodega next door has an amazing French roast." I smile up at Phyllis and continue cleaning up the tiny slivers of glass. Man, Ziggy really broke that cup good. *Opa!* I chuckle.

"Wow. Is she always this unprofessional?"

My head snaps up. Marjorie glares at me while her kids run amok, throwing magazines on the floor. One's found a pen from my desk and is drawing on the wall. "Can you…" I motion to the burgeoning artist.

Marjorie ignores her kid, crosses her arms, and moves closer to Phyllis. They just stand there, glaring at me. I don't know who I dislike more between the pair of them. Same crappy attitudes, but at least Phyllis doesn't come with a posse of destruction.

"Sarah, I've got Marjorie in for the next hour and a half. Keep an eye on her kids."

What the hell? "Um, no?"

"Excuse me?" Phyllis straightens to her full height. She's taller and larger than I am, but she's too addled to intimidate me. "Look, bitch, Marjorie is my friend, and…she's a client. You need to do your very best to see that she gets the most relaxing Inner Space experience we can provide for her."

"What's this?"

Ziggy's appearance behind me explains Phyllis's sudden professionalism.

"Slight disagreement, Ziggy. Phyllis's client is here, and Phyllis asked that I watch her kids while they're in session." I raise my eyebrows and smirk at Phyllis, knowing Ziggy can't see my face. He'll back me up on this at least. I'm his receptionist, not a babysitter.

"Well, what's the issue?"

He can't be serious. I have thirty-seven things to do, none of which will get done if I have to sit here and watch Marjorie's hell-spawn—now tearing pages out of the magazines and tossing the pieces about like confetti. "The laundry won't get done if I'm stuck to the desk."

Ziggy gives me the look an indulgent parent gives to a child. "The laundry can wait, Sarah. It's not the end of the world if the towels don't get folded the very second the dryer buzzes."

They all laugh and I try to look affable, taking my seat behind the desk. Ziggy disappears into a room as his next client shows up. Drizella and Anastasia head into a room, and I start trying to mitigate the damage the kids have caused. Unfortunately, I need a mop, because one of the kids figured out how to work the cooler and has been flinging tiny cups of water all over the floor.

Kids suck.

"Excuse me?"

I look up at the tall lady with a blond side-shave. "Yes?"

"I'm here to see Phyllis for a massage. I'm a couple minutes late."

Crap.

Five minutes before my shift ends, Fern walks into reception. "Sarah, I think we need to have a talk about your performance today."

I haven't technically done anything wrong, but unease still stiffens my limbs and heats my face. "Okay."

Fern hauls a chair next to me. "We have to be really careful with the schedule when we're booking people."

Her use of "we" doesn't escape me, though we both know she's referring to me alone. "I wasn't the one who booked Phyllis's friend. Callie was in the schedule. I pulled her file last night and put it in Phyllis's tray. Phyllis brought her friend Marjorie in today out of the blue."

Fern frowns and closes her eyes as if she's in actual pain. "Sarah, we're a team here. When you make a mistake, we all make a mistake."

"But I didn't make a mistake."

She waves her hands around me. "There's that defensive energy again."

"I'm not trying to be defensive. I'm trying to explain what happened."

"No, you aren't trying to explain the truth. You're trying to be right."

I feel my eyes become two different sizes. "It's the same thing."

She stands. "You need to decide which is more important: being right, or being here."

"But Phyllis double-booked the clients."

"Perception is reality, Sarah." She walks to the cooler and pours a cup of water.

"What does that even mean?"

She takes a few deep breaths and comes back to her chair. "It means that to you, Phyllis booked the appointment. And it means to Phyllis, you are the one who booked it. You perceive your version to be the right one. So does she."

"Yes, but one of us is telling the truth."

"When there are two radically differing opinions, the truth always lies right in the middle."

What? "Not always."

"Always."

It bloody well does not always lie right in the middle. Sometimes people are just lying or wrong. How do I respond to this?

My mind spins and Fern continues. "What you really need to do in these situations is ask yourself, 'What am *I* doing to make these situations worse? What can *I* do in these circumstances to make the outcome better?'"

Slam Phyllis's stupid face into the counter and run screaming from the building? "I see what you mean, Fern."

"Just try to keep that in mind. Instead of gathering this prickly, defensive energy around you, try to be soft and welcoming."

I smile and nod because I can't unclench my jaw enough to speak.

"You may go now. See you tomorrow."

No time is wasted as I grab my purse and get the hell out of there as fast as possible, eschewing the subway. I need to stomp off some of this frustration, and a nice, long walk is a good start. Everything started out so well today, and now it's like the color has been sucked

from it. How can Fern and Ziggy completely disregard
the truth when that's all they talk about?

The blaring horns and sirens going off are a welcome
change from the stupid Tibetan singing bowl CD my
hippie bosses had playing, and I welcome the cacophony
like a long-lost friend. The muggy air coats my skin,
making my tank top cling to me. That makes a few guys
catcall and another tell me to smile—but something in
my eyes shuts them up and makes people give me a little
breathing room on the normally crowded sidewalk.

Heat radiates up from the asphalt in hazy waves, and
a trickle of sweat tickles my spine. Six blocks and too
much sun later, I feel no better about my conversation
with Fern.

The complete lack of logic crawls beneath my skin
and chafes against my bones. Guess they mean their personal truths, which is another way of saying, "I believe
what I believe in, and *my* version of the truth is *everyone's* reality."

Perception, my ass.

I cram myself on the subway with the rest of the
working crowd. I really should have taken a cab.

When I get home much later, my feet ache and my
annoyance hasn't faded. I slam the door and shove the
dead bolt into place, then kick my shoes off, liking the
way they sound hitting the wall. To the bottom of my
toenails, I know that Phyllis double-booked on purpose,
but Fern would hear none of it.

Pete doesn't pick up when I call, and I don't bother
leaving a message. I'd just spew everything onto his voice
mail and not get the benefit of his sympathetic comments.

I'm typing in my computer's password before I

realize I've turned it on. Skype loads with a cheery
zoom. He's online. And he's left me a message.

Him: Message me when you get home.

Seeing that message from him puts a dent in the
frustration.

Me: Hey.

His status was Away, but it changes to Online immediately. *How are you today?*
Shitty. I delete it before sending and type something
else. *Is your other clinic hiring?* Deleted unsent. I hate today.

*Him: What's wrong, Sarah? I can tell some-
thing's up.*

What do I even say? The truth? Isn't that overwhelm-
ing? My phone rings—a call, but it's Jack. I don't
answer. We parted on a high note, and I don't want to
spoil those feelings by unloading all my hippie bullshit
on him. Besides, that's a bit more domestic than I care
to get with him. We're sleeping together, and that's all.
We're not each other's support systems. Leaning on
him when I have problems isn't the smart thing to do.
Instead, I reply to Blake. *Work.*

Him: Ah. What did they do now?

I love how he automatically assumes I wasn't the one
screwing up. Feeling like he's on my side wraps me in

warmth and security. *Evil coworker brought an evil friend to work. Friend had three evil kids who destroyed reception for two hours while I was forced to watch them.*

Him: That sucks. You're not a babysitter.

Me: That's what I said! Unfortunately, boss didn't agree. And there was a scheduling mishap because of the coworker, which was resolved, but somehow I got in trouble for it.

Him: I hate hippies.

I like you. I hit Enter, then blush. I hadn't meant to type it, even though it's true.

Him: I like you too.

Me: Thanks for letting me vent.

Him: That wasn't venting. That was barely a leak.

I laugh. *LOL.*

Him: What are you up to tonight?

Is he going to ask me to meet up in person? Do I want that? *Licking my wounds.*

His reply seems to take forever. *Care for some company?*

Online, or in person? Which do I even want?

Him: Online. I don't think we're ready for in person yet.

Relief and disappointment spiral through me. Then again, he didn't say anything about online.

Him: So. What are you wearing?

I giggle. *A sweaty tank top I really need to strip out of.*

Him: You're bad. What are your plans for the weekend?

Why, you want to come meet the nightie? He's really not joining in this sexy talk, despite my prompts.

Him: I think the nightie and I should wait awhile. In person or online.

Well, he closed that door firmly. *Oh.*

Him: Are you mad?

No. A little. Mostly I feel rejected.

Him: I'm sorry. It's not that I don't want to share that with you as well. It's just that all most people focus on when going out is sex, and they mistake a physical connection for something

more. I want something deeper with
you, Sarah, to truly know you on more
than just a physical level. And I want
you to know me.

That's true enough. Jack and I had a very physical night again, but that's all it was. I guess getting to
know Blake before doing anything naughty is a good
idea—and what I initially wanted. Jack must have
passed me some of his libido through osmosis.

We're going out? I hadn't thought of it like that.

I'm not seeing anyone else. He doesn't ask if I'm
seeing anyone else, but for the first time, I wonder if
I'm dating two men instead of sleeping with one and
talking with another. It's something I've never done
before, and it makes me feel a little strange.

If I'm now dating Blake, what does this mean
for Jack and me? Is there even a Jack and me? We
had sex once. Well. Three times, but that's hardly
dating. It feels weird to be exclusive with someone
I've only spoken to a few times online and met in
person twice.

I send a *:)* instead of a real response. He smiles back.

For now, we're happy.

And he's right. It will be better if I get to know more
about him. I type, *So you know all about me, but I know*
next to nothing about you.

Him: We talked for hours the other day.

Me: Not about you. You know what I mean.

Him: Ah. What did you want to know?

Where should I start? Is your name Blake? *Do you have a job?*

Him: Yes.

Me: Well? What is it?

Him: If I tell you, you'll know for sure who I am.

Me: OMG Is your first name Barack?!

Him: Oh no, you guessed!

I grin. *What DO you do?*

*Him: I'm...an entrepreneur of sorts. I work with
     my hands.*

The massage therapists are independent contractors, so they are technically entrepreneurs. And Blake's hands are frigging amazing. *You're not a drug dealer, are you?* Of course he isn't, but I don't want to be ambushed by a secret coke habit.

Him: Definitely not. I'm not into that scene.

Me: Me neither. Any kids?

*Him: Nope. Do you want kids? You know,
     someday?*

*Me: After today, it will take a few years to forget
that all kids aren't tiny terrors.*

Him: That bad, huh?

Worse. And there were three of them. I shudder.

*Him: I wouldn't want three. Maybe one, but I'd
rather have two.*

*Me: Yeah, I'm an only child. I'd have loved to
have a sibling. I'll never be an auntie.*

*Him: Well, if your spouse has siblings, you'll be
an auntie-in-law.*

I shrug. *Yes. Do you have any siblings?*

Him: A brother.

Me: Are you guys close?

Him: Very.

That's nice. I like to think if I had a brother or sister,
we'd be close, but you see sibling rivalries and fighting
all the time. They're bound by blood but too different to
be close. Or too similar. *A partner in crime would have
been nice.*

Him: It was.

Me: Were you the good kid or the bad one?

Him: I plead the fifth.

Ooh, Blake was a bad boy. Now he's stable, which is even sexier. *:D*

Him: Were you ever a bad girl?

I grin. *Who says I'm still not?*

Him: Touché. So what are you going to do about those hippies?

Me: I still don't know.

Him: Either way, don't let them get you down. I hate that they made you feel bad.

Maybe they did, I write. *But you made me feel better. Thank you.*

Him: Anytime. Have you eaten yet?

No. I wasn't hungry when I got home. But my stomach is rumbling now.

Him: Want to order something and watch a movie with me?

Me: But I thought... Oh, you mean online?

Him: Yes.

I like this idea. We don't have to order from the same place, so I still get to decide what to eat, and since he won't be here, I can eat like nobody's watching. That is the real dream—not dancing like no one's watching. *I like the sound of this. What are you going to eat?*

Him: I think I'll get Indian.

Mmm. *Ooh, that sounds good. I was going to get sushi delivered, but I like the sound of Indian.*

Him: Since I've sort of chosen the cuisine, would you like to choose the movie?

Me: Sure! Do we want an old classic or something we've both never seen before?

Him: You decide.

Maybe I'll go with something new. What if he hates one of my all-time favorites, and then every time I watch it, I'll think of his disparaging comments about it? Then again, I'd rather watch something I've seen since I can't give my full attention to a new movie if we're chatting about it. I open Netflix in a new window. *I have a hankering for something…eighties.*

Him: Perfect.

Me: Maybe not when you see what I choose.

Him: Oh?

Invisible test time. If he reacts poorly to this movie, that's a major strike against him. *You've got Netflix?*

Him: Of course. What am I streaming?

Me: Dirty Dancing.

Him: Okay.

I wait a minute, but he doesn't say anything else. I bite my lip. *Thoughts?*

Him: Actually, I like this movie.

Me: You do?

Him: Yes. The music is great, and I secretly wanted to be Johnny when I was younger. Took a bunch of dance classes on the sly to impress the ladies. Bro would have been merciless if he knew about it.

Blake can dance like Johnny Castle? He just gets better and better. *That's sexy.*

Him: Hey, I said I took them. Never said I was any good at it.

Me: I don't believe that for a second. I bet you can move those hips like nobody's business.

Him: Fine, you're right. I was being modest.

Me: Knew it! So, will you take me dancing sometime?

Him: I promise.

We order food and chat until it arrives. Mine comes only five minutes before his, but he insists I start without him. I totally already had, but it was nice that he was considerate of my comfort. The next two hours are spent eating and laughing and talking, hanging with Baby and Johnny at Kellerman's.

It's the perfect end to a crappy day.

Chapter 19

I GLARE AT THE WATERCOOLER, HATING THE STUPID stones inside that make up the filter. It's another hippie thing, some weird water system that has three different kinds of rocks or something. I don't understand how rocks can filter water. Ziggy said something about the attunement of the water on a cellular level, and I kind of glazed over. The water tastes okay, but the system looks like fish should be swimming inside, and I have to pour water in to top it up every day.

My stomach's a huge ball of resentment because I'm alone at work. I'd much rather have had the day off, like I thought I'd get, but on Friday evening, Fern told me that Phyllis might have a client on Sunday, so I had to come in at nine.

Phyllis screwed up Saturday for me too, opening her schedule, then acting incompetent so Ziggy and Fern volunteered me to come in to support her emotionally. Saturday's appointments never showed up—and I suspect they never existed, because Phyllis was the one who added them to the schedule—and she never made it to the office either. By the time I got home, it was two thirty, and I was tired and cranky and just crashed on the couch.

Phyllis is doing this on purpose, but I don't know
why. She shouldn't feel threatened by me. We don't
work the same job, so there's no way I could be viewed
as a replacement.

Today is Monday and I'm alone at the office because
Fern and Ziggy decided everyone needed a day off to
"ground and center their energies outside the office." Really,
I suspect it's because there were only three clients booked in
the schedule and they wanted another day off. Everyone but
me got one, since they wanted someone here to answer the
phones again. They acted like they were doing me a favor
when they said I could leave early—at three.

The Internet is down in the building as well, so I can't
talk to Blake online, and he wasn't in on Saturday when
I came. I wonder where he is. What does he do on his
days off?

My battery is nearly dead, but at least my phone has
Internet. I don't care that it's too soon. I want to see him.
Want to meet up? I'm at work but leaving early.

Ten minutes later he replies. *I don't know. I wanted
you to know me better first.*

Me: Please? You make me feel better.

Him: I can't say no to you. Where and when?

I name a coffee shop a few blocks from my apartment. Home turf, an hour and a half from now.

Him: I'll be there. But...

Me: What?

Him: Keep an open mind, okay?

*Me: If it makes you feel any better, I already
know who this is.*

Him: You do?

Yes. I knew right away. I'm so sleuthy.

Him: That's both a relief and terrifying.

See you in an hour. Oh, Blake. What are you so
worried about?

························——···········

I show up a few minutes early and grab something decaffeinated. I'm already vibrating out of my skin. I can't
believe I'm doing this. Blake and I have talked for hours
and hours, but this still feels like meeting a stranger for
the first time. Now that the disguises are gone, will he
like me? Everything's different in person. What if he
doesn't like me, if he only likes the idea of me?

And what if I don't like him in person when it's more
than casual flirting at work? What if, in retrospect, I
invented more chemistry than there really was? Then
again, if the way he worked the knots out of my neck
is any indication of what his hands can do, I think we
might be okay. He'll come in, and we'll chat and…what,
jump into a relationship? What if he's a bad kisser?
What if he had an ulterior motive for wanting me to get
to know him online before in person? Does he have a
criminal record? Is he into kinky shit?

What if Blake isn't what he claims to be?

And worst of all, what if we don't get along and I lose the amazing relationship we've been cultivating online? Who would I have to talk about the hippies with? To tell about my day? Who would talk with me about my stupid nightmares and share his with me? Losing that would be devastating.

I can't do this. My gaze flies from man to man as they approach the café, ratcheting up my nerves with every footstep until it's finally too much, and I bolt.

It's better this way. We need more time to get to know each other. He was right and I was wrong—and why is this so scary? By the time I get back to my apartment building, the reality of the situation sets in.

I've stood him up.

I'm an awful person, and he's never going to forgive me. I'm the one who pushed a meeting, while he wanted to wait, but here I am, strolling off my elevator, sweating and shaking, and bumping into… "Jack?"

"Hey." Just that one word reminds me of the last time we were together. My thighs tingle.

"What are you doing here?" I step past him and unlock the door, motioning him inside.

"You've sort of been avoiding my calls since we…"

"Ah. I haven't been avoiding you, Jack." I close the door and kick off my sandals.

"Then why haven't you picked up?"

"I've been busy dealing with crazy hippies. They had me go into work today, even though they gave everyone the day off. And I had to go in on Saturday."

"Oh." He runs his hands through his hair. "I thought maybe you had second thoughts about us."

Us? I set my keys on the counter. "Jack, there is no 'us.'"

He moves closer and traces my cheek with his thumb. The look in his eyes breaks my heart. I like Jack, but I can't risk this. "I know you're scared, Sarah. But you feel the connection between us. I know you do."

"It was just sex."

His eyes darken. "It wasn't 'just' anything, and you know it." He steps closer, invading the space between us. He tangles his hand in the hair at the nape of my neck and presses his lips just above the artery—bastard biology giving away exactly how fast my heart is beating.

It wasn't just a connection I felt between us. It was more like we heat-sealed together and obliterated the rest of the world when we touched.

"You do things to my body no one's ever done." Covering his hand with mine, I press a kiss to the inside of his wrist. "But, Jack…what we have is physical only." My other hand wanders around his hip and pulls until we're pressed to each other and I'm breathing in his peppermint breath, wanting to feel it on my skin again and hoping he agrees to the terms I've set.

"Fine. If that's what you want, I'll give it to you."

"Mmm. Please do."

He tugs and my leg rises, wrapping around, and he grabs my thigh, pulling me in tighter. His lips part as though he has something to say, but only a sigh comes out. Then his lips are on mine, and I taste the coolness of mint on the warmth of his tongue. Everywhere he doesn't touch burns jealously for his hands. I'm feverish, shaking, and weak with desire, but I seize him by the belt wrapped around his low-slung jeans and tug him toward the bedroom.

We don't make it to the bed.

It isn't until Jack's mouth works its way down my throat and chest that I realize my shirt and pants are gone. It's so easy to lose myself with him. Grabbing his hair, I force his head back until he looks into my eyes. I kiss the little mole at the corner of his eye and reach down to remove his shirt. While he kisses and nibbles my collarbone and heads south, I yank hard, taking his belt off and smacking his ass with it.

"Hey." He unclips my bra. "None of that."

"Or else?" I slap him again.

He moves bullwhip-fast, bending, twisting, and grabbing my waist, but he's upside down.

"What are you doing?" I figure it out quickly, when he straightens and my head points toward the floor, my stomach pressed to his, my shins resting against his collarbones. I hook my elbows around his calves. "This is teaching me a lesson? Giving me a head rush?"

He adjusts his grip, hitching me higher. "Not exactly."

My hips twitch involuntarily when his mouth makes contact between my legs. He works me through my satin panties for a minute before slipping his tongue beneath the fabric.

"Please." I brace my hands against the floor.

"Please what?" His tongue circles my clit and my elbows buckle and it's a long moment before I can speak.

I moan. "I don't even know."

His laughter sends vibrations through his mouth and against my clit, and I come, hard, dizzy from what he's done as much as from the blood rushing to my head.

Slowly, gently, he turns me around and sets me on the bed. I lie there spinning for a moment, breathing heavily.

"Still want to spank people?"

"If that was supposed to be a deterrent, you've failed spectacularly."

He chuckles softly.

I point behind him at the floor. "For real. Can you pass me that belt?"

He crawls over my body unhurriedly, like a panther sneaking up on its prey, and lazily runs a hand up my side. I spread my legs just as he settles on top of me, gasping when he presses his hard length against me. He's still in his jeans, and the material chafes me through my panties in the best possible way.

We grind together, locked in a kiss, arms and legs and hands sinuous and hungry. Jack sucks my tongue, and I bite his lip in retaliation and scratch down his back for good measure. His thumbs flick across my nipples and tease them through my bra, then his hand dips down to my waist, hips, the swell of my pubic bone, underneath the waist of my panties.

"Oh God." I feel it, but he says it when he slides two fingers up and down, feeling how wet he's made me, rubbing the pleasure-soaked fingers across my clit. But when he suddenly plunges those fingers deep inside and starts rhythmically pulsing them against *that* spot right there, my voice drops an octave and my back arches.

"Jack."

"Yes?"

God, I love that smile. "I want you inside me."

"And I want to make you come again first."

"I need you to fuck me. Right. Now."

His pupils dilate and his breath hitches. I cry out as he withdraws his fingers, but his lips crush my cries as he slides my underwear off, then breaks the kiss when he stands and removes his jeans and boxers. I can't resist reaching over and stroking his cock. His abs flex, and the veins on his lower belly become more pronounced.

"Are you going to get a condom on, or are you just going to stand around with your dick in my hand all day?"

"For that? You're getting fucked hard."

"Promise?" I trace one of those veins toward his cock with my tongue, slow like cold syrup dripping from the bottle. He twitches in my hand, and I trace my lips from the base of the shaft to the head, keeping my eyes on his as I take as much of him as I can into my mouth. What I can't suck I stroke with my hand, so every inch of him is being touched. I swirl my tongue faster, suck harder, and when he pushes me back, triumph ripples through me.

He gets a condom from the nightstand and rolls it on, never looking away from me once, dark and delicious promises in his eyes. I know I'm in trouble when he kneels on the bed and pushes my knees up and apart in a position that spreads me wide but still allows him to get close. He squeezes my ass, then he strokes my thighs and pushes into me with one slow movement.

That first gentle slam into home is the best, like a relief, but all I want is more. And Jack gives it to me. Deep thrusts, shallow thrusts, all while rubbing my clit. Wanting him even closer, I throw my legs around his hips and squeeze until he moves on top of me, missionary-style. His pubic bone rubs against my clit, and I feel myself tighten around his cock while he drags himself out and pushes back in.

"Harder," I urge him.

"I don't want to hurt you."

"You won't."

And he slams into me with a force that drives me over the edge in three more pistons of his hips, and I scream his name while he keeps pounding into me, riding me through the pleasure until he stiffens and comes a moment later. I close my eyes and squeeze him tightly. Senses completely overloaded and satisfied, I nearly doze off with him still buried inside me.

Chapter 20

FRIDAY FINDS ME RIDICULOUSLY EXCITED TO GET MY check and get the hell out of Inner Space for the weekend—especially since Phucking Phyllis ruined my last one, and Fern and Ziggy ruined Monday. Even at the law firm, I never counted down the days, hours, minutes until the workweek was over. But when I glance at my net pay, there's a problem. Ziggy wanders out into reception. I decide to tackle the small issue first. "Ziggy? I'm short on my check."

"Yeah, that's from when you came in early." He answers that like he was waiting for me to bring it up.

Wednesday, I'd stayed up way too late talking to Blake online. I guess that threw me off when I set my alarm, and I stumbled through my morning routine an hour early. But I came in and realized I was horrifically early and got right to work. I'd done dishes, cleaned, and typed up a couple of insurance forms before Ziggy came in at nine thirty. "But I was working the whole time. You came in and saw me. You even had me doing things for you."

He nods. "Yeah, but we didn't ask you to come in then. It'd be different if we asked you to come in early or stay an hour late, but we didn't. So that's on you."

My left eye twitches. "Right, but that's not the only issue. You guys didn't pay me for that Monday you had me come in—or the hour you had me come in to check on Blake." The Monday they had me work so I couldn't get Dad's pills.

Ziggy looks baffled. "If you have an issue, you'll have to talk to Fern."

This is absolutely unacceptable. "Okay."

"You may not be happy with the situation, but this is what's happened, and it couldn't have happened any other way. Just breathe into it." He breezes out the front door, taking an early lunch.

So. Violently. Annoyed right now. Twelve hours isn't a small amount—at least not to me.

Needing to burn off some energy, lest I crane-kick the phone through the front window and run after it screaming with glee at my newfound freedom, I head to the back room and begin folding sheets.

Elise, a new massage therapist, rushes into the back. "My client's here early! It wouldn't have been a big deal, but I'm late too, so I put her in a room and she's getting undressed, but I feel terrible about keeping her waiting."

I nod in commiseration. "They're never early unless you're running late."

"For real. Crap!" A thunk, and the sound of something spilling.

I turn and survey the scene. Laundry soap is *everywhere*. In the sink, on the counter, inside the laundry basket, in the garbage, and on the floor. All over the floor.

"I'm so sorry, Sarah! I tried to get a towel and bumped it with my elbow."

The best I can fake is a weak smile. "It's okay, Elise. You go see to your client. I'll clean this up."

She looks like she wants to cry, which makes me feel better. She didn't do it on purpose, so there's no point being mad at her.

"I promise, I'll—"

I hold up a hand. "You'll do nothing. It was an accident. Just go take care of your client. I'll clean this up."

"You are the nicest person ever. Thank you." She hurries out of the room, and I grab the broom and sweep up the soap, tipping it into the garbage.

Honestly, with the number of crumbs and bits on the floor with the powder, you'd think I don't sweep every day, but soon enough it's cleaned up. How ironic is it that I'm cleaning up cleaning supplies? What if it had been floor cleaner? That would have been even more ironic. Or convenient—just add water. On the downside, there's only enough laundry soap left in the box for about three and a half loads. Fern or Ziggy will have to pick up more tonight or tomorrow morning before we open.

Ziggy pokes his head in. "Sarah? The phone was ringing."

"Sorry, Ziggy. One of the therapists accidentally knocked the detergent off the shelf, so I've been back here cleaning it up and didn't hear it." No way I'm landing Elise into it. She's too nice and I want to keep her here.

He looks around as if trying to see the mess, but I've already swept it up. "Oh. Well, did you put it back into the box?"

"Uh, what?"

"Did you sweep it up and put it back into the box?"

He's kidding, right? "It fell on the floor."

"Right, but that happened before, and we just swept it up and tipped it back into the box. Saves money."

"There was dirt in it."

"It's soap."

It was on the floor. I've told him. How can I be clearer? "Most of it fell into the garbage."

"Oh. I'll pick up more after work."

I feel my eyebrows do something unattractive to my forehead when I walk out of the kitchen and head back to reception. What the hell? Are they going bankrupt? Is this why they've shorted me an hour and are trying to squirm out of paying me properly? Phyllis's sabotage aside, is my job secure at all, or have they mismanaged this place right into the ground? Maybe they're just supremely cheap.

"Sarah?" Fern has snuck up on me while I was lost in a cloud of rage and worry. "Ziggy says you wanted to discuss your check."

"Yes." Keeping my voice mild is the way to go here. They made a mistake, no big deal—as long as it's rectified. "You guys shorted me twelve hours on my check."

Fern laughs. "This can't be right, Sarah. And we're not paying you for the hour you came in early."

"The big shortage is from the Monday you had me come in. Remember? I needed to get my dad's heart pills that day?"

She grabs the nearby calculator. "That's only eleven hours total."

"Right, but the day before, you had me come in because Ziggy had booked someone with Blake but hadn't told him."

"You know." She begins punching the buttons. "I honestly never thought you were so materialistic, Sarah. Don't we take care of you here? Good hours, relaxing work environment. You're practically family."

This is how they treat family? "I'm not asking for anything extra."

Fern digs in her handbag and comes up with a checkbook. "You're young, Sarah, and still have time to make something of yourself. But you'll get nowhere in this life—or after—if you give in to the trappings of this money-hungry society like everyone else." She fills out the check, clearly angry judging by how hard she's pressing the pen to the paper, and I try not to gape at her words.

They had me type up the invoices, so I know that Fern and Ziggy's little workshops cost eleven hundred dollars *per person* for a weekend. They do two or three per month, times about eight participants each time, which equals who the hell are *you* calling materialistic? Not to mention the weekend retreat they throw at some nearby resort in the middle of nowhere, which costs four thousand dollars per person, and they don't run it unless there's a minimum of ten people in the class.

They've done two this year and had five last year. Call me crazy, but if they were really all about the energy and making the world a better place, they wouldn't charge such exorbitant prices for their workshops.

Fern hands me the check, and it's the amount they shorted me—minus the hour for Sunday, and the extra hour I came in early. Her smile is tight. "Think about the life you want. The life you need. You're worth more than money, and I shudder to think about how long it's going to take you to figure that out."

She's right that I'm not just a dollar sign, but unfortunately, my landlord doesn't accept interpretive dance as payment. No appropriate retort finds me before she leaves. I got what I'm owed and what's right, but it still somehow feels like I've lost.

Chapter 21

I ALMOST TURNED JACK'S INVITATION DOWN, BUT THAT felt like letting the hippies win, so I agreed to go out with him. And as an added "screw you" bonus, I bought a new dress to wear tonight as a tip of the hat to my *materialistic* generation. Have the hippies never heard of stimulating the economy? My plan for the future includes rocking this dress and dancing my ass off with Jack.

Right after his set.

At his club.

And fine, maybe I bought the new dress to show the women at Frisk—show Maxine and Shiny Hair—that Jack's with me for a reason.

His response when he picked me up in the cab and saw me was worth it. I'm surprised we made it out of the apartment, given how intensely he kissed me—against the wall of my lobby.

"We'll continue this later," he'd growled. I've never felt such raw hunger for someone before.

The fact that we couldn't give in to the raw, physical lust has made this entire night feel like drawn-out foreplay. Jack's splayed hand on my lower back when he guided me to a table in the VIP section lingered just long enough to burn its shape on my skin through my dress.

In retaliation, I made sure to brush my ass against him when I slid into my seat.

He left to get our drinks, giving us a needed breather. It picked up as soon as he got back to the table and sat across from me.

His eye twitched when the straw slipped between my lips. My nipples tightened when he traced patterns in the condensation on his bottle.

If he hadn't gone to do his set, I may have gotten in trouble for doing something frightfully indecent under the table with my foot.

I'm still debating what we can get away with in his booth—but he's working, so I keep my ass in the chair.

My eyes resentfully drink in the sight of all the girls getting way too close to Jack around the DJ booth. So much for my self-control. Would the situation feel better or worse if we were in a committed relationship instead of just friends with benefits? Do I even have the right to feel possessive without the title of girlfriend?

A sexy brunette runs her hand up his arm, and my blood pressure rises with her grabby little paw. This is a huge reason why Jack and I can't be anything serious. I'm too possessive for this to work. We're only sleeping together, and I feel like that stranger's touching what's mine.

And what's happening when I'm not here? We've never had a discussion about exclusivity, so I have no right to be upset if he's banging ten chicks in ten boroughs. It's his business and none of mine. Maybe this is all he wants with me. Come to think of it, after the blowup in my apartment, he's never broached the subject of being something more.

With a sigh, I turn from the booth and head to the bar. I can't get sad over Jack. We were only going to be a temporary thing anyway.

There are inset lights in the bar, blues and silver making the granite sparkle. The whole place is tasteful but expensive, upscale but not pretentious. People are dressed to be seen, and I'm pretty sure I see a pop star in the corner booth, but I don't want to stare and seem too impressed.

I am, after all, dating the man who owns this place.

No, not dating. Seeing. Is there a difference?

I order a screwdriver—a girl's got to get her vitamin C—and head back to my empty table. Sliding onto the seat, I take a deep breath, then a deep sip, and relax. Jack and I are about fun, having a good time with no strings, and if I start letting feelings creep in, it's just going to complicate the hell out of the arrangement and sour things unnecessarily.

Not wanting to engage anyone near me, I pull out my phone to text Pete about the singer in the corner.

One text message from Blake, sent a minute ago.

I bite my lip, filling with regrets. The last time we spoke was just before I stood him up. He's going to be mad and disappointed in me. I brace myself, waiting to be reamed out, and open the message. *Miss you like crazy. Want to meet tonight instead?*

Do I? I'm just so glad he isn't mad that I stood him up and have avoided him since. My buzz has lifted my mood, and I look back to Jack, who's dancing in the DJ booth, giant headphones pressed to one ear as he seamlessly mixes two of my favorite songs together. I know he's doing it for me—I mentioned liking the one song in his car on the way over—and a smile spreads across my face.

He turns in my direction, and I swear I can feel the warmth of his gaze. I have to look away.

Miss you too, I type. *But not tonight.*

I try to focus on my words to Blake, but I can't get Jack's hungry look out of my mind.

Fuck it.

Slipping my phone back into my purse, I grab my drink and head to the dance floor. Time to drive my friend with benefits a little crazy with some dancing.

⸺⸺⸺⸺⸺

Jack's fingers lightly trace dizzying patterns on the inside of my thigh. I want to climb on top of him but remain still, savoring it. He leans close, trailing the tip of his nose up my jaw and barely touching my ear with his lips. "You nearly killed me in that dress on the dance floor." His ragged whisper teases my skin and pleases my heart.

Mission accomplished. We may not be exclusive, but I still want him to want me more than anyone else in the club. And the way he escorted me from the building like he couldn't wait to be alone with me—in front of a few employees—made my heart purr. We may not be exclusive, but his employees know I'm important to Jack.

I stifle a moan, too aware of the cab driver's eyes in the rearview mirror to relax fully, but Jack's hand and voice are doing plenty to distract me. Jack had a couple of drinks, so we left his car parked at the club. I regret the loss of privacy, but it's probably for the best.

He breathes in my ear. "When we get back to my

place, I'm going to take your panties off with my teeth, bend you over, and fuck you while you're still wearing that dress."

Unf.

Not soon enough, he's tugging me from the cab by the hand and leading me up to the door of his house on the Upper East Side. It's a nice place—understatement of the century. Hardwood floors, comfortable furniture, dark walls. The whole place smells like smoky vanilla, and I wonder if it's a candle or something he cooked recently.

I haven't seen it in a while—we usually hang in public or at Pete's—but there are some big upgrades with the floors and decor.

He locks the door behind us and seizes me, crushing my body to his, kissing me hard and fast with an aggressive tongue and teeth that nip. His hands slide down my back to cup and squeeze my ass. I tense with pleasure and press harder against him. My hands wind around his body, stroking up and down his back before settling on the nape of his neck as I try to make the kiss deeper, harder. He lets me help pull his shirt off.

Jack's erection presses into me, and he wrenches away with a smile. "I believe I made you a promise in the cab."

Warmth spreads through my body, starting at my stomach and radiating everywhere as I remember his words with stark, happy clarity. "You did."

His hands stroke down my thighs before scooping me up and setting me on the kitchen island. "Lie back."

I start to obey but prop myself up on my elbows to watch when he grips my panties in his teeth and pulls them down my legs and over my high heels. The granite is cool beneath me, but his eyes burn a hole in mine as he kisses his way back up my calves and thighs, not once looking away. His hair is silky between my fingers, and I sit up fully and am fisting it when his hot mouth makes contact with my clit.

Watching him go down on me is the hottest thing I've ever seen, and I can't look away. He pushes two fingers inside me, and my back arches. I fall back, unable to stay upright beneath the fury of pleasure, though I'd give anything to keep looking at him. I've never understood the appeal of a mirrored ceiling until this moment. I'm dying to watch him, unable to move.

He presses his teeth into the sensitive skin around my clit and gently sucks at me. A jolt of pleasure slides the room sideways, my heart beating at the lightning bolt of fear of sharp teeth near my sensitive places, but "God, that feels good."

I know he knows. He somehow knows my body better than I do, and a moment later, I'm writhing around, soaking his hand and crying his name. A few gentle licks to let me recover, and he pulls me from the island to my feet and turns me around…and bends me over.

"I've only delivered on half of my promise."

My knees buckle, but the biggest smile claims my lips. Normally, I'd be too short, but the added height from my heels matches us perfectly. The air is cold on my ass and thighs, even cooler when he backs away to undo his jeans and push them down just enough to put on a condom. He hitches up my dress and slaps my ass. I squeak and start to straighten up, but he spreads me wide and thrusts inside with one steady movement, and my body screams *God yes* as my arms shoot out to grab the opposite edge of the island.

The cold, beveled edge of the island rubs my clit as his hard cock plunges in and out of me. His body is muscular and hot and slammed up against my back. The coolness and heat and friction are too much, and then he reaches around and squeezes my breast, stimulating my already-hard nipple. His free hand lavishes attention on the other, and all I can do is grip the edge of the island and brace myself as he grinds me six ways to Sunday.

He leans over and kisses the back of my neck, and my pussy begins to flutter, the muscles deep inside seizing and clamping down on his cock as an orgasm starts.

"Come with me." He continues pumping for a moment. Then his hips press tightly to me, and the tip of him hits a place that makes me go rigid and shake, then go absolutely limp with pleasure.

No movement but the racing of our hearts, the heavy breathing, and Jack's hands gently stroking my shoulders and running through my hair.

"Mmm. You're trying to kill me with this dress. Admit it."

I smile. "I had no idea you were into girlie girls."

"I'm into things that show off your incredible legs."

"You're a leg man?"

He nuzzles the back of my neck, making my eyes roll back. My pussy tightens around him again; he's found one of my hot spots. "I'm a Sarah man." He pulls out of me, which stimulates places that are wet and already throbbing, and I moan and clench my thighs when I feel his half-hard dick start to go rigid again.

"God, Sarah. You're going to kill me."

He might kill me too. I could live with him inside me and forget about the world outside, forget to eat or sleep or breathe. "Take me to your bedroom. You fucked me on something hard. I want to return the favor on something soft."

He presses his erection against me. "It won't be soft."

"God, I hope not."

Chapter 22

"WE'VE GOT SOMETHING FOR YOU THAT WE THINK WILL solve your"—Fern looks me up and down—"dilemma."

Dilemma? I follow her to the back room where there's a pile of fabric on the counter in blinding shades of red, orange, and yellow. The colors are so saturated and bright that I have to blink and look away. Fern's expectant smile confuses me.

I'm clearly missing something. "What?"

She tsks. "They're smocks! Now you won't have to worry about what to wear every day. Isn't that fabulous?"

No. Oh God, no. She holds one up and spreads it out, and I see it is indeed a smock.

"Put it on," she encourages with a smile.

I balk, but there's a stack of them, so at least I won't be alone in this travesty of fashion and individuality. With a smile, I take it, head to the bathroom, and put it on as I try to compose myself in private. Looking in the mirror, I can see it's even worse than I thought. The color scheme is like a reverse partial rainbow. The neck, shoulders, and sleeves are bright yellow—a color that's always made me look sallow and ill. The strip of orange cuts my boobs in half and continues down to my belly button. The bottom of the smock is bright red.

The lights reflect the colors into the room around me, and they shine up into my face. As if the horizontal striping wasn't unflattering enough, I look radioactive. The material is stiff, and the boxy pattern completely hides my shape, but I discover a tie at the back and pull the drawstring a little tighter. It brings in the waist but makes the shoulders and sleeves flare out more dramatically.

Now I look like a fluorescent linebacker.

I loosen the drawstring, returning to being a rectangle. And I'm going to have to wear one of these every day? What's brought this new uniformity on? Why would Ziggy and Fern, champions of freedom of expression, suddenly decide uniforms are the way to go? They're not corporate enough to resolve any conflict between Phyllis and me, or learn labor laws, but they decide that uniforms aren't impinging on individuality?

With a sigh, I head back out to the kitchen.

"It looks wonderful! So bright and cheerful." Fern's eyes light up when she sees me.

"They certainly are bright. But…" I gnaw my lip, deciding how best to proceed.

Her smile dims. "What?"

"Is this going to be an everyday thing?"

"Yes."

"And we all have to wear these?"

Fern crosses her arms. "The material is a little stiff for the massage therapists to work in and move freely."

Tell me about it. "I need to move too, doing the laundry and making the beds," I point out.

"We didn't feel that it was fair to expect the massage therapists to wear them because they are technically independent contractors, and this new policy wasn't in place when they started."

"It wasn't in place when I started either."

She purses her lips. "No, but you're a different type of worker."

"So…"

"It's for the employees. To look more professional."

Is she saying I don't look professional because I haven't been parading around in a kaftan or wearing jewelry made from shells and crystals? "But I'm the only technical employee."

"Yes."

"So I'm the only one who has to wear a smock?"

"Not necessarily. We're leaving it up to everyone else's discretion. They can choose to wear one if they like. We bought enough that everyone can if they so choose." She stands up straight and her nostrils flare. "I'm sensing a lot of negative energy from you."

Goddamn right you are. I take a deep breath and struggle to keep calm. "It's just that—"

"We spent a lot of money on these uniforms, Sarah, in an effort to make you feel more comfortable here."

"I get that, but—"

"Not that we can't afford it. We could keep this place running for another two years, even if no new clients walked in the door. We're doing just fine financially, so don't even worry about that."

Tell that to the laundry soap. "I never said you weren't. But—"

"And if you're going to continue to be defensive, there isn't a place here for you."

What? "Fern, no, it's not that at all!"

"Then what is it?" Her voice is as dead as her eyes.

Damn it. I've got nothing. "Is it all right if I wear jeans with these? Or is that too casual? My black skirts definitely don't suit these new bright colors."

She nods. "Of course you can wear jeans. We want you to be comfortable here. You know that." She chucks my cheek like I'm a child getting over a tantrum. "Feel free to take another home as a spare, maybe in a smaller size?"

"Sure, thank you." I'm so tense I expect my face to shatter when I force it into a smile.

Phyllis's grin is brighter than my smock the first time she sees me when she comes in just after lunch. I'd tell her to shut her mouth, but she doesn't say anything, just stares at me as long as possible on her way past.

I mutter a quiet insult at her back, wishing I could scream it in her face. Everything she does annoys me, especially since I'm pretty sure she's trying to make me lose my shit and get fired.

The phone's been quiet, so I wander to the back to fold some towels. Fern and Phyllis are in the kitchen, sharing a plate of fruit.

Phyllis licks her finger. "I mean, I use the cup. Tampons are terrible. Inserting things into your body? No way, such a violation of your root chakra. And pads are just awful—all that waste going to landfills, I can't stand the thought of it! If only they could recycle all that waste." She actually shudders, and I suppress a grin, thinking she might have killer cramps right at this moment.

I hope her boobs hurt too.

Fern takes a bite of star fruit. "Very true. What do you use, Sarah?"

Jesus Christ, have these people not heard of *boundaries*? I blink and turn to Fern, not wanting to say anything, but unable to run from the room screaming. "I, uh… I'm on the shot, so I only get my period once every three months, but I use tampons. But they're the applicatorless kind, so that cuts down on waste in landfills."

"You're on birth control? Oh no, that's just so awful. You should quit that as soon as possible. Like, today." Phyllis takes another bite of dragon fruit.

"Since it's a shot I get four times a year, I can't exactly do anything about it right now. It's not like a pill." And even if it were, it's none of her business.

"You could *not* get the next poisonous shot instead of continuing."

Fern nods. "They change who you are on a cellular level, Sarah. It's like saying you don't want to be a woman anymore. Do you want that?"

"I'm pretty happy as I am."

"Complacency," Phyllis mutters.

I can't let her win. "What's the cup?" I know what it is, but there's no way I'm appearing inflexible in front of Fern—especially after the birth control comment.

Phyllis patronizingly explains the cup. While I can see how it would be good cost-wise and in reducing a bit of pollution, the thought of shoving a plastic cup into myself and then emptying it out, cleaning it, and reinserting it a couple of times a day grosses me out and doesn't sound worth the effort. I'm all for good ol' clean, disposable cotton.

Fern nods. "It's wonderful. You girls are so spoiled nowadays with all your options. It's no wonder you end up choosing the wrong ones." She eyes me.

Maybe I can turn the tables. "What do you use, Fern?"

"I have welcomed the crone phase of life, having ceased menstruation three years ago. But back when I was your age, we had belts that we fastened cloths to. And when they were soiled, we'd rinse them out in a bowl of water, let them dry, and use them again."

If I could hug the twenty-first century I would. "Ah, that makes sense." Still sounds gross, but they didn't have anything better.

"And that water, filled with the menstrual blood, is full of amazing earth-mother energy," she continues.

Oh God, where is this going?

"So we'd take that bowl and we'd water our plants and things with it."

My cheeks twitch in an effort to arrange my features into a mask of polite interest instead of the disgust rampaging through me.

Phyllis nods. "So amazing. There are so many applications for menstrual blood. I read online that to fully bond with a partner, you can brew up a tea, sort of an elixir, and add your menstrual blood to it. You get him to drink it near the full moon but don't tell him what it is—you know how men are about menstruation…especially ones who are against women being fully in their power. When he drinks it, it adds some of your own feminine energy to his system."

My mind boggles while Fern nods. They think slipping their lover some period-blood tea is going to bond them? "Isn't that a health and safety issue? I'm pretty sure feeding someone your bodily fluids can't be good. Especially when any kind of blood is involved."

Phyllis laughs. "Oh, Sarah. Traditional medicines

have used methods like these forever. They're perfectly safe. The only thing they can hurt is a closed mind."

Okay. How about another tactic? "I think I'd rather talk to my partner."

"Sometimes talking is just that—talking. You've never bonded, synergized with someone on a cellular, energetic level, merged with them energetically."

"You've got me there." I have no idea what the fuck those words mean. I know what they mean individually, but when paired together, they become nonsense.

Phyllis continues. "We can give parts of ourselves to others, or even imbibe them ourselves for amazing health benefits. Haven't you ever heard of placenta soup?"

"What?"

Fern takes up Phyllis's point. "When a woman gives birth, they can either make the placenta into a soup for her, or dry it and grind it into pills. They're fabulous for helping her rebuild blood lost giving birth."

What. The. Fuck. "Blood transfusions and iron pills do that. We have iron pills for replacing iron."

Fern frowns. "This is something holistic. Natural."

"Iron pills *are* natural. Saving a placenta for stem-cell research that could treat a child would be a way better use." The words spew from my mouth, judgmental and loud.

Phyllis sets down her plate. "It's done in nature all the time. Animals eat their placenta to build up their nutrients and become strong after giving birth in the wild. They even lick their juices from the babies. Everybody knows that, Sarah."

"Um, no." I clear my throat. "They eat the placenta so any nearby predators won't know that there's a baby and come to eat it. They eat it to hide the smell of the blood. They clean the young off for the same reason, not because they need vitamins."

Phyllis sighs. "You really can't admit when you're wrong, can you? You're not an expert at everything in the world, you know. How many years have you studied these things?"

"I'm pretty sure if eating the placenta was still the best thing new mothers had going, doctors would continue to prescribe it as the optimal treatment—real doctors backed up with peer-reviewed studies."

Phyllis shakes her head, and Fern frowns. "Judge if you want, Sarah, but it's holistic, natural, and women have been doing it since the dawn of time. Who are you to scoff at thousands of years of something that's helped women through the ages?"

Same way I scoff at anything that is pseudoscientific snake oil and can cause more harm than good. Still, my cheeks burn and I feel bad.

Fern sets the plate down. "I didn't know you were so judgmental, Sarah."

Phyllis's smile is triumphant as she walks out of the kitchen, leaving me with Fern's disapproving stare. She even looks a little hurt. Too late, I realize she and Ziggy have a twelve-year-old, and she probably ate the placenta. She was feeling judged personally.

"Fern."

She shakes her head and walks out, leaving me drowning in a room rapidly filling with my shame and uncertainty.

Chapter 23

AFTER THAT, I'M NOT HUNGRY, BUT I STOP AT THE store for some chocolate and wine. Supper of champions. The first thing I do when I get home is pour a giant glass and log on to talk to Blake.

> Me: Am I a bad person?

Luckily he's online, and his reply comes right away. *Am I made of bananas and optimism?*

> Me: I'm being serious.

> Him: Ah. I thought we were asking ridiculous questions. Now, what are you talking about?

I sigh and debate logging off. Blake knows me better than anyone, but he still doesn't really know me. I barely know me. What's the point of talking about it? *Bad day at work.*

> Him: Hear me on this. You are absolutely NOT a bad person. Tell me what happened.

Where should I start? The smocks? But were the smocks what brought this on? Were they really all that bad? Because now that I think about it, not having to worry about my clothes making me stand out is a good thing. One less thing for them to criticize me about. And they seem to criticize me to make me a better person in the long term. They aren't really picking on me. I should focus less on the external and more on what I'm doing for the world.

> Me: I guess I feel like maybe I've been too hard on them. Like maybe I'm the crazy one and they're basically kind people trying to make the world a better place.

> Him: Okay, I'm going to need you to back up. Start at the beginning of the day. Leave out no details.

> Me: Are you sure? Because there are some details of today that can't be unknown. You'll want to scream at the floor and then wash your brain with acid. Ugh! See?! I'm doing it again! I'm judging them and being a snarky bitch.

> Him: You aren't. It's your frustration talking. Just tell me what happened.

So I take a deep breath, a deep swallow of sparkling wine, and start typing. Sticking to the facts and not adding any judgmental comments, I spill every awful detail of the day and add my reactions and why I think I was wrong. I backtrack and tell him about perception being reality and how tired I am of Ziggy telling me to "breathe into it" instead of doing anything about a situation. Blake doesn't interrupt at all, and when I've finished, there's no response, which makes me reach for more wine and chocolate. Is he disappointed in me too and trying to think of something to say? I can't take the suspense anymore, so I type another response before he's answered.

Me: Are you still there?

Him: Uh, yeah. Just stunned.

Me: See? I told you I'm a raging asshole and—

Him: YOU are NOT the asshole in this situation!

My fingers hover over the keys as I wait for him to finish typing. I don't want to feel like a jerk, but the bleak feeling weighing my shoulders and heart tell me that there's nothing he can say to make this better. The truth is, I'm a horrible person—but I don't want to feel like I am.

Him: The smocks suck. Uniforms are bullshit, and it's brutal that they went about it in such an underhanded, passive-aggressive way. If they wanted to implement uniforms, they should have just come right out and told you they wanted

*you to wear one. Acting like they were
for everyone when they only want you to
have one is just mean. Besides, you're
gorgeous and could rock a paper bag,
so the way you look isn't an issue if you're
worried about that.*

Me: *I guess, but they were thinking of me, on
some level.*

Him: *Disagree, but I'm not even done.*

I smile and feel a little lighter. His next response
takes a minute.

Him: *Second of all, your ovaries are none of
their fucking business. Your body is
none of their business. I can't believe
they told you to stop a valid personal
choice that is none of their concern. No, I
can believe it because they are assholes
who think they know everything about
everything and can presume to boss
people around.*

Me: *:)*

Him: *Still not done. Them having no boundaries pisses me off. It's invasive and inappropriate and makes me cringe thinking
of you being trapped there for hours and
hours every day. I want to go over there*

and give them shit. I'll swap the decaf tea
bags for caffeinated! I'll put GMO veg-
gies in the fridge. I'll pour fake satanic
symbols onto the floor with refined, white
sugar then steal you away and never
take you back.

My insides are getting tingly. He always goes out of his way to make sure he asks how I'm doing, but the best part is he truly listens and remembers everything I've said. He truly cares.

Him: Damn it. I hate thinking of you there all
alone, immersed in their bullshit, letting
them make you think you're a bad person.

Me: But maybe they're not all bad.

Him: Period. Blood. Tea.

Me: Okay, that was supremely messed up.

Him: I puked in my mouth a little bit. Seriously, if
a woman ever did that to me, I'd sue her.

Me: Yeah, that was nasty.

Him: I don't know how you controlled your face
and didn't freak out when they told you that.

Me: It was hard. And like I told you, I didn't. I
was mean and hurt Fern's feelings.

Him: Screw Fern. She can just "breathe into it."

I snort, but a teeny twinge of guilt slithers through me. *Maybe their views aren't totally bad though. I still think I might be viewing things with a bias, you know?*

Him: Uh-oh. You're starting to identify with your captors! Stockholm syndrome!

Am I?

Him: Sarah, they aren't good people. Maybe they aren't horrible people, but that doesn't mean they are GOOD. They bought into their own bullshit, thinking it's the truth. They won't solve any of the conflicts between you and Phyllis, but they'll lecture you about anything they disagree with? No way. They are the ones in the wrong here, not you. Don't ever think that you're a bad person. The fact that you feel bad that you MIGHT have hurt Fern's feelings shows me how good a person you truly are.

Hope swells in my chest. *You really think so?*

Him: I know so. You're direct. And that's tough when you're in a place where they view their own perception as reality. I mean, how narcissistic and messed up is that?

Yes! That part I can't defend at all. *Perception ISN'T reality. REALITY is reality.*

> Him: Keep that in mind. The reality is that they
> are loopy hippies and are living in a
> dream world. Some of their things are
> good—self-improvement, recycling, etc.
> But the rest is crap. Don't buy into their
> granola, fair-trade world.

His reference to the sugar makes me smile. *Thanks for listening to me.*

> Him: Always.

> Me: I feel like all I do is bitch when we talk,
> spewing hippie bullshit all over you.

> Him: Not true at all. Besides, I love that you
> can talk to me about your problems.
> You need to talk about things instead of
> holding them inside. Do you talk to other
> people about this?

Not really. Pete doesn't get it, and my girlfriends seem to only see the humor of the situation, which is frustrating as hell. Except for Naomi, but she ends up profusely apologizing when all I want to do is vent, and then I end up comforting her and trying to assuage her guilt.

> Him: Then I'm glad you're able to talk to me

*about it. I love that you share parts of
your life with me.*

Me: *Parts? I've basically been spilling my guts
to you about everything in my life since
the first time we chatted.*

He lets me be myself. He knows me better than anyone
else in the world right now—because we talk about now.
It makes me realize that I might not know my friends
very well right now either. I know them as they were the
last time we really talked, but when was that?

Him: *It's not often we sit around baring our souls
to someone, talking about the things that
really matter. We ask how their families
are, their partners. How work's going? Did
you see the latest episode of that show?*

Me: *Exactly! It feels incredibly shallow after
being able to indulge in the conversations
you and I have had. It's gotten to where I
don't even call anyone else to talk.*

I pause over the next words but type them anyway.

Me: *I head straight for you now, not bothering
to even try to talk to anyone else. You're
always here for me, and I really appreciate it. I feel like you really listen to me.
Like you're not just waiting until I stop
talking so you can speak.*

Him: *Same here. I like seeing the world from*
your eyes. I'm the one who's thankful
you've let me into your thoughts.

And *heart*.

He keeps typing, and I wait for his words. *The thought*
of you feeling bad...knowing someone hurt you...makes
me crazy. I wish I could protect you from hurt.

Me: *Me too.*

Him: *Sarah, I really like you. I feel like with you,*
I can share things about myself that no
one else knows. It's easy to talk to you.
It's hard for me to open up to people, but
with you it feels natural.

Me: *I feel the same way.*

Him: *I miss you when you're gone.*

Me too. I look forward to his conversations all day.
I'm sorry I didn't show up. The words are hard to write,
but that bandage has to be ripped off. *And I'm sorry I*
couldn't meet you again the other night.

Him: *It's okay. Full disclosure? I didn't show up*
the first time either.

The fact Blake didn't show up makes me feel better—
and curious. *Why didn't you show up?*

Him: Scared it was too soon. It felt too early.

*Me: That's my fault. I pushed you into agreeing.
And then bailed on you. I'm such a jerk!
You were right about the situation.*

Him: Thank you, but you're not a jerk.

*Me: But you asked me if I wanted to meet up
the other night?*

It's a while before he replies. *Maybe it's not too
soon anymore.*
My heart slams into overdrive. *I feel a bit...conflicted.*

*Him: Because everything is perfect right now,
and safe, and because we haven't met
yet we can continue to be ourselves and
idealize everything?*

Get out of my head! I smile.

Him: Go out with me.

Me: You want to go on a date?

He replies right away. *I want you to be my girlfriend.*
Oh.

*Him: I know it seems sudden, but I... Ugh. I'm
just going to put it out there. I've fallen*

*for you. In a big way. And I don't want
to lose you to someone else because
I didn't let you know how I feel. I've
wanted to tell you for ages but never felt
like the timing was right.*

Wow.

Him: Say something.

I wait for a bad feeling or refusal to rise, but nothing comes up. Just a feeling of happiness and a shy
optimism, like maybe this could really work out.
Because he knows me. He understands me like no
one else does. Jack's face flits through my mind,
but I push thoughts of him away. He gets my body,
but we never really talk. Our relationship isn't even
a relationship. Not like mine and Blake's is. Jack
and I have incredible sex, but it doesn't go further
than that.

Blake and I have conversations that feel like forever. He's perfect for me on paper and in reality...
which means I can't see Jack anymore. Because if
I continue sleeping with him while feeling this way
about Blake—and Blake feels this way about me—
then I'm as bad as Mom. And I never wanted to be
with someone who treated me the way she treated
Dad. I swore I'd never be like her.

*Me: It's not that I don't want to, but...it's compli-
cated. I'm not saying no, but I need time
to think about it. Okay?*

*Him: Guess we should figure a day to meet
     in person.*

Definitely. I want to give us a chance, but if I dove into exclusivity, I'd have to say good-bye to Jack—and I'm not quite ready to do that. Am I? *I'll talk to you later, okay?*

Him: Okay.

Time to make a phone call.

He answers on the second ring. "Hello?"

"Hey, Jack."

"God, I love hearing your voice."

I can't do this over the phone—that's not fair to him. I'm going to have to do this in person. "Listen, do you want to come over? We need to talk."

"Definitely. Should I bring supper?"

"No, that's cool."

"Something to drink?"

I swallow down the nerves. "No, I'm good."

"All right. I'll see you in an hour?"

"Sounds good. See you then."

"Bye."

Maybe things won't be perfect between Blake and me, but I have to choose one man or the other.

Jack and I don't really talk, other than foreplay. He doesn't ask about my day. With him, I'd always be a little bit alone, left when he's off having late nights to deal with work—or play? Could I ever truly trust him to settle for only me when shinier options shimmy around him every night? Even if I could trust him and get used to his business, he's not emotionally available to me like Blake is. I don't know where he's at unless our clothes are off. What kind of relationship is that? We don't talk to each other. I don't even know if I mean more to him than friends.

And Jack doesn't seem to want more than what we have together. Blake does. He wants a full, real, grown-up relationship. He asked me, and that has forced me to make a decision.

It's time to move on with the man I see a future with.

Chapter 24

"I KNOW YOU SAID NO TO SUPPER, BUT I GRABBED A couple of panini from that bodega you like, just in case."

"Oh. Thanks." Taking the bag with a smile, I move to the kitchen and grab a couple of plates for us. With the conversation to come, I'm so not hungry. Now we'll have to sit through a hellish supper before I can tell him we can't sleep together anymore. "Cola?"

"Sounds good."

While I'd feel more comfortable drinking my way through a vat of wine, I owe it to Jack to do this as tactfully as I can and while sober. Or mostly sober—I've had a glass of wine since I got home.

"You made it sound sinister on the phone. 'We need to talk.'"

"I didn't want you to get the wrong idea and come in here kisses blazing."

He takes his plate with a smile and follows me to the living room, settling opposite me on the couch. "I can see that. The last time we spoke was intense."

I smile. "There wasn't much talking at all. You nailed me over your island. I rode you in your bed."

He looks surprised. "I meant after."

It had been an amazing kiss when he dropped me off.

He'd looked at me as if he wanted to have a long talk but hadn't said anything. "A few things have happened to me since I saw you that night, Jack." Things involving a sexy massage therapist working his way into my heart and asking me to be exclusive. He said he's falling for me and wants more. I want more too.

"Like what?"

My sandwich tastes like sawdust. Why are the words so hard to find? It's just Jack and me—we've been friends forever. The only difference is we'll be going back to the way we used to be. And taking us back to where we were proves I'm a good person. I refuse to lead them both on and then tear their hearts out. "Nothing bad. Don't look so worried. Eat your sandwich. You're looking skinnier than usual."

"I haven't been sleeping well." He resumes eating.

His unusual confession throws me off. "Why not? Everything okay? Is Pete okay? I haven't heard from him much lately."

"I haven't heard much from him either." He narrows his eyes. "But he's been really quiet. I don't like it."

"Me neither. Things feel wrong when he's not there being obnoxiously loud."

"Do you miss living with him?"

The Coke burns a cold trail down my throat, making my eyes water. "I loved spending time with him, and I miss him, but no. I definitely like having my own place better."

"I like you having your own place better too."

I want to launch myself up his body and bite that lip, but no. I have to think of Blake now. It wouldn't be fair to him to sleep with Jack. If I'm going to be

Blake's girlfriend, I have to be exclusive. But is that what I want?

Jack sips his Coke. "I can't stop thinking about how sexy you were the other night. You've never been so unrestrained."

Unable to sit still any longer, I stand and pace.

He sets his sandwich down. "What's wrong?"

Everything. Nothing. "You can't talk to me that way anymore."

"What?"

"You heard me."

Jack's at my side in a second. "Why?"

"This shouldn't be so hard. We were never anything serious." I'm speaking more to myself than anything else, but he answers.

"We were friends. And now we're more."

I shake my head. "We were friends and we slept together. But that's it. That's all it ever could have been."

"What, so you think I'm good enough to fuck, but not good enough to have a conversation with?"

I wring my hands. "No, it's not that." And *he's* the one who never lets *me* in.

"Then what is it?"

I didn't want to tell him. I didn't want to tell anyone about Blake and me. It's too soon, too nebulous to talk about with other people. But it feels right. "I've met someone."

"What?"

"And we really connected. We met online a few weeks ago. You don't know him."

"Online?" He looks like he doesn't know whether to laugh or leave.

"Yes."

"So you're stopping us because of some random guy you met on a dating site who you might have feelings for?"

"It wasn't a dating site." Not that that matters. "But, yeah. I have to give him a chance, and it's not fair to be with you both. I refuse to be that person."

"You'll give him a fair shot but I get shut out before even getting a chance."

"I'm not shutting you out! I never shut you out."

He steps closer, taking my hands. "Then let me in."

My eyes close. *Now* he wants to talk and share more than a bed? His thumbs running against the backs of my hands are driving me crazy. "I did."

"No, you didn't and we both know it. I can make you scream my name in bed, but I can't get you to call me and talk to me about your day."

I didn't know he wanted more. I was waiting for him to want more when all along I was the one keeping this physical only. Right? But if he wanted more, he could have used his fucking words. I have to face facts, so I force myself to look at him. "Our relationship isn't— wasn't—like that. We both know the score. All it was ever going to be was something casual and fun, or you'd have said something."

"It was never just sex to me."

"It wasn't to me either." Shit. I don't mean to encourage him, but I can't stand the betrayal in his eyes. Not when he does mean so much more to me than sex. "I thought you were content to carry on the way we have been."

"You're wrong. We could be great together. We *are*

great together." His hand caresses my face, making me shiver. "Tell me you don't feel the connection between us."

I should choose Blake, but I still want Jack too. What's wrong with me? "I can't." My voice is barely a whisper.

He licks his lips. "What we have is real." He pulls me into his embrace, and despite myself, I wrap my arms around him and squeeze tight. I don't want to let him go either. "It's powerful."

"Jack, I—"

"I'm what you need," he whispers into my hair. "I'm not just a walking cock. Don't pretend I mean nothing more to you than that."

God, I'm dying. I welcomed Jack into my bed and he's crawled underneath my skin, burrowed inside me, and it would be easier to tear out my bones and watch them walk out the door than to say good-bye to him now. I'd written him off as a possibility because I thought I should, but it doesn't feel right to end it now.

"You're looking for something better when I'm right here. I've... It's not easy for me to express myself. But, fuck it, I'm falling in love with you, Sarah."

His words suck all the air from the room. My lungs expand and contract, but I can't get enough air.

So I nod, and he smiles and pulls me closer, and his lips find mine and melt the barrier between us I was trying to carefully build. I let him lead me to my bedroom because I want him. I need him.

Blake was wrong about me. I'm a terrible person.

Chapter 25

I HAVEN'T TALKED TO BLAKE OR SEEN JACK IN FIVE days, despite both their efforts to contact me. How can I talk to either of them when I'm sort of betraying them both? Speaking to Blake is impossible until I break up with Jack, but I told Jack I'd give him a chance—and whenever we're together, everything else in the world burns away.

That should tell me something, but if Jack is the one, how come I still feel this amazing connection to Blake? When we talk, no one else in the world exists. Our conversations are the weird, amazing ones that are about everything and nothing. They eat up hours of my days, and I can't imagine going the rest of my life not talking to him.

I'm not technically exclusive with either of them, but that doesn't make me feel any better. I'm being torn in half, and neither man is the clear choice. So I need to back off and stay away from both of them until I can give all of myself to one of them. Otherwise, it's not fair to any of us, and I'm no better than my mom.

Every night, I lie awake, tortured with the knowledge that I'm going to hurt someone. I already am hurting someone—I just don't know who I'll say good-bye to. The bags under my eyes have swelled to epic proportions, and my nerves are shot. I've made pro and con

lists for both men. I've had dreams about them both—
the few times I've managed to pass out—and I can see
a happy future with either of them, each in their own
separate ways.

Unfortunately, I have to make a decision—and fast.

But it would be easier if I could split myself in two
and be with both of them.

Shit. I realize the phone has been ringing for who
knows how long, and I scramble to answer it. "Inner
Space, Sarah speaking."

"How much for a butt massage?"

"Pete?"

"You know it."

Paranoia has me throwing a glance over my shoulder
to check for hippies or Phyllis, but the coast is clear.
"How are you? Where have you been?"

"Oh, I've been around. Not feeling well, blah blah.
I'm better now. I'm more interested in what you've been
up to, my little seductress."

"Huh?"

"Are you really going to pretend you're not boinking
my brother?"

I cringe. "He told you?"

"He didn't have to. He's been way too happy lately,
and he's mooned over you for ages. I put two and two
together, and he admitted you two had begun seeing
each other recently."

Great. Now Pete's going to hate me too when he
finds out about Blake. If Blake is the one for me. *FML,
I don't even know who I want.* "Is it cool if I call you
later? The other line's ringing." Lie.

"Sure. We've got to do drinks soon and catch up."

"How about you cook me dinner instead?"

"Now that sounds like the Sarah I know, trying to mooch food. Call me later and we'll bang out details. Unless you're too busy banging my—"

"Bye, Pete."

He laughs. "Love you."

I hang up and sag. Great. Now I'm going to have to avoid my best friend as well, or the guilt is going to eat me alive. I literally can't handle one more thing going wrong right now.

As if summoned by a choir of demons, Phyllis strolls into the waiting room and leans against the counter, leaving a shiny forearm print of oil before taking a seat in a chair to do her notes until her client emerges. She discusses homework stretches with her client while I process her credit card. When my part's done, I head to the back to clean up Phyllis's room, which looks like it was hit by a tropical storm.

But I put it right, hauling the sheets and towels to the back room, and start a load of laundry. The load in the dryer finishes then, so I fold the towels I pull from it, replenishing the dwindling stack on the shelf and catching sight of my reflection in the mirror on the wall—and the dark circles under my eyes. Both Jack and Blake have noticed my absence the past few days, and though neither has pressured me to get together, I'm feeling the stress of the situation.

It's only going to get worse the longer I go without making a decision. If only the world would stop and let me think about this for a year or two. Maybe I don't deserve either man, but the fact remains: I have to let one of them go.

I've lusted after Jack for so long that maybe it's nothing more than a habit, a default position. We have intense sexual chemistry, but could it be more than that? Just because he's not as irresponsible about the future as I thought he is doesn't automatically mean I should be with him. He's a great guy, but do I mostly want him out of habit? What if all we have is sex, and my fears turn out to be true?

And Blake and I have these amazing conversations I've never had with anyone before. He's hot and sweet and charming, but what if we don't work in person? Is he so appealing because he's safe? I can talk to him about things, but if it gets too intense, I can turn the computer off. I won't be able to do that in person. Will it be so appealing when I don't have the power to literally pause the relationship whenever it suits me?

Fern is chatting with Phyllis when I get back to my desk.

"We're expecting a larger crowd than last time, which will be fabulous for the energy."

"What's this for, Fern?" Might as well engage her.

She turns to me. "Our Intensive Awakening workshop. We're holding it at Salt Spring Lodge this year."

"And you're expecting higher numbers? That's good." *For your bank account.*

She nods. "It speaks to the collective consciousness and how people are screaming to evolve. As an energy worker and light warrior, it's incredibly satisfying to realize I'm a part of it."

"We all are," Phyllis says.

"Yes. How is your Reiki going?" Fern touches Phyllis's forearm.

"Very well. I've found it a little difficult working from the head down, but the more modalities you have under your belt, the better able you are to help others."

"True. But remember, dabbling can be dangerous for your progression. It's better to choose a couple of things and become great at them than to be adequate at many things."

"You're so right. I still have so much to learn."

Ugh. Phyllis's false humility makes me want to vomit. Just the other day, I heard her bragging to her friend Elizabeth that she was a leader in the healing war and one of the greatest healers in North America. I guess Fern doesn't teach humility at her workshops.

"What about you, Sarah?"

"What about me?" I stare back into Phyllis's glossy eyes.

"How many courses have you taken?"

"University and specified training. I'm a paralegal."

"No." She laughs. "School can only get you so far. I meant energy courses."

"I haven't done any."

She closes her eyes and sighs. "Why are you here?"

"To work?"

"Yeah, but is that all? Because the rest of us are here to work and learn and grow and hold the space. We're here to put good energy into this corner of the world and elevate its vibration. You won't even have a treatment with any of us, and you've never even asked about Fern's courses."

"I sort of have a personal space thing."

"If you were truly a good fit here, you'd see why such rigid boundaries aren't a good thing for any of us."

Phucking Phyllis.

Fern's eyebrows are raised, and I find myself wanting to be a part of things, if only so they stop dismissing me like I don't understand anything.

"I did learn how to do ear-candling."

Fern smiles. "Oh, that's a good one. Where'd you learn that?"

"My ex worked at a health food store." Actually, he and Phyllis would probably get on swimmingly.

"What else did he teach you?"

Not to trust people who talk about vitamins all day because eventually they'll leave you for an amateur female bodybuilder so they can talk about carb-protein ratios? "He was really into sacred geometry."

Fern looks impressed. "That is interesting. Did you study it much? I just got a merkaba crystal last week."

I shake my head, now moving into bullshit territory. "I didn't like the way they were so exclusionary with the teachings. The way they hoard their knowledge turned me off. Sort of like with Reiki—no offense, Phyl—but they sort of do the same thing, from what I know. I think that all knowledge should be shared. We should help people up, not try to hold them back to feel better about ourselves."

"I agree completely," Fern says with the biggest smile I've ever seen on her face, at least when directed at me. Phyllis's mouth scrunches like she just sucked on an onion while Fern continues. "Have you ever thought about trying our program?"

Damn it, I didn't want her to think I'm too into these things. "It's so expensive. I couldn't afford to do it."

"Nonsense. For you we'd make an exception. It would be worth it to have you there joining in, being part of the team. It would be fabulous for the energy around here!" She holds her hands up in the air and smiles, then turns to Phyllis. "Wouldn't it be fabulous?"

"Yes, but…" Her expression turns cunning. "Sarah hasn't exactly said yes to anything yet. Maybe she doesn't want to."

My face heats up. "It's not that I don't want to. It's that I really can't afford the course, and I'd feel bad if you paid."

"Sarah, let Ziggy and me worry about that."

Think fast, Sarah. "It's not just the course, Fern. It would be the days off work as well."

She nods slowly. "I see what you mean. Let me think of something and get back to you."

"Thanks for understanding."

"Not a problem. We'll make it work."

"She doesn't want to make it work," Phyllis snaps and walks toward the counter.

"I already said I'm open to it."

"That sounds really nice, Sarah, but until you walk the talk, your words are just breath-scented air."

"Breath-scented air?"

"It means you aren't getting off that easily. Some of us have worked our asses off to fit in around here, and you think you can just prance in here with your goth-black wardrobe and fancy hair and be one of us just like that? Without putting in the effort?" Phyllis snaps her fingers in my face just as Blake walks in like my dimpled, avenging angel.

He frowns and crosses the reception area, concern written all over his gorgeous features.

"Phyllis, can I talk to you for a second?" Fern takes

Phyllis by the upper arm and leads her away from the desk as Blake steps behind me.

"Everything all right, Sarah?" He keeps his voice low so only I can hear it.

It is now. I want to throw myself in his arms and shout "Take me away!"

"I'm okay. What are you doing here?"

He trails his hand across my lower back on his way to the computer. "I finished early and decided to swing by to check my schedule." His touch bolsters me. I'm not alone here. I have a sexy ally who cares about me. I hate that I can't say anything to him about us, not in front of Fern and Phyllis, but I lean into his touch, grateful for his support. He's always there for me like fate is trying to tell me something.

Blake narrows his eyes at Phyllis and Fern in the corner. "Are you sure you're okay? I'll be your getaway driver if you need to escape," he whispers.

I suppress a giggle. "I'm good. I just need a new job far, far away. We'll talk later, okay?" I don't want to get too friendly in case I tip Fern off about us being more than coworkers.

"Okay. Don't let the hippies get you down." He turns his back to them and winks so only I can see, forcing me to smother a smile. He leaves and I focus on Fern and Phyllis's conversation again.

"I'm surprised at you." Fern crosses her arms. "Where is this coming from?"

"She's always getting away with this, Fern. She's not one of us and can't possibly understand the fight we face every day to bring people to the light."

"All the more reason for us to bring her along and

make it easier for her. Evolution waits for no one. Maybe she's never been in a safe enough place to grow the way she was meant to." Fern strides to me and rests her hand on my shoulder. "As an energy worker yourself, I'm surprised that you would come down on her for not knowing better. You do."

Phyllis looks stricken. "You're right. I've failed."

"Just breathe into it." Fern nods at her and I grin. You know, that phrase isn't quite so hateful when it's directed at someone who's been a pain in your ass. "And, Sarah, I've got it." She heads back to the desk. "You can come to the course for free, and we will just extend your hours for a while so you can make up the difference."

That wipes the smile from my face. "How do you mean? The retreat's in a few days, and it's almost the end of the month."

"We'd be taking four days from your check. So, to make that up, you can come in early and get caught up on laundry and answer phones. Oh! And we can have you come and babysit our boys on Sunday."

"So I'd be working twelve-hour shifts all week, and then babysitting for you all day Sunday?"

"Isn't it great when things come together? It's perfect! Ask and you shall receive," she trills.

Phyllis is pissed and Fern's thrilled, so that can't be a completely bad thing, right? And who knows, maybe the time away at a quiet retreat will give me some perspective and stress relief so I can make a decision about which man is the one. On the other hand, it looks like I've been sucked into attending their course. "Are you sure Phyllis wouldn't like to go instead? I'm so new, and she would get more out of it than I would, surely? I'd hate to take such an amazing experience from someone."

Phyllis's triumph returns. "I've already done the course three times. You're right. Because you're so new, it will be a fabulous new addition to the energy at the retreat. So fresh. You'll learn so much. I remember the first time I went. It completely blew my mind! I came back an entirely different person. Maybe you will too."

That's what I'm afraid of.

Chapter 26

LATER, AT HOME, I'M PACING AROUND MY LIVING ROOM with a comically large glass of white wine. The added stress of Fern's course makes my head throb with every beat of my heart. Making a decision between the two men in my life would simplify things so much.

If it's about a physical connection, that's not fair, because Blake and I have only touched a couple of times, and they were regrettably platonic. That said, the one time he practically melted me with his hands, so who knows how great our chemistry could be if we made love. There was something there, or the potential for something there, so Jack and my amazing physical relationship wins, but it's not by one hundred percent.

And the emotional connection I have with Blake should be the clincher, but I've had moments of that with Jack too. And I haven't really talked much with him or given him a chance to be more than sex. He was right about that.

Jack has the physical edge with the potential for more emotions. Blake has the emotional edge with the potential for more chemistry. What's more important in a relationship in the long term? I'd say emotional, which would mean Blake is the one, but Jack and I started as friends, so I know we'd get along well long-term.

I pace around my coffee table, waiting for a bolt of clarity to hit and tell me which man is the one. They both deserve an answer, but I don't know what to do. My stomach's been killing me for days.

Time to talk to the one person who will tell it like it is and kick my ass into gear.

Pete picks up on the fourth ring. "Hello?"

"Hey, it's me."

"Hey, what's up?"

"Calling to work out the details of our dinner date, and also I have some issues right now that I could really use your keen observation on, oh sage one."

"Okay."

Now that I can fully vent, I don't even know where to start. I'm overwhelmed by choices and hippie bullshit. I guess I'll start there. "Everything is a mess right now. My bitchy coworker I told you about has gotten way worse, and I'm pretty sure she's trying to get me fired and making me look bad whenever she can. Ziggy and Fern hate me and have no boundaries, and have made me start wearing these god-awful smocks to work every day. They're a horrid shade, like half of a rainbow, and make me look sick and the fabric is stiff and makes me look about as curvy as a refrigerator. I got railroaded into doing one of their stupid New Age courses, which is four days long! And it's way out in Jersey, so it's isolated, and I read on the pamphlet online that we're completely cut off from the outside world! It's going to be like *Survivor* without the film crew, but full of hippies trying to stare into my eyes and break down my boundaries and make me talk about uncomfortable things."

"Wow."

"I'm not even done yet. After the course—which freaks me out because I'm pretty sure it's a cult—I'll be short on rent, so they're 'helping me out' by letting me work twelve-hour shifts all that week and then baby-sitting their children on Sunday! Can you believe that? Twelve-hour shifts for a week after doing their hippie crap. I'll be wrecked."

"Well—"

"And that's not even touching on my personal life, Pete. I swear, it never rains; it pours. You know that I've been seeing Jack, but we're just, well, physical. I can't be with him for obvious reasons, not least of which is the fact it would ruin the friendship. Or, at least, I thought there were other reasons we couldn't be together until very recently and now I'm not so sure. But our chemistry is amazing. I'm trying really hard not to get into specifics and gross you out because he's your brother—"

"Thank you, I appreciate that."

"—but I really like him. And he's asked me to give him a fair chance at being something more than friends with benefits. And I really want to." I'm going to wear a hole in the varnish from pacing on it. "But there's this other guy I met online, and we have this amazing connection. We didn't really meet online. Technically, he works with me. Well, not with me; he's that massage therapist I told you about, but he's not a hippie, and we have these amazing conversations, and I think I'm falling in love with him too. I don't know what to do, Pete."

He clears his throat and is quiet for a minute. "Wow. Holy first-world problems, girlie."

"What?" He sounds so uninterested that I get a weird

feeling in my chest. "Okay, are you mad at me because you think I'm cheating on Jack? Because Blake and I have barely even touched—and we've never kissed. Or even hugged. I'd never do something cruel to Jack. You know me better than that." I need his validation that it's not really cheating despite the gnawing in my gut telling me it is.

"It has nothing to do with that. Jack's a big boy, and you're a big girl. But your problems are so fucking meaningless. You have a job and two guys who want to be with you, and you think those are problems?"

Shock springs tears to my eyes. "I can't believe you're talking to me like this. We always talk to each other about our lives."

He sighs. "You know what? Maybe I'm being harsh, but it's the truth. Today, I worked on someone whose hair was falling out from cancer—a regular client who's full of life. She's an emergency room nurse who busts her ass every day helping people. She's one of the best people I've ever met, best attitude, brightest smile in the world. She started chemo a couple of weeks ago. Today, when I was washing her hair, it started falling out in the sink in these huge, sickening clumps that stuck to my hands and clogged the sink, and she apologized and cried over a disease that's killing her."

The tears that gathered for myself fall for a stranger, burning my face. I feel an inch tall. "Pete, I am so sorry. I can't imagine how scary and sad that must have been."

"No, you can't imagine it. This woman, a bright spot in my salon who I see every two months, might die. She's really sick and she could be gone, and the only way I'd know is an obituary. So I just can't muster the same amount of worry for your situation."

I don't know what to say. "I'm so sorry."

"Look, I know I'm being harsh, but just make a decision and stick with it. In your case, nobody's dying, Sarah. You can change any of the things you just told me. You have the power to do that. My client doesn't. She'd probably love to have any or all of your 'problems' right now instead of the things she's facing. I don't know. I'll talk to you later."

He hangs up, and I'm at a loss because he's right, but that still doesn't help me make a decision. It just makes me feel even shittier about myself than I did ten minutes ago.

Chapter 27

HOW DO I KNOW YOU'RE NOT SOME CURVY NORWEGIAN HOUSEWIFE? I ask, hoping to provoke Blake into giving me a little more. After eight days, I've caved and answered Blake's last message, asking if the hippies chained me to my desk and he needs to come rescue me. Just knowing he's here helps soothe me—something I don't deserve right now but desperately need.

No reply for a moment. Not a good sign. Have I offended him? Then, *Check your email.*

The photo quality isn't great, taken with a webcam in a dark room, but the sliver of his skin I can see is still damp and he's wearing nothing but a towel clinging to his hips. A hand-written sign says "Norwegian housewife" and covers his abs. Damn. All that's visible is a very prominent bulge behind the towel. *Damn.*

Wow. *Oh my God.*

Him: Yeah?

Me: Mmm-hmm.

Him: You've seen what I'm wearing. Are you going to return the favor?

Man, I shouldn't, but I need a distraction right now. And Blake definitely fits the bill. *I'm not wearing anything sexy.*

Him: Can I be the judge of that?

My heart pounds and I bite my lip, but I trust Blake, so I angle the laptop down and take a picture. I send the shot of me in a tank top and panties back to him.

Him: Holy shit.

My face is going to start a fire. *Yeah?*

Him: You couldn't have picked a sexier thing to wear. I wish I was there right now.

My fingers fly over the keys, and I hit Enter before I can talk myself out of it. *What would you do if you were here right now?*

Him: You don't even want to know.

Shivers cascade across my skin. *Oh, but I do.* Are we really going to do this?

Him: You'd feel me standing behind you. I'd gently move your hair to kiss the back of your neck.

Me: I really like that.

Him: I'd kneel beside you and kiss the delicate

*skin just below your ear where it meets
your jaw. Do you know that place?*

Yes. *Yes.*

Him: Touch that place. On the right side.

I do. *Then what?*

*Him: I'd reach down, and through the tank top,
I'd gently palm your left breast. Are you
doing it?*

My skin burns, nerves hyperalert as though it's
Blake's hand, not my own, moving to my breast. *Yes.*

*Him: I'd run the pad of my thumb over your
nipple, maybe use my thumbnail over the
material to tease it until it's hard. I'd make
it hurt just a little bit, then squeeze and
release it, and move my hand…down.*

Heat flows through me and gathers between my legs.
They're just words on a screen, but I'm already wet. *And
then what?*

God, Sarah. I need to hear your voice. He sends a
request for a voice chat and I click Accept, fingers fumbling like I'm drunk. I feel drunk.

"Are you there?"

*Him: I'm going to keep typing, but I need to
hear you.*

I want so much more. I want his voice too, but I'll take what I can get. "Okay." My voice is barely louder than a whisper. I'm afraid to speak too loudly and shatter whatever this is that's happening right now. "Please don't stop." I'm afraid I'll chicken out, and I need this so much tonight, need to feel a connection with someone who cares about me. Life has rubbed me raw, and I need someone who treats my heart with delicate hands.

> Him: I can't stop, Sarah. I'm so hard. I want you
> so bad right now it hurts.

A moan escapes my throat at the thought of him looking at my picture, thinking of me and touching himself. "Please, don't stop."

> Him: I'd pull the chair out, turn you in it so I could
> kneel between your legs, stroke your thighs
> up and down, getting closer to your clit
> each time until I just barely brush against
> it. Slowly slide your panties off, Sarah.

Like I'm under a spell, I comply. "They're gone."

> Him: Are you wet?

Without even touching myself, I know the answer. "Yes."

> Him: I'd kiss a trail down your chest and belly,
> and I'd lick and suck at your clit until your
> hips were jumping all over the place.

My hand starts to move between my legs.

Him: Agonizingly slowly, I'd finger you, watching your skin flush and burn until you begged me for more.

"I want you inside me." Desire loosens my tongue and my reservations.

Him: I'd make you come first, then I'd pull you with me to the floor and take off that little tank top and bra, and cover every inch of skin beneath it with kisses.

How can I be so close already?

Him: I'd move back down and tease your clit more, then when you couldn't stand it any longer, I'd thrust my hard cock inside your tight, wet pussy. But I'd go slow to make it last, so you could savor every inch of me filling you.

I slide my fingers inside, imagining it's his dick, feeling myself clench around my fingers, gasping at how sensitive I am, how close I am to coming. "Yeah. More."

Him: God, your voice is doing things to me. I couldn't take it a moment longer. I'd fuck you as hard as I could just to see how loud I could make you scream my name. Just to fill the room with your pleasure.

Incoherent noises come from my mouth.

Him: Say it, Sarah. Come with me. Say my name.

"Blake," I moan. A few more seconds and pure heat crashes over me. "God, Blake!" My back arches and I shake with the intensity of my orgasm. When I come back down to earth, a shyness slightly taints the moment. "I've—" Oh. He's disconnected the voice chat.
I'm going to sleep well tonight. I smile.

Him: I should be going too.

Me: All right. Good night.

Him: Good night.

I disengage and take a long, long bath. I cannot believe I just had cybersex with a coworker. But when I brace myself for the shame that should follow, nothing happens. Blake made me feel too good for me to make myself feel bad about what just happened between us. It's strange being so uninhibited and intimate with someone I haven't even kissed.

But amazing too. It's a whole new layer, a type of intimacy· I've never had before, and I want more of it. Am I really in love with someone I've never kissed?

Yes, I really think I am.

So strange that this is my reality.

I've dried off and applied lotion when someone knocks on my door. Damn it. Who the hell is that at this hour? Thankful for my fluffy robe—which covers a hell of a lot more than a towel would—I pad over to the front door and peer through the peephole. As soon as I see his face, I throw open the door.

"Jack?"

He shakes his head and slumps against the door frame, eyes focusing on the floor.

"What's wrong?" Did someone die? "Tell me what's wrong. Is Pete okay?"

"Pete's fine." His voice is raw.

"Then what? You're scaring me."

He just shakes his head.

"What happened?" He doesn't resist when I pull him inside my apartment and close the door, locking it behind him.

"There are things I have to tell you. Things I've done that I'm not proud of. You have to know I'm not this type of person. I'd never normally do something like this."

This isn't my Jack. The Jack Devine I know is strong, cocky, fun, and alive. He doesn't stand like he's defeated and look like this.

I step closer and wrap my arms around him, expecting him not to respond, but he clings to me, coming alive at my touch. Did he sleep with someone else? I've been in an online relationship while we've been seeing each other and didn't tell him. He doesn't owe me an explanation. "It doesn't matter what you've done, Jack."

He pulls back and strokes my arms and back like he's memorizing my body. "Sarah, I needed to tell you—" He's struggling to find the words.

"I'm here." I'm the worst person in the world. Because I love Jack as a friend—and as way more than a friend. I'm awful because my body is still warm from what Blake and I did earlier, but Jack's eyes are breaking my heart, and the only thing in the world I want is to make him feel better, to take away the stark loneliness in his expression. By any means possible.

"Sarah, I've done—"

"It doesn't matter. That was the past. This is now." Maybe it's to assuage my own guilt at not telling him about Blake. All I know is that I can't stand Jack hurting.

His eyes close when I palm his cheek and stand on my tiptoes to kiss him gently—so gently it's more the idea of a kiss breathed against his mouth.

"I can't find the words now," he admits, his words almost lost against my lips.

"It's okay. You don't have to. Let me make you feel better, baby," I murmur.

He gasps as though a live current zings through him at the endearment. His hands knead their way down my back and cup my ass as his kiss grows deeper, more urgent, aggressive, and I respond in kind.

Jack always knows just how to touch me to drive me crazy, to drive all other thoughts from my mind. As if I can absorb him if we are close enough, I press our hips together and wrap my arms tightly around him. Why is it never enough?

He scoops me up and holds me close, walking us through the hall and into my room. He sets me on the bed and keeps his gaze on mine while undoing the belt of my robe, parting the material to reveal my naked body. The shivers that dance across my skin are as much from the cool air as from the expression on his face.

"I'm going to make you come harder than you ever have before."

I'm supposed to be making him feel better, but there's no way I'm going to protest that. I nod.

Bathed in the glow of the light spilling onto my bed from the hallway, Jack decorates my skin with kisses and caresses. With each kiss, the broken sorrow in his eyes fades until it's just me and my Jack in the room, his pain no longer the third party driving us together with dizzying intensity. His caresses turn from gentle to passionate, and soon he's lighting my skin on fire with ruthless pleasure.

Shrugging out of my robe, I sit and he lets me strip his shirt from him, unbuckle his belt, unzip his jeans slowly. His throat is warm beneath my kisses, his chest warmer under my tongue. With a few sensual movements, he's moved me up the bed and stretched out beside me, spooning my side, giving his hands access to *everything*.

His hands, his mouth, his eyes treasure me and claim me. He touches me like I'm his, and oh God, I am, but there's a tension humming through his movements that makes me want to show him how much.

I reach over him and grab a condom from the nightstand and roll it down his cock. Kneeling over him, I position him right where I want him. The fleeting thought of Blake and my earlier actions flits through my mind but disappears as I lower myself onto Jack and watch his expression change as I push down, impaling myself on his hardness. He moans and grabs my hips, holding me in place as though us just being locked together like this is all he wanted.

"Do you feel that? How perfectly we fit together?" He pushes up and I gasp and nod, unable to form words. I trail my hands all over his abs and V-muscles and up his chest.

His gaze singes my skin. "What feels better than this, Sarah?"

"Nothing," I moan.

His lips curl into a dangerous smile, and with firm pressure, he guides my hips around, proving me wrong.

Nothing feels better than *this*.

I lean down and kiss him. Then I begin rocking up and down, back and forth. His hands roam all over my hips and thighs and breasts. Soon, I'm unable to maintain the slow pace, and my hips start circling wildly as I pump up and down, bracing myself on his shoulders, on the headboard, on the wall when he tells me to go harder.

He thrusts his hips up as I push down, cock rubbing a place inside me that slams my eyes shut and throws my head back.

"God, Jack, you feel so good." My moans would be embarrassing if I didn't feel so fucking right with him inside me.

He flips me over and drives into me hard, harder, and the sensation of new places being rubbed from inside makes my thighs tense as I brace myself. But his fingers find their way between us, and there's no way to brace for the depth of the pleasure he pistons into me. "Who makes you feel good?"

I moan his name, pull him down to me for a kiss, bite his lip, and suck his tongue while I come. He stiffens and pounds into me a few more times before pulling me up so I'm sitting on his lap, moaning and shaking and smiling with him still inside me.

He grinds his hips in tight circles, drawing out my orgasm. My hips twitch and my belly flutters as he wrings every bit of sensation he can from my body, and when I don't think I can take any more, he stiffens and comes.

"I've missed you," I whisper.

"I've missed you so much." He holds me tight, but the urgency that brought him to my door has eased, and I'm glad—though still curious.

After, we lie there under the covers not talking, taking in what happened. I'm still waiting for him to talk about what brought him here tonight. I don't wait long.

He flips onto his side so we're facing each other. "What are you most scared of?"

The usual glib comments—clowns and so on come to mind—but I answer with the truth since he's trying to open up to me. "Something happening to my family. The people I love."

"Because of your dad?"

Each of my dad's heart attacks has been scarier than the last. "Yeah. You'd think they'd get easier to deal with because we've been through this already. He's recovered every time and been okay. But it's not like that at all. Every time it feels worse, like he's a cat using up his nine lives, and *this time* will be the last. Like there are only so many narrow misses we can have." And how it's mostly because of stress that his heart's bad. Whose heart will I break before this is over?

Jack presses a kiss to my forehead and snuggles me closer.

Death is final, but it's not the only thing I worry

about with my loved ones. "But not just them dying. I worry about Pete too, especially after that asshole followed him from the bar."

Jack clenches his teeth. "I still can't believe that happened."

"I had a nightmare the other night that I hadn't followed the guy out of the bar. That I hadn't gotten in his way and forced him to stop following Pete. I—"

"Wait, you got in his way?"

Oh, right. I'd left that part out that night when I told him what happened. "Yeah."

"Sarah, what if he'd hit you, hurt you?"

"I wasn't even thinking about myself. I was trying to help Pete."

He clutches me close. "God, you're amazing. And reckless. And the best friend my brother could ever ask for, though he doesn't even know it."

"I never want him to know it either. As a woman, I get it. We're taught not to walk down dark alleys. Don't go out too late when you're alone. Don't let your guard down around strangers. Hold your keys like a weapon. Don't leave your drink unattended. Always be ready to fight. Even when we're okay, there's always that awareness in the back of our minds that we could be attacked.

"Pete's a guy, so he wouldn't have that—but because he's gay, if he runs into bigots, then he's extra vulnerable. And if he's walking around worried that someone's following him to hurt him for something he can't change?" I shake my head. "I don't want him feeling that. Knowing what happened—what almost happened—at the club that night will do absolutely no good."

"He's been in some situations like this before, but not

for years. Not since we were in school. The world's a better place than it was even a few years ago. Or I thought it was."

"All the more reason to let him feel like that's firmly in his past."

"I agree."

He's always been Pete's protector, looking out for him, defending him even when Pete has no idea. How many other fights has Jack gotten into that Pete never knew about? Jack's like Pete's personal superhero, working from the shadows to keep his twin safe. I kiss his cheek, liking the way he's letting me in. "What about you? What are you scared of?"

He stares at the ceiling. "Time." He takes a breath like that revelation was taxing.

"You're afraid of dying?"

"No. I'm worried that my time will run out before I get to do the things I want to. Not getting the chance to experience things I need to. The funny thing is, I haven't even discovered what most of those things are yet."

"So you'll need time for that as well."

"Exactly."

Was that part of what freaked him out so much tonight? He got to thinking about time and how we're all just zooming along in our lives, and it got to be too much for him all at once? Maybe he almost got in a car accident. He needed me to distract him for a while from the ticking of the clock in his mind. "Then I'm glad you're wasting some of your time with me." I kiss his nose.

"Time with you is never a waste. Lately it's the only time that makes sense to me."

His words creep from his lips into my heart and squeeze. Unable to speak, I kiss him again.

Chapter 28

MY HEAD HURTS, AND I HAVE NO APPETITE. PROBABLY because I'm stuffed with the guilt of leading Blake and Jack on and not making a decision. Blake is usually the one I talk to about my problems, so it's weird that my first inclination is to talk to him to sort this out, because I can't.

Nor can I continue to drown in pleasure with Jack. It makes me feel amazing at the time, but when he's gone, I crash and feel like crap again. And since Jack has been opening up emotionally, and Blake and I connected sexually, things are more confusing than ever.

Maybe we can move to a commune and all be hippie, happy lovers? Somehow, I don't think Blake or Jack are polyamorous. I wonder if cheating is genetic. Either way, that's no excuse.

"Are you planning on doing any work today, or are you going to just sit there looking stupid?"

"Excuse me?" Disbelief that Phyllis would say this at all, never mind in front of two clients in the waiting room, disintegrates any snappy comeback.

"You heard me."

"I don't feel like this is a discussion to be having right now."

"Whatever." She looks at her client. "Come right on in, Steph." Steph follows Phyllis into her room, and the door closes.

What the hell? I try to compose myself and not make a scene in front of the remaining client, but I can't handle this today. "Meryl? Will you come with me? I'll get you settled into a room for Ziggy."

Meryl follows me with a small smile. She's one of Ziggy's regulars, a regal, elderly woman who, Naomi told me, wears fur coats if the weather dips below fifty-five degrees, which I take to mean Meryl comes from money. That, and she's got a boy toy, though he's in his late fifties himself.

"Ziggy will be right in."

"Sarah?"

I turn back to her. "Yes?"

"Don't let her push you around. And don't trust her as far as you can throw her either."

"She's not all evil. I think."

Meryl laughs. "Girls like her never change. I'll say no more. But I like you. You're a hard worker and a lot nicer than the other girl they had working the desk."

"Thank you." This time I don't have to force a smile. "You have no idea how much I needed to hear that today."

She pats my shoulder, and I leave the room. She's right. Screw Phyllis—she was supremely unprofessional, and I'm going to talk to Ziggy or Fern about it the first chance I get. Grin-and-bear-it time is over. Fern saw the other day that Phyllis has an attitude with me. Maybe if I tell her about this, she'll understand that wasn't an isolated incident and Phyllis will get put on probation or something. It's too much to hope that she'd be fired outright, but I can't see Fern letting go of something that could potentially cost the business money. Phyllis and Fern seem close, but Fern cares about the business.

My first chance comes at lunchtime. Phyllis cut out early, and Ziggy's client left a couple of minutes ago. He ran to grab a sandwich from the grocery store. It's better to let him eat something and then I'll tell him. I get impatient and snappy when I'm hungry and someone's preventing my food intake, so I'll wait for a few calories to hit his stomach. He comes back and rushes past with a bag throwing off the scent of melted cheese, bacon, and turkey. I give him exactly five minutes, then walk back to the kitchen and peer inside.

"Ziggy?"

He swallows and looks up. "Yes?"

"I wanted to bring to your attention some behavior that I think is inappropriate for the workplace. Phyllis insulted me in front of clients, berating me and being verbally abusive."

"Ah." He dabs his mouth with a hand towel (because napkins are evil). "That's not what she said happened when she texted me before lunch."

Bitch! "What did she say?"

"She said that you were fooling around online during work hours, and when she reminded you that that is inappropriate, you resorted to name calling."

"That's not what happened at all."

"Phyllis doesn't lie, Sarah. No one in this office tells lies. We're very selective about our employees, and there are no liars here. We'd feel the energy immediately."

"Then I guess you made a mistake with her because she hates me and is lying about me."

He looks awed. "She said you'd say as much. Fern and I know that perception is reality and that the truth of the situation lives in the middle. Either way, this is something we might want to look at working out etherically with Phyllis at the retreat this weekend."

Etherically. The hippie way of feeling good about not actually doing anything. "I'd prefer we sat down and worked things out right now, to be honest. Maybe you and Fern could mediate so we could sort this out once and for all."

"We don't want confrontational or defensive energy here. It's best that you work it out with her this weekend."

"I thought Phyllis wasn't coming this weekend." Great, just what I need: to be trapped at a hippie retreat with a woman who might try to slit my throat in my sleep. No thanks.

"Oh, she's not. You'd work on it etherically, energetically. Your spirit will talk to hers and work things out between you. It's very powerful."

I want to kick him right in the root chakra.

"Was that all?"

"Yeah." Disgusted, I turn and walk out. The phone's ringing when I get back to my desk. "Inner Space."

"You know, you've really got some nerve. But did you actually think you could beat me? Honey, you've got to up your game."

"Phyllis? Something I can help you with?" I inject as much sarcasm as humanly possible into my voice since the waiting room is now empty.

"The sad thing is, you truly think you're going to win. You're not. You're a pathetic little nothing. You have nothing to fall back on if you—no, make that *when* you get fired. You're a receptionist. Do you know how fucking insignificant you are? How replaceable you are?"

"I'm a paralegal. I have the shiny degree and everything."

"Yet look at where you are. Wearing a smock and changing used bedding. Doing laundry and dishes for people who know how disposable you are. Did you need a degree for that too?"

I don't hang up because then she'll think she's getting to me.

"Ziggy and Fern will fire you. I'll make sure of that. And then, ten minutes later, they'll have hired someone to take your place at the desk. You're nothing."

"If I'm nothing, you sure spend a lot of time talking to me about the same crap. Who are you trying to convince? Me, or yourself?"

"That's cute. But the thing you really should be focusing on is what you're fighting for. Seriously. You love Inner Space so much you're willing to tangle with me? Sweetie, I'm an orange belt and a firecracker. I eat little bitches like you for breakfast. I've stabbed bitches bigger than you."

That I do believe.

She continues. "Watch your back. It would be better for your health if you quit. Besides, you don't even want to be one of us. Why are you fighting so hard to stay?"

I laugh when it hits me—I've gotten under her skin just as much as she's gotten under mine. She isn't antagonizing me for something to do. She really wants me out of here because, in her mind, I'm her nemesis.

With a triumphant smile, I hang up on her. The annoying part of the conversation is that she's right. I don't want to be one of them. The thought of doing

Fern's course makes me itchy, but for some reason, I'm going along with it and fighting to stay here. Why haven't I been looking for another job as hard as I could have been? Have I just been sucked into the competition with Phyllis?

············——————··········

Later, at home, my phone rings. Call display shows Pete's number. I answer with a heavy heart.

"Hello?" God, I hope he's not calling to ream me out more. Today has been filled with too much *everything* already, and I can't take more. I'm at saturation point.

"You okay?"

Yeah, like I can bitch about anything after a client's hair came out in his hands. She and Pete have way worse things to worry about and deserve more sympathy than I do. Hell, my situation doesn't require sympathy at all. "I'm fine."

"Liar. Look, I'm sorry for being a bitch the other day. You needed me, and I wasn't there."

"Pete, you had a shittier day than I can even fathom. I'm the one who's sorry."

"All the sorrys in the world won't fix things. And all problems are relative, right?"

"I guess. But really, it's fine. You don't need me unloading all over you again."

"Bitch, please. There were starving kids in Africa when I called you and pissed and moaned about not getting floor tickets to Gaga. Right?"

"Yeah."

"And there were women being subjugated all over the world when I called and cried over Thomas standing me up after I'd spent all day making him that picnic lunch—and then when I bawled all over your living room when we broke up two days later, right?"

"Yes."

"So, spill. I want to hear all about this massage thera-pist who isn't a hippie who you have delusions about being just as cute as my brother. My *twin* brother. Who you are sleeping with, which must mean you think I'm the bee's knees."

"I was hoping you wouldn't pick up on that."

"I always knew you thought I was hot. How long have you been in love with me?"

I smile. "Jack is hot. You're too groomed."

"Denial. Anyway, tell me about this online fiasco."

With more coherency than during the other night's phone call, I walk him through each relationship from beginning to end, blushing at the naughtier parts. The great thing about Pete is that he only interrupts to clarify things. Ten minutes later, I'm flushed and still confused but feeling lighter.

He's quiet for a minute when I finish catching him up. "I really wish you'd have told me this all along."

I sigh and flip around on the couch so my feet touch the wall. I trace invisible patterns with my toes. "Me too. Things might not have been in such a big mess."

"No, they'd still be in a mess. But I was right the other night when I said you need to choose. I know you're freaking out about history repeating and becom-ing your mother, even though that is utter bullshit and you're nothing alike. So you need to choose which guy to be with as soon as possible for your sanity's sake."

"The thought I'm just like her has been dancing

through my conscience. The reason I called you in the first place was because I need help choosing between the two of them. Carrying on with them both isn't right at all, and I hate myself for it more every day. I already know I need to make a decision; I'm just terrified of making the *wrong* one."

"Unless you date them both in an open relationship. Poly is in."

"I thought about that too, but I'm not built like that."

"I don't know about this Blake, but neither is Jack, so that option's out."

"So who's the one? How do I know?"

He hums. "Who's the first one you think of every day when you wake up?"

"Blake."

"Who's the last one you think of at night?"

"Jack."

"Sarah! You're not making this easy."

"I'm torn. I can't help it! I think of them both, dream of them both, want them both. Pete, I think...I think I love them both, and it's killing me. The more time that goes by, the more the lines are blurring."

"How?"

"Blake and I sort of had cybersex the other night. And Jack and I actually talked instead of just having incredible sex. I can see myself with either of these guys and being completely happy. I just don't know which one I need to be with and which I have to say good-bye to."

"Who gives you a more visceral reaction when you think of him?"

"Jack. No competition. But I haven't slept with Blake, so I feel like that might not be a fair comparison."

"Then you need to think about who is better for you outside the bedroom. Sex eventually cools down. So you have to decide who is the one you can rely on no matter what. Who do you call or turn to when you have problems?"

"I can rely on them both, but the one I think to call when I need to talk is Blake." Always Blake. "Not being able to talk to him as much while I decide between them has been awful."

"Then, Sarah, I think he's your answer. The man you turn to when you have a problem is the one. And as much as I'd love for you to be legit family and marry and make gorgeous babies with my brother, sex isn't love, no matter how hot it is. You've been friends all along, but on the periphery. Not friends like you and I are. So mostly, all you have is sex. And it's probably amazing because he's my brother and there's no way my twin could be anything less than a sex god."

"But I haven't given Jack the chance to be there for me. Ugh! I love them both. I never knew that was a possibility. I always thought that was some bullshit people used to cheat on their partners." I can tell myself I'm different than my mom, but I don't know what her intentions were. I just saw the fallout. Maybe she felt as conflicted as I do right now. Maybe cheating is genetic and I've been doomed from the start. But I don't *want* this. "But now I'm smack-dab in that situation and I totally get it and I'm miserable. I always thought love was infinite. But it's not. I need one person to give myself to completely. Just one. Right now I'm being torn in half emotionally, and I can't keep this up."

"The real question is who do you love more?"

I bite my lip and tell the truth. "I'm not sure."

Chapter 29

IT HAS TO BE CLOSE TO SIX IN THE MORNING. WITH A violent shiver, I push the air from my lungs, trying to see my breath and feeling surprised when I can't. Sitting up as quietly as I can, I grab my hoodie from my bag and put it on over my pajama top. How the hell am I supposed to flit around in the morning filled with love and light when I've slept for maybe forty-five minutes—freezing my ass off—and am absolutely starving?

Visions of a hot breakfast float through my mind. Buttery waffles drowning in heated syrup. A side of crispy bacon. Scalding hot coffee with lots of cream and sugar to replenish the calories I've missed by not eating for most of yesterday…all served by a hot, naked waiter with a hot, Scottish accent…

Part of the Awakening includes an all-day fast on day one, which is really only three hours, since we arrived just before six and got to leave the circle at nine p.m. It wouldn't have been bad, but Fern and Ziggy drove me here right after work on Friday, so I didn't get supper. They wouldn't stop at a fast-food place so I could grab a bite. Not even a drive-through. Instead, I got a rant about GMOs and hydrogenated oils corrupting my soul star. Whatever the hell that is. They munched happily on road snacks and never offered me any. I didn't want to ask for some, afraid of what might lurk within the granola clusters, so I arrived at the workshop hungry and annoyed.

Tightly wrapping the itchy wool blanket around my shoulders, I glare around the room. It's definitely not the glossy-brochure retreat experience I'd hoped for. Screw our own rooms; we don't even have our own beds. Seven of us are crammed onto straw mats in a small room. Not even an air mattress in sight. My pillow has the size and comfort of a lump of unleavened bread. I wasn't expecting much, but this is ridiculous. Are Ziggy and Fern making everyone slum it so they can take home more money?

So far, the workshop itself hasn't been quite as invasive as I thought it would be. The twenty-two of us—twenty participants plus Fern and Ziggy—sat on the floor in a circle and introduced ourselves. We had to state our intentions for the course, meaning what we hoped to get out of the workshop. That took up a fair amount of the evening, because some people crammed a life story into an intro that was supposed to be a minute long—and, of course, nobody reined them in.

For homework, we have to come up with a problem in our lives, and Ziggy and Fern will show us how to fix it. That sounded awesome, except that my biggest problems are Ziggy and Fern and their lack of management skills. And Phucking Phyllis. Ziggy has been "holding space," whatever that means. He's basically the ultimate creeper—seeing everything, hearing everything, but saying nothing. I'm glad I don't have to listen to hippie crap from him as well as Fern.

Fern has actually surprised me. From the moment we got here, she's sort of blossomed and turned into a nicer person. Her eyes are warm, her smile's bright, and she's relaxed like I've never seen. Maybe this is what she's supposed to be doing. I've never seen her this happy at Inner Space. I don't know if it's the teaching or the energy stuff, but she's like a new person. If she was like this every day, maybe we'd get along better.

When the rest of the group found out I work for Ziggy and Fern and spend hours and hours a day in their venerated presence, they looked at me like I was a guru by association, which is weird and creepy. I never knew how much people in these circles look up to my bosses. To me, they're just my pain-in-the-ass hippie bosses. Maybe the children of celebrities feel like this when they get old enough to realize just how famous and influential their moms and dads are.

It feels kind of nice, but I don't want to get swept into BS. By contrasting these happy-go-lucky versions of Fern and Zig with the ones I know better, I'm able to keep my feet on the floor and the stars from my eyes.

Breakfast is the most disappointing thing I've encountered in recent history. It's grayish, lumpy, and flavorless. Calling it oatmeal would be an insult to oatmeal. This is something poor fairy-tale children are forced to eat in abusive orphanages. Despite the hunger gnawing at my stomach, I'm only able to choke three slimy bites down. We were given weak herbal tea, but it's more scented than flavored. I finish mine anyway, enjoying the heat. The others are talking among themselves, but I can barely focus because I miss coffee so badly.

"If you've all finished enjoying your meals, we're

ready to begin." Fern beckons to us from the adjoining room and we all follow her inside, once again settling on the floor in a circle like we're about to have a rousing game of duck, duck, goose.

"Now, I'd like everyone to take a pen and one of the pieces of paper Ziggy is handing out, and write down the challenges you are facing in your life right now. Be specific."

"Do you have any more paper?" a man quips, and we all laugh, though the sound is tinged with nerves. No one likes spending time looking their fears in the eyes.

"That's excellent! I love how ready you are to lay it all out there. Good for you!" Fern's eyes twinkle at him. "Remember, these issues are things you want to sort out this weekend. These can be fears you want to discard forever. Don't hesitate; we're in a safe place. Nothing leaves the circle. No one will know whose problems are whose. It's completely anonymous. We're going to write out our fears and burn them in a bright flame, releasing them from our lives forever! Doesn't that sound great? It's amazingly cathartic. Trust."

Okay. Well, if we're just burning them, I guess this one is an activity to participate in. If Fern and Ziggy try to get me to do trust falls or anything like that, I can always fake stomach problems and hide in the bathroom. I'm picking my battles here.

After a moment, I begin to write, accompanied by the sounds of scribbling from the other participants.

I'm scared of being stuck in this sort of limbo forever. I'm sort of seeing two guys right now. It's really complicated. But I know I need to make a choice. My heart can't take this situation anymore, so I guess I'd like

to leave indecision behind and make the right choice.
I pause to think of my life and keep writing. *I hadn't really noticed, but because of this situation, I've kind of abandoned friends. I don't want to be one of those girls who ditches her friends, so I want to be able to make new friendships and better maintain the old ones I've neglected.* Ugh, what the hell. *I'd also like for Phyllis and me to get along better, because I'm tired of it being tense at work, even though it's pretty much her fault why we don't get along.*

Surprisingly, I do feel somewhat better for having written it all out. Everyone finishes writing at about the same time, so we sit and wait for Fern's next instructions. "Fabulous. Now pass them up to the front, and I'll prepare them while you all participate in this guided meditation by Ziggy."

Papers passed, we all turn to face Ziggy. Perfect. I can gap out, and it will look like I'm participating. I focus on Ziggy's monotonous chanting.

I rotate my shoulders, working the tension out.

I wonder what Blake's doing right now. It's Sunday, so he could be giving a massage at Inner Space. Now *he's* someone I wouldn't mind getting a massage from, that's for sure.

No matter what choice I make, someone will be hurt. Including me.

Saying good-bye to either of these men will hurt for a long time, even with the other by my side loving me, being loved by me. Is this how my mom feels? She meets someone and falls in love. It knocks her out of line, but then she always stays with Dad because he's her One? Or does she stay with him because she's afraid of the unknown, and it just hurts Dad more when she should do them all a favor and go be with the other guy?

Am I hesitating to make a decision to move forward with Blake because I'm afraid of leaving my safe little niche? Is Jack my rock—he's been in my life for years now, comfortable and safe—but not really the one I need at the end of the day?

But Jack isn't safe, is he? Blake is the safe choice. Blake's the steady raft drifting slowly down a lazy river on a hot summer day. Jack's the pulse-pounding white-water rafting trip. That type of excitement isn't meant to last forever. It's meant to be had in doses because there's the very real danger of being thrown overboard and drowning.

And at this point in my life, I'm supposed to find something long-term and safe. Something nice. Something lasting. Right?

Either one of them could be the man of my dreams. It just depends on the dream I'm looking for.

My shoulder is touched, startling my eyes open. "Yes?"

Ziggy laughs. "We're done. Everyone's back in circle. You went really deep into that meditation, Sarah. We've been calling you for a bit. Great job!"

I blush, but instead of making fun of me, the rest of the participants smile and look envious.

"I wish I had your concentration and focus," the girl next to me says.

I smile and duck my head.

One participant raises her hand. "Is there going to be a break soon? I need to check my messages." I think the lady's name is Valerie, and she's a CEO for some big company I can't remember the name of.

Fern shakes her head. "Actually, there won't be a chance for that. While you had breakfast, and then when you were in circle, we had people go through your bags. They've confiscated all watches, phones, and electronics. All the trappings of the outside world. If any of you have anything that hasn't been confiscated, please hand it to Ziggy now, and he'll give it to the people holding your things."

I left my phone safely stowed in my purse in the room. Does this mean someone went through it? No, they wouldn't do that.

Fern holds her hands up at the murmuring of the group. "This is about being serious and focusing on yourself. The Internet will be there when you get back. Your families will be there when you get back. We do this at every retreat. Someone's collected your phone from your bag, but it's completely safe. We want you to go back to the world a better version of yourself, and that can't happen if you're clinging to the old you. The old you is white-knuckling technology at the cost of your soul. I'll give you a moment to reflect on that."

A man steps forward with his watch, and a lady hands her phone over, but I'm stuck on the idea of someone I don't know—and didn't give permission to—pawing through my things. If this situation were a horror movie, I'd be rolling my eyes and not letting myself get too attached to the character playing me. Because who lures people to a retreat, starves them, makes them sleep in a cold room on a floor with blankets thinner than one-ply toilet paper, and then goes through their bags and confiscates anything they can use to communicate with the outside world?

Serial killers and cultists.

Naomi told me this retreat was a cult.

And there's no way in hell I'm drinking anything brightly colored around here at lunchtime. This is how you break people down, break down their resistance to your agenda. I read a book about just this sort of thing. The first thing is to isolate you. Then take away your comforts, and by getting you hungry and tired, the leaders wear down your resistance.

They make sure you're never alone—that way you don't have time to think about the stupid crap they're trying to feed you. I can't believe I was falling for this. I'd actually begun talking myself into believing the experiences weren't totally stupid! It's asinine and surprisingly effective. You get so tired and hungry that you just go with it, not even thinking about arguing.

If I stay and participate in the rest of the course, how broken down will I be by the end of it? What will it do to who I am, what I believe? It's like police getting a false confession with the suspect under duress. I've found myself wanting to please Fern and Ziggy, wanting to fit in with the group even though I don't share their values. And that shouldn't be a bad thing. We should be able to believe what we want—the only reason I'm here is because I got railroaded into coming.

In group, I'd searched for things to say, ways that my experience might be more than just me struggling to relate. Another day of this and who knows what they'd have me doing? The course is called "Sex, Evolution, and You." When does the sex come in? I like to think I'm a strong-minded person, but I'm so tired and hungry, I can barely focus. Hell, I'm not even as mad as I should be at this violation of my rights. I always thought that underneath it all, Fern and Ziggy were good, moral people. But they aren't.

Normally, if someone had told me they'd gone pawing through my things and taken my personal belongings, I'd be flipping tables demanding my shit back. Instead, I'm sitting here meekly wondering with the others when I'll get my phone back. My keys. Holy shit, they've taken my life.

I don't know who has my stuff or where it is, or what exactly they're doing with it. There's nothing to say they are trustworthy or good people. Are they copying my information down, scrolling through my texts and emails?

I need to get my phone back. And I need to get the hell out of here. It's all too much, too invasive, too crazy. And if whoever's going through my texts and emails shows them to Ziggy and Fern, I'm pretty much fired. I unlocked my phone to lend it to my dad six months ago and never bothered putting the password back on.

No, it's vital I get my phone back. My employment, and sanity, rely on it.

"I need my phone."

"People lived for thousands of years without mobile devices. We'll give them back in a couple of days at the end ceremony." Fern leans in as though imparting a big secret. "You know, some people don't even want their phones back at the end. They'll have grown that far in just those few days."

"But I'm waiting on an important email." I plead with my eyes, but Fern's not buying it.

"Nothing is more important than your enlightenment, Sarah."

"Pretty sure someone dying would count. Emergencies happen all the time."

"No one's going to die." Fern turns to the rest of the group. "Do you see how tightly she's clinging to technology? She's going to crazy lengths, stressing herself out over something that doesn't love her back. Something that is actually hurting her. And why? It's an inanimate object. What does she get out of this abusive relationship?"

An older guy raises his hand. "It lets her stay connected to the martyr mentality so she doesn't have to grow."

"Exactly right. As long as someone on the phone needs her, she doesn't have to fully plug in here with us. Our brains are fabulous at making excuses for the things that hurt us."

Like her and Ziggy and Inner Space?

She smiles. "Sarah here is naturally a very defensive person and puts barriers around herself so she can shut everyone out and not challenge herself, not grow. We've had issues with her doing this at work."

What the hell is she doing talking about my life outside the course? "That is none of anyone else's business." A few of the other participants mutter and look at me like I've disappointed them.

"She has no real friends to speak of, and her interactions with her coworkers are strained at best."

How does she know that? I never shared that information…but I did write it in the form. Tears of outrage sting my eyes. "What gives you the right to talk about my private life, things that I haven't shared?"

"We're here to help you, Sarah. Your issues with Phyllis are just the tip of the iceberg."

Oh my God. She read what I wrote. That's how she

got those "insights" into my life. She's no better than a fake psychic doing cold readings, but in this case, she's gotten a huge tip-off straight from the sources. It's disgusting and just another way to fool people into thinking she's insightful and wise. She and Ziggy are going to use whatever advantage they can to make the weekend seem insightful and spiritually fulfilling.

Fern takes a big, cleansing breath. "She's not in a committed relationship. In fact, she's seeing two men right now and unable to choose between them. She's a cheater."

If I get indignant, then I'm likely to get confrontational and shout and talk myself right out of my job—in front of all these people who would back up anything Fern and Ziggy say.

Even though I'm mad that Fern and Ziggy are taking advantage of all these people, would the participants be happier knowing they paid a lot of money for a scam?

No. Shouting about Fern and Ziggy being liars and cheats wouldn't do a damned thing to help anyone. These people want to believe, so nothing I tell them will help change their minds or make them see the truth. They'll find a way to justify Fern's actions. Just like Ziggy and Fern's *perception is reality* crap.

And yet, I'm unable to stop the words. "You read my response! You're using what I wrote down against me. I thought this was a safe place—that nothing would be thrown back at us. Did you read all of our forms? Is that how you seem like a wise woman? By cheating?"

"Oh, Sarah. *You're* the cheater." She turns back to the group. "Do you see? I give her this amazing opportunity for personal feedback, free of charge, unlike in a group session, and she gets emotional and lashes out. Plays the victim when she should be embracing the experience."

"The intake forms were supposed to be anonymous!"

"Yes, but I recognized your handwriting. You should be thanking me. We're finally going to get to the root of your issues and rip them out of your soul! Tear down those boundaries, Sarah. Tear them down. This is a safe place."

Safe place, my ass. I'm done. Shaking my head, I stand and speed walk from the room.

"Yes, I think while Sarah takes a moment alone to calm down, we should also take a quick break, stretch a little, get some water into us. *Everyone* be back in ten—" Her voice fades as the door swings shut behind me. Fern's delusional if she thinks I'll be back. I am grabbing my phone and getting the hell out of here.

Chapter 30

WHERE WOULD I STICK STOLEN BELONGINGS IF I WERE a crazy hippie with no boundaries? In my room? No, too obvious. Besides, Fern and Ziggy were in the room with us when the belongings were taken. That means they have someone in on it with them—a sympathetic staff member? So that person would be the one with the stolen items. Someone in a position of power, but not an owner—they wouldn't want to get their hands dirty in case someone got mad.

Front-end staff. It has to be someone in administration. Low enough that they'd do what Fern and Ziggy wanted to keep the guests happy, but important enough to be able to bend the rules and go into our rooms. Fern and Ziggy wouldn't have trusted a housekeeper with this—it had to be front end. Maybe they're all in on this, true believers of Fern and Ziggy and their weird cult.

The irony that a receptionist is the most likely accomplice isn't lost on me.

My first stop is the room where we had slept. When I get my phone back—and I will get it back—I'm not sticking around. Best to pack my meager belongings now and then hightail it when I get my phone. I'll figure out the logistics later, such as how the hell I'm getting home, and if I'll still have a job when I get there. If I still *want* that job when I get there.

My feistiness flags when I jam my clothes into the small backpack I brought. How could Fern reveal my problems like that without asking my permission? She can't have thought that would have been okay with me, and it certainly has to be some kind of breach of... *something*. It was sneaky and opportunistic—and how dare she call me a cheater? I sit on the mat I slept on, head spinning.

This crosses a major line. If she's willing to do that here, she's going to do this when we get back to work as well, isn't she? Casually bringing up my personal life in front of clients and, worse, Phyllis.

Maybe I'm overreacting. Everyone else in the group was cool with this. Am I making a mistake? I wish I could talk to Blake. He'd know just what to say to make me feel better about this and help me find my next move. I miss him. Tears spring to my eyes, and I sigh. I wish we were together right now. He always makes me feel better. No matter how bad everything seems, he knows just what to say to make things okay.

And there it is.

In the midst of sleep deprivation, low blood sugar, and hippies violating my boundaries, I've stripped away the layers of indecision.

I think of Blake first when I need support. Support is the foundation of a long-term relationship. Maybe a candle isn't as exciting as fireworks, but it's better to carry with you to find your way ahead. If Jack and I broke up, I'd lose Pete too. How could I ever look at my best friend's face and not see his twin who broke my heart? Jack's been opening up, but Blake made himself emotionally available from the start, and that's important.

Blake is the one. I need to get home and tell him that as soon as possible.

Feeling light enough to float, I jump up, bag in hand, and leave the room. I have a receptionist to see, a phone to find, and a life to live.

I tiptoe past the conference room and hit the communal bathroom before making my escape, because if life has taught me anything, it's that you should always go when you have the chance. The resort isn't big, but the hallways twist and turn, so I have to hike around a little to find the front desk. A young, bored-looking brunette is typing something onto a screen I can't see.

I clear my throat. "Excuse me. May I use your phone? I wanted to double-check an appointment."

"Sure." She passes me the cordless phone and goes back to her typing.

Excellent. I take a couple of steps away from the desk, ostensibly for privacy, but really, I want to be able to hear my phone when it rings. I dial my number. The *Game of Thrones* theme song rings out in the lobby. Surprised, I look at the receptionist.

"I'm sorry. Someone left their phone here while they're in a course." She looks at the top drawer. The song stops when my voice mail kicks in. I don't leave a message, staying silent for a moment instead.

"That's fine." This is hilarious. She's apologizing to me, thinking I'm annoyed that the noise is happening during my phone call. I fake a conversation confirming my "appointment" and give the phone back to her. Now I have to get her away from the desk.

I lean closer. "Sorry, but I think one of your toilets is leaking."

Her head snaps up. "What?" I know that face. That's the face I make when something barely falls under my jurisdiction at work and I don't want to deal with it, but there's no one else to handle the situation.

"Yeah. I can't be sure. I was in the other stall, but I thought I heard dripping. And saw a puddle," I add when she looks like she's going to ignore the leak.

"Crap. That's the second time this week."

I make a sympathetic face. "Do you have a pen and paper I could borrow? I need to write down my appointment time."

"Sure." She rummages around and hands me a pad with the hotel's information on it, then stands. "If you're good, I have to go check on that leak."

"I'm perfect, thanks." I begin writing, and she huffs and heads toward the bathroom.

As soon as she turns the corner, I race behind her desk. Nothing else was missing from my things, so as soon as I grab my phone from the drawer, I speed walk outta there, trying to look casual while formulating my next move.

Thankfully, it's warm, and I flop onto a nearby bench once I'm outside. I'm stuck in the back end of Jersey with no vehicle and no friends. Blake? No. I don't want to go into things with him rescuing me. That would set a precedent and the tone for our relationship in a way that I don't want. I'm not a blond-haired princess in a video game; I don't need to be rescued.

Not by Blake, at least.

But I've missed a text from him while the hippies had my phone.

> Hey, Sarah, it's Blake. I know it's not my place to interfere, but things didn't look so good at Inner Space. Screw those hippies. I've got a job opportunity, if you're interested, with a friend who's head of HR at a women's magazine. Let me know. I've emailed the details. It's yours if you want it.

My heart soars at this blinding light at the end of the tunnel. My fingers tremble while I check my email, sending back an immediate "YES" when I see the description and the starting pay. I call his number, but he doesn't answer. Now I really want to get home.

Pete doesn't pick up when I phone him four times in a row. Even though I'm overstepping the bounds in a huge way—especially when I shouldn't be calling him except to say good-bye—I call Jack.

"Hey, I was just thinking about you." His voice is warm and brings back memories best left in the bedroom of my past.

"You got the distress signal?"

"What's happening?" The humor leaves his tone.

"There's been a situation with the hippies. I need a ride, but I'm still at the resort."

"What's the address?"

I tell him.

"I'll be there as soon as I can."

"Thank you."

Chapter 31

OVER AN HOUR LATER, JACK PULLS UP AND EXITS his car, and as happy as I am to see his friendly, familiar, non-hippie face, I realize again with stark clarity that I wish it were Blake, because he's the one I really want to talk to right now. Blake's emotional support has edged out the molten chemistry between Jack and me, but that doesn't make me feel any better.

Still, I can't help smiling at him, sadness swelling because I still love him too and good-bye isn't going to be easy to say. "Thank you."

He takes my bag. "What's going on?"

"I'll be better as soon as this place is just a speck in the rearview mirror. Total violation of my boundaries. And no sleep. They took my phone, had someone paw through our bags *without* our permission while we were in the course, taking things so we wouldn't be distracted by the outside world."

"What the hell?"

"So I left the course and stole my phone back." I grin, feeling a bit like a badass.

"What about Fern and Ziggy?"

"What about them?"

"What did they say when you told them you were leaving?"

I pause and bite my lip. "Oh, I haven't exactly told them."

"Sarah!" He laughs. "You have to tell them you're leaving."

"Maybe I told them etherically..."

"You what?" His forehead wrinkles in confusion.

"It's something they do, where they basically meditate and imagine telling the person."

"Sarah."

I guess sneaking off isn't the best course of action, but I don't want to deal with them anymore today. "I'm scared I might say something I'll regret. Or wave my new job offer in their faces while flipping the bird."

He tilts his head. "That's fair."

"Sarah, what's going on?"

I get a crick in my neck as I whip my head toward the entrance of the hotel. Shit. Maybe I shouldn't have joked about that etheric crap. "Hi, Ziggy."

"You can't just leave the program. We've given you plenty of time to cool off from your little performance in group, but it's time to come back now." He squints suspiciously at Jack.

"Ziggy, I'm sorry, but it's just not for me. I gave it a fair try, but it's not something that I'm comfortable continuing." That's about as diplomatic as I can be under the circumstances.

Ignoring Jack, Ziggy stops in front of me and crosses his arms. "There are three days left. A lot can happen in those days that I think you'll want to stick around for. You've been doing well so far. Don't let the phone get in the way of your enlightenment."

He's trying to entice me back, but I don't give a tiny crack of a rat's ass about the rest of the course. What I've seen already has been more than enough. His eyes don't have bags or dark smudges under them like mine do, and that makes me wonder something. "Ziggy, do you and Fern sleep in a room with a bed?"

"Well, yes, but—"

"That's what I thought. Sorry, but I can't stay and drown in the hypocrisy anymore." They lie around comfortable and well-fed while we starve on the path to spiritual growth? No thanks.

"Hypocrisy?" He puffs up, and his face flushes. "If you value your employment with us, you will tread very carefully, Sarah. We've forgiven so much already, taken more than others would of your defensive behavior and disinterest in fitting in with us. We've made many allowances to your ways. Many."

Jack laughs. "It's a job, dude, not a religion. You take yourself way too seriously. She shouldn't have to become one of you just to get a paycheck."

"She belongs to us. As long as she works for Inner Space, she will be whatever we say she will be."

Wow. "Thanks for making it easy for me, Ziggy. I don't know what possessed me to think I needed to take so much bullshit from you guys in the name of fitting in or keeping the peace. Maybe there is some kind of energy field around the reception area that made me forget who I am. I quit."

He makes a weird barking sound. "You can't just

quit, young lady! You owe us two weeks' notice at the very least."

"So you can make my life even more hell than usual? No thanks. If you were going to fire me, would you give me two weeks' notice, or would you sneak in my replacement for an interview on the weekend and just tell me not to come in on Monday? I'd rather not find out. I owe you nothing."

Ziggy looks around as though searching for an excuse before his eyes light up. "You owe us for the course."

My degree finally gets some use. "You gave me this for free. I have copies of the paperwork. You can't suddenly decide to charge me thousands of dollars for it after the fact. There's no way I'm paying you a goddamned cent, and nothing you say to the contrary would hold up in court."

"Listen here, missy. You will—"

"Hey, Ziggy?" Jack interrupts with a smile.

"What?" Ziggy snaps.

"Breathe into it."

The vein in Ziggy's forehead swells to epic proportions as I freely laugh.

"Come on, Sare." Jack grabs my hand and leads me to the curb, opens the passenger door, and shuts it behind me. A few seconds later, he slides behind the wheel and slams his own door. "Crazy fucking hippies."

"I can't believe you told him to breathe into it. You're my hero."

"They're delusional. What truly awful people. It wasn't my place, but I couldn't help it."

The comfort of the car seat and the heat of the sun on my face makes me sleepy, but I have a more pressing need. "We have to stop for some food."

"Where?"

"I don't care. Something quick, hot, and greasy, with as many preservatives in it as possible."

"Yes, ma'am." He steers the car down the street, and my mouth salivates at the sight of fast-food restaurants. "Sure you don't want to eat fresh?" He points at a sandwich shop.

My glare could melt glass. "I said greasy."

He laughs.

I'm scrabbling at the door before the car is in park and heading inside, practically drooling at the smell of food. Verboten food full of preservatives and nitrates and chemicals. Processed cheese. I stroll up to the counter. "Can I have a cheeseburger with no onions, no pickle, extra cheese, extra bacon? And six chicken nuggets. And large fries. Do you have extra-large?"

The guy at the counter looks a little stunned and shakes his head.

"Then give me a large and a small. And I want a Coke. And a chocolate milk shake. Do you have any pies?"

He shakes his head. "We sold out at lunch."

"Damn. Okay, that's all then. For here."

He rings up the order, and I swipe my bank card. Jack makes it to the counter. His smile grows bigger as more and more items are set on the tray.

I hope he doesn't think I'm sharing. "Aren't you getting anything?"

"I ate already. Need some help carrying that tray?"

"No, I'm good, smart-ass."

He orders a milk shake, I suspect only so I'm not eating alone, and we head to a table. All I can smell is the bacony goodness. My cheeks are barely in the chair before I'm tearing into the burger and stuffing my face with fries.

It takes four nuggets, the large fries, and half of the burger before the hunger haze lifts and my awareness expands to include things other than my empty stomach and my tray of food. Jack's eyes are big as I swallow my bite. The past few minutes can't have been pretty to watch.

He steals a fry. "Didn't they feed you up there in hippie Siberia?"

"Gruel." There's only time for one word as I shovel in another bite of juicy burger.

Jack grins, but he doesn't realize I'm serious. Unfortunately, my stomach has shrunk, and I fill up way too soon for my tongue's liking. The food is delicious, and I could eat for hours if not for my protesting stomach. Despite being stuffed, I pick the bacon off the burger and cram it in my mouth for my final bite.

"Full?"

"Yes." I pat my stomach.

"That's good. You were all big eyes and sharp teeth for a while there. Now you're looking more relaxed."

"Maybe too relaxed. I'm so sleepy."

"You can sleep in the car. Come on. Let's get you home. What's this about a new job?"

Suddenly, the food in my belly doesn't feel so great. "A friend, Blake, hooked me up." I give him the details about the job.

The drive takes forever, but I can't tell him while we're driving. At some point I doze off, because I wake up to his hand gently stroking my cheek.

"Sarah, wake up. We're here."

I blink, stupidly leaning into his touch. He's parked us in the shade of one of the tall trees that line my street, but it's still so bright and warm that I could easily slip back to sleep. Four kids on bikes zip by, laughing, and I sit up, checking my face for drool. Man, I was really out.

A group of teenagers crowds the steps of the apartment building across the street. Jack leans closer, and his lips curl into a gentle smile.

I pull back. "I need to go inside."

He takes the key out of the ignition, but I stop him from leaving the car with a hand to his arm. It's not fair to him or Blake to continue like this. Not even one more kiss. I've finally made a decision and need to honor it.

"We need to talk."

He goes very still. "Okay."

The gentle haze of sleep deserts me, leaving behind painful reality. "We can't do this anymore. I can't do this anymore."

He grips the steering wheel so tightly that his knuckles go white. "This again? Why not?"

"Jack, I know it sounds like the oldest cliché in the book, but it's really not you. It's me."

"Don't do this, Sarah."

"We're amazing together, but not in all the ways I need."

"What we have isn't just sexual!"

"I'm sorry."

"Is there someone else?"

I nod.

He slumps in his seat. "What's his name? Blake?"

"He's the one who got me the new job."

"I offered you a job too."

"I know. It just wasn't the best fit for me, Jack."

"I can't believe this." He won't even look at me. I know I'm the one hurting him right now, but it kills me that he won't look at me.

"I know. But believe me when I say it wasn't easy, and you mean so much to me." Tears drip down my cheeks, and I try to hide them because I don't have the right to cry while breaking up with him. Jack's the injured party, but I can't help it. My heart's still breaking in two, and half of it will leave in his car with him and trail around behind him forever. A piece of me will always belong to Jack.

He nods.

I squeeze his hand and leave the car, forcing myself not to look back. His car rumbles and drives away, and through the uncertainty, I feel a little lighter now that I've made a definitive decision. I made the right choice for my future. It's time to move on with Blake.

Chapter 32

THE WHOLE SITUATION MAKES ME FEEL LIKE CRAP, but if nothing else, the hippie weekend made me realize that Blake is the one I need to be with, the one I want even more than Jack, which is saying a lot. If Blake and I had never met, who knows what Jack and I might have eventually been?

But I have to focus on the future, and that means telling Blake I'm ready to meet *right now*. I don't know if Jack and I will ever be able to be friends again. I don't know if Blake and I will work in person. But I know I want to give him my full heart and a fair chance. He's the smart choice, and it's time for me to grow up.

Being so out of my depth with Fern and Ziggy eroded my self-confidence in ways I hadn't expected and can only see now that I know I'm not going back to Inner Space. I wanted to fit in so badly that I overlooked how shitty they truly were to me, and it made me doubt my decision-making abilities, even when it came to Blake and Jack. I was so paralyzed about making the wrong decision that I wasn't able to make any decision at all. Then seeing the way Fern and Ziggy cheated people and lied to us at the retreat was like a bucket of cold water poured over my body.

I need to be true to myself, but I need to keep other people in mind too and not justify my own bullshit like Fern and Ziggy do. Maybe I'm making the wrong choice in the long run, but I don't think I am. And even if I am, that's what life's about. At least I'll have put myself out there and tried to do the right thing, tried to be a good person.

Jack and Blake deserve someone who's going to give them one hundred percent. I can only give that to one man. I refuse to give less than that to one man.

The weight of my mom's history falls from my shoulders. I'm not like her, and I never will be. I made the best decision, and I'm sticking with it. A smile takes over my face, and I turn my computer on and wait for it to boot up. Then I spring up and look around in the fridge. Do I have anything I can make for a dinner? I find a baking chicken and vegetables. Homey and perfect. I log on to Skype and message Blake, though he's away.

> Me: I want you to come over tonight. Online isn't enough anymore. I want us to be a real couple, live and in person. Come over for dinner. I want to see you in 3-D.

God, why do I feel so nervous? We've talked so much, and I'm making the right decision. But what will it be like in person? Will the conversations flow as smoothly, the truth come out as freely when the screens and anonymity are taken away? My nerves are like honeybees, buzzing beneath my skin. I push away from the computer and pace around, wondering, savoring the sharp, sweet sensation. What if our sexual chemistry pales compared to Jack and me? It doesn't matter. Some relationships are a slow burn. What we have is so satisfying that we'll make it work.

My computer chimes with a reply.

Him: What time?

Seven? That gives me just over two hours. I send my address.

Him: I'll be there.

Shit. Is that enough time to get ready? My gaze ping-pongs around the apartment. It's okay, but not perfect. *See you then.*

I log off and run around tidying things that are out of place or embarrassing. He wouldn't judge me for all the chick flicks in my DVD stand, but I move some of the cooler movies and classics to the top to display them more prominently. Half an hour later, after dusting and sweeping and vacuuming, I catch sight of my reflection while scouring the bathroom.

Shit! I forgot all about myself. Flat hair, pale skin from lack of sleep. Dark circles beneath my eyes. I have a situation here and might need more than an hour to fix it. My chest rises and falls as I breathe way too heavily—and suddenly I start laughing.

I don't have to do a damn thing.

Because it's Blake, and he loves me. He doesn't give a shit what I look like. He loves me for who I am, not my looks, and I feel the same way about him. With us, what's on the inside has always driven our feelings. It's substantial, and no matter what, we have an amazing foundation to build upon.

So I head to the kitchen and take my time preparing supper, putting the chicken in the oven. Then I head to the bathroom and step into the shower. He loves me for who I am, but I still want to look nice. I'm just not going to drive myself up the wall aiming for perfection.

Not liking damp hair, I blow-dry and rub some shine serum into my hair, leaving it at that. Wanting to skip decisions about coordination, I choose a simple but cute blue jersey dress and apply some light, clean makeup—undoing the evidence of the hippie weekend. Clear lip gloss, an extra coat of mascara. It's the most relaxing date preparation I've ever had, and it makes me even happier.

By the time I'm done, it's almost seven and the doorbell rings. Right on time. I throw open the door and smile at…Jack? No, he can't be here right now. Blake will arrive any second. "What are you doing here? You can't be here right now."

"You look beautiful." He looks me over head to toe and pushes past me into my apartment. "Expecting company?"

"I am, actually." He's being uncharacteristically rude, but I did just break up with him after having him drive to a retreat center in far Jersey to get me. I owe him a few minutes and want to give him time—but not right now, with Blake on his way.

Jack paces in the same pattern on the same place in my living room that I walk when I'm burning off excess energy or trying to work something out, and it slams me in the heart. He's so right for me. He's conflicted and walking exactly where I do when I'm tangled up in knots.

"There are some things I have to tell you, and you might be mad, but you need to keep an open mind."

"Another chance" twirls around my legs and slithers beneath my feet, unbalancing me because I do want to give him another chance. Jack's an amazing man, and I was an idiot to think he'd cheat. He's no closer to being my mother than I am. He deserves someone who appreciates and loves him on every level. I can do that. I see him for who he is, and I know I could trust this man with my life—with my heart. "Jack."

The timer goes off on the oven, shattering the moment. Shit! The chicken. "Hang on." The oven clock tells me Blake is now six minutes late, but I know he'll be here soon, so I turn the oven off but leave the chicken inside so it stays warm. My emotional connection with Blake is the smarter choice. I can't forget that, but I owe it to Jack to hear him out.

Jack's still pacing when I return to the living room. I sit on the couch and wait for him to speak.

"Sometimes we do things…when we truly love someone…"

"Jack, please don't think this was an easy decision for me. It was about what he gave me emotionally."

"Fuck it." He pulls out his phone and fiddles with it. Impatience itches my skin, but I try to give him time to collect his thoughts. My phone buzzes, and a chime sounds from my computer that I left on when I started cleaning.

My hand twitches, but I can't get it while Jack's here and so upset. That's beyond rude. My phone buzzes again—probably Blake telling me why he's late.

"Aren't you going to get that?" Jack asks.

"I didn't want to be rude and talk on my phone in front of you," I say pointedly, hoping he'll take the verbal nudge to start talking, but he misses the irony of the situation and continues screwing around with his phone. With an eye roll, I move to my desk and grab my phone. If Jack's not going to talk to me, I can at least see what's happening with Blake. Maybe it will give me an idea of how much time I have to give to Jack before Blake shows up.

The missed message is from Blake. *I'm right here.*

The door steals my focus like a flower turns to the hot sun. Blake's outside that door right now. I swallow hard, suddenly nervous, and not just because Jack is still here. Why hasn't Blake knocked? I walk over and stare out the peephole, but the hall is empty. I open the door and look up and down the empty hall.

My phone beeps with another message. *I'm in your living room.*

He's… What? Shaky legs carry me back to the doorway, and I stare at Jack who smiles weakly and presses a button on his phone while looking me in the eyes. My world trembles.

My phone receives another message, and it's a long moment before I can look at it. *It's Jack.* "What?" My brain stalls.

"I'm here for dinner, Sarah. I'm your Missed Connection."

Chapter 33

IS THIS A TRICK? IS HE DOING THIS TO SABOTAGE BLAKE and me? But no, Jack's not like that, and besides, how the hell would he have Blake's Skype account? "What the hell is going on? What do you mean you're my Missed Connection?" The impossibility of it pings through my mind. He can't be. But he's here and knows about the Missed Connection, and he's walking toward me, swallowing my reasons with the intensity in his eyes. What about Blake? "You can't be."

"Why not?" His voice is soft.

Because I'd have known if it was you. "Because…it can't be you."

"It wasn't me when we ate Indian food and watched *Dirty Dancing* online? When I told you I took secret dancing lessons so I could be like Johnny? When you'd come home from work and talk to me online about your days and let me be there for you? It *was* me all along."

I shake my head. "No."

"Are you disappointed?" Jack stops just inches away.

"I don't know how I feel." I can barely breathe. I can't believe it. "But I have your number. It's not the same as my Missed Connection."

"You're the only one with this phone number. I

wanted you to get to know me for real with no preconceived notions." He scrolls back, showing me the messages from "Blake" over the past couple of months.

My hand clutches his phone—and the truth. He's my
Missed Connection, and I don't know how to feel about
this. "Why didn't you tell me?"

"I wanted to but never found the right time."

"The right time would have been anytime in the past
two months, Jack! We talked almost every day. You
could have told me every day that it was you. Or, I don't
know, maybe when I was downstairs breaking up with
you to be with…you."

"So you could tell me how we could never be a
couple because we were too different and the best I
could be to you is casual sex? And I didn't know if you
were breaking up with me for the Missed Connection or
someone else. Not for sure. Not until you messaged me
after I left."

I can't even deal with the thought of there being
someone else besides Jack and Blake in the equation.
The doorway is too crowded with Jack, me, and all my
emotions crammed into it, so I push past Jack and walk
into the living room. *Jack* is my Missed Connection?
"Start from the beginning."

"It was the only way I could get you to open up to
me. I knew I'd never be anything but a hookup to you.
And maybe it was the only way I could open up to you
as well. I'm not the best at expressing myself. God, I'm
making it sound as though the whole thing was a sordid
scheme. It wasn't." He runs his hands through his hair.
"It just sort of happened, and then I was so, God, so
happy you were letting your walls down with me that I

couldn't stop. Just getting to talk to you every day was like an addiction. Our conversations were the best part of my day."

Mine too. "Were you ever planning on telling me the truth? How long would you have continued the charade?"

"It wasn't a charade. You have to know that all of it was real, Sarah. I got so wrapped up in you, in the relationship we had online, that I justified it any way I could to keep talking to you. It was new for me too. I didn't want you to know it was me for sure and freak out, push me away. But I know I let it go too far."

"Did you get off on it? Knowing that I had no idea it was you? Did you think about it when you were f-fucking me?" Outrage chokes my words. Like my thoughts, nothing is flowing easily, and I wrap my arms around myself, feeling way too exposed.

He looks horrified and takes a step closer. "I'd never… I wanted to come right out and tell you so many times but I was afraid I'd lose you. Maybe it was delusion, or wishful thinking so strong it made me stupid, but I honestly thought you knew it was me—or at least suspected."

"I had no idea."

"I know that now, but I didn't know for a while. I figured that out the night we…the night we were online and…voice chatted."

Oh God, he means the night we sent each other the pictures and…

He gnaws at his bottom lip. "And I never intended to… I wanted our conversations online to be about everything but sex, but I couldn't resist. Maybe I was subconsciously trying to show you it was me—to provoke you into confessing you knew it was me. You hadn't responded to me in person or online for days. By then, I'd wanted to blow the whole thing apart and bring it into the open for so long, but I didn't know how to tell you.

"And we crossed the line that night, but it felt right. I was swept away by you. It was like a dream—our online emotional connection was enough for you to fall for me. You let me in, found out who I am inside, and it was enough for you. I wasn't just a body, a rich catch like I am to everyone else."

Despite hauling in a deep breath to protest, I say nothing. He's probably right. I had written him off as a sexy body. A bad boy. I'd fallen for the hype and couldn't see past his looks and what I kept thinking of as his nonstop party lifestyle.

"But then, when we…we connected in that way online as well, and you cried out another man's name… I'd felt like you were finally seeing me in our conversations and I'd be able to reveal myself. I'd planned on telling you the truth. Then you…" His hand balls into a fist and he presses it to his forehead like he is trying to banish an awful memory. "That night I realized you'd been falling in love thinking I was someone else, and I lost it. I came over, needing to be with you, needing you to see *me*. Needing to be the one in your arms and in your thoughts. Needing *my* name to be the one you sighed. I was going to tell you that night, but you said it didn't matter. I took the easy way out and didn't confess. I should have."

I still remember that awful look in his eyes that night, but I had no idea it was because of me. I can imagine the pain that caused Jack. I'd have been devastated if our positions had been reversed. He had tried to tell me something, but I'd assumed he felt guilty about hooking up with someone else and shut him up with my body. "But how could you string me along like that for so long? Pretending to be two different people?"

He shakes his head and steps closer. "I never pretended anything. I've been honest all along, other than not outright telling you it was me. I've never lied once."

I think back over our online talks and he's right. He never pretended to be anyone other than himself, never gave a fake name or picture. Still. "Do you know what it's been doing to me, thinking I was hurting two people by not choosing between you and…online you?"

"I'm sorry. I never meant for you to get hurt. I just wanted you to give me a chance. The anonymity made it possible for me to be who I am. No preconceived notions, no club or bad-boy persona to get in the way. Still, I'm sorry. I never should have let it go on this long."

Mind racing, I step away from him and sit on the arm of the couch, holding up my hand for him to not talk for a moment. I can't believe Jack would go to such lengths to win me over. Is he proud of himself for this? For fooling me? For getting his way? Because I had no idea, and now he's won and the truth is out. He has to be ecstatic.

But he's standing here, larger than life…head down, arms crossed like he's trying to hold in emotions that are trying to blow his body apart. He doesn't look particularly proud of himself at all, nor very happy about any of this.

So there never was a Blake. Correction, there *is* a Blake, but he just gave me a chocolate bar, rubbed my shoulders once—which was probably more about getting me for a client, not a girlfriend—and told me about Fern and the float. He was concerned about me that day at Inner Space, but not because we were in a relationship. It was because he's a decent guy. And he got me an amazing job—my escape from the hippies.

He didn't leave me a Missed Connections post.

He hadn't admired me from afar.

He wasn't the one who was there for me every day when I needed someone to talk to, when I got overwhelmed by Inner Space and Phucking Phyllis.

But he saw the Missed Connections up on the computer at work that day. How did Jack find out about that? "How did you know about the Missed Connections? I hid that from everyone. It's been my guilty pleasure for months."

"That time right after you moved, when I brought over the things you left at Pete's?"

That was the day Fern called me, making me go into work on a Sunday. "Right."

"You got a phone call and went into the bedroom to take it. Your computer was on, and I saw the Missed Connections section was open. That night, I went home and started reading through them, wondering what someone like you saw in them. At first, I'd thought it was some online dating site. I didn't know if it was something you always read or if it was a one-time thing that you happened to be checking out, but I was intrigued by the whole thing. I posted for you, and you replied a couple of days later."

"Oh."

"But…can I ask you something?" He doesn't look like he really wants to know the answer.

"I guess."

"Who's Blake?"

"He's a massage therapist at Inner Space, but he only works on the weekends."

"And you guys have a thing? Is it serious? I know it's really none of my business by any means, but... never mind." Jack's face is pale and he doesn't quite meet my eyes.

"What? No! The timing is what made me think you were him online. I've only met Blake a few times. Seeing the ad is what made me think it was Blake."

"So you're not together?"

"No. We've never...we've never dated or kissed or anything." Strange that it's not harder to realize Blake was never a part of my life. He was never the guy I was talking to, and it's telling how easy that is to take, how easy it is to say good-bye to him, even though I thought I was in a deep, committed relationship with him for months. It was Jack all along. It's always been Jack, even when I thought he was someone else.

But what does that mean? It's still Jack.

I've been in a relationship with him for a while now. Hell, I've been in two relationships with him, and the only bad part was when I knew I had to say good-bye to one side of him. Deciding who was better for me was a nearly impossible decision to make. The scorching, panty-melting, sexy Jack or the sensitive, supportive, incredibly good listener, online "Blake."

But there's only one Jack, and he's everything I've wanted, everything I've had these past months, all in one tight package.

One package with a heart that matches my own. His

past is in the past, and I'm the only one who didn't see that. I've been his present since we started talking. The thought of not having him in my future is worse than any traces of doubt I have about this working long-term. It's worse than the lie of omission he's so openly apologizing for.

"I'm sorry, Sarah. I'm so, so sorry."

He's done something wrong, that's for damned sure. But he's also done something right. "Jack?"

"Yeah?" He meets my eyes.

"You should probably go."

"Okay. God. Okay, if that's what you want. I know I have it coming. I just hope someday I can be your friend again after all—"

"You should probably *go* take the chicken out of the oven before it dries out," I interrupt.

He should never have hidden the truth from me. But if he hadn't done that, would I have known how incredible he is on the inside? I don't think so. I'd have missed out on the most incredible man I've ever known.

His shoulders sag, and he shakes his head like he can't believe it. I smile and nod when he reaches for me. He runs his hands up my forearms, up to my shoulders, and stands in my space with a fierce love shining in his eyes. Even when he thought I might be seeing another man, he didn't confess the truth, waiting for me to make the choice instead. Even though it hurt him so deeply. It wasn't just about what I needed or wanted; he wanted to be more to me than a casual lay. And he is.

I squeeze his biceps. "What you did was dishonest and sneaky. And perfect. You made me truly see you.

Who you are on the inside." There's so much love in his eyes that it's like staring at the sun, but I don't look away. "And that's pretty hard, considering how distracting your appearance is."

"So, you're saying I've got a chance?"

"Jack, you don't need a chance. You're it for me. But I want to be clear. Your personality? The true you, the person I got to know online, is who I fell for."

"You proved that by choosing well. Me." He smiles.

"I'm sorry I never let myself really see you before. I'd be an idiot to let fear get in the way of us."

His smile dazzles me, and he rests his forehead against mine. "Thank you, Sarah." He captures one of my hands and kisses my palm. "I love you."

"But just to be clear: you're *also* the hot guy with me, because sweet baby Jesus, Jack, the things you do to me…"

He closes his eyes and bites his lip. "I love you."

I laugh. "You already said that."

"I wanted to hear it again." He gives me a big-eyed expression that kicks me in the heart.

"Oh, well, in that case…I love you." I take a step toward the bedroom and pull him with me. "I love you." We cross the threshold. "I love you." When we reach the bed, I lie down and pull him on top of me. "I love you."

"I could listen to you say that all night." His breath is warm against my neck. "But right now I'd rather hear you scream my name."

"If you're not naked in three seconds…" I gasp at the sharpness when he nips my neck.

"What will you do?" He kisses me deeply and I wrap my arms and legs around his body, grinding against him, shamelessly wanting more, unable to answer his question.

I reach between us and rub him through the fabric of his jeans, reveling in his sudden intake of breath. "I'll drive you crazy until you give me what I want."

"What do you want?"

"You. Just you."

He straddles me and pulls off his T-shirt. When his hands land on the hem of my dress, I lift my hips and let him work it over my body and head. He stands and takes off his jeans while I remove my bra, neither of us looking away from the other.

Jack lays kisses down my body, but I can't wait anymore. "No."

"No?"

I urge him down until he's half lying on me and hook my leg around him, pulling him closer to where I want him. "I need you." My chest is going to explode if I don't have him inside me right now. "*Now*."

"Not yet. I waited so long for you to know it was me, and now you do and it feels like too much all at once. I don't want to rush it." His fingers burn a trail down my belly and rub my clit like he said he wanted to do that night we Skyped and I thought he was someone else. It was him then, and him now, and it's always been him. But I can't stand the feelings. I want to cry from the frustration of not being joined with this perfect man. Surprise is on my side. I sit up and am able to push him onto his back and climb on top.

"You nearly tore my heart in two by giving me an impossible choice to make. I made it, felt bad that you wouldn't be in my life anymore, and then I find out that both of my dream guys were you?" I caress his face. "When I say now, I mean *now*." I reach below me and stroke him a couple of times.

His hands still my hips as I rise above him. "Don't you want to get a condom?"

"I'm on birth control. It's just you and me, right?"

He smiles. "Yes."

Covering his hands with mine, I slowly ease down onto his cock, working my hips at the tight fit, sighing at the heat of him sliding inside me with nothing between us.

"I love your mind, but goddamn, Sarah, those hips give your personality a run for its money." He grips them, sitting up and running his hands back to cup my ass. His change in position has brought us together again, and I rest my forearms on his shoulders and use his body for leverage, rising up and pushing down on him again and again and again.

"I can't believe it's you," I moan. "You're perfect."

His eyes crinkle at the edges, but he kisses me before I can see the smile. He kisses me so deeply, tongue stroking mine so perfectly, that I freeze and pull back. He knows my body better than anyone. We're kissing and he's inside me, but the thing that makes me happiest, turns me on the most, is that he knows my heart better than anyone.

And I know his.

His fingertips trace the contours of my cheek. "Be my girlfriend."

"I already am. I was willing to give up the best sex of my life with the guy I've had a crush on for years just for the man who stole my heart online. You're that man. That's what matters."

"You've had a crush on me for years?" He looks way too pleased.

I stretch up and kiss the happy grin off his face. "I love you, Jack."

"I love you too." His eyes are tender as he flips us over and pulls my feet over his shoulders.

Who he is *inside* is what really matters to me.

But I love when he does *this* too.

Epilogue

I BLOT MY SWEATY PALMS ON MY BLACK A-LINE SKIRT, feeling tragically unhip compared to the leggy receptionist in next year's Blahniks who showed me into Melanie's office five minutes ago. The scent of stale coffee and correction fluid hits the back of my throat as I inhale deeply and sneak another glance at the clock on the wall.

The door opens behind me. "Sarah?"

I stand and turn, heart pounding. I need this job. "Yes."

She's about my age. Trim but curvy. Her glossy brunette hair is twisted into a bun, but the severe style only showcases her classic bone structure and high cheekbones. She's striking even with minimal makeup. She looks up from the stack of papers and holds her hand out. "I'm Melanie."

I shake her hand, glad I blotted mine a moment ago. "Nice to meet you."

"Have a seat." Melanie slides into her chair behind the desk and appraises me. Her eyes are a fascinating shade somewhere between yellow and green and framed with thick, black eyelashes. "Thanks for being early."

"Lateness is a pet peeve of mine."

She smiles. "Blake said you were working reception at a spa?"

I nod.

"Sorry to say that there won't be any chanting or"—she waves her hand dismissively—"tea leaf readings around here."

"Thank God." The words fly out of my mouth before I can stop them. I cringe, but she laughs.

"You weren't into that New Age business?" She pronounces *New Age* so it rhymes with sewage.

No job is worth putting myself through another Inner Space. The few days away have given me time to decompress and realize that the things Fern and Ziggy did to me were shitty, but they're not bad people. For someone who's into the same philosophy they are, working with them would be a dream come true. Maybe that's not quite right—but it definitely wasn't the place for me, and I shouldn't have stayed as long as I did. Some people aren't completely bad; they're just terrible to work for. I can't subvert myself for a job—it's not worth it. Never again. So I swallow and decide to tell the truth. "Not at all. Don't get me wrong. People should be able to believe whatever they want to, but they ran things a little too casually there for my tastes."

"We run a pretty tight ship here at H2T. What were your responsibilities at Inner Space?"

"All the front end. Booking, billing, scheduling, bookkeeping, filing, archiving. Light cleaning. I made up all the rooms between clients, did all the dishes and laundry."

She looks down, and I notice she's focused on my résumé. "You're a paralegal? No wonder you were bored there."

"You caught that?"

Her lips quirk into a grin. "Four years as head of

human resources? I'm pretty good at reading people. I'm not going to ask why you want to work here. If the stories Blake told me when he recommended you for the job are true, then it's no wonder you wanted out."

"I don't want to speak poorly about a former employer, but...well, chances are, you wouldn't believe me anyway. But Blake's a good guy. He'll have told you the truth."

"Blake's a great guy." Her cheeks redden slightly, and she shifts in her chair.

Wait a second. "Are you two...?" I ask before common sense kicks in.

Luckily, she isn't offended. "What? No. He's just my big brother's best friend. We keep in touch via email, the odd call. There's nothing there. He hasn't even seen me in years." She tucks a few stray hairs behind her ears and picks at some invisible lint on her sleeve.

Methinks she doth protest too much. "He and I are just friends too."

She sits up a little taller, and I know I've said the right thing. Melanie is majorly into Blake. Maybe I can invite them to Jack's club one night and see if I can nudge them closer together.

"At some point, I might employ your paralegal skills, but that's not what the job is. We have a somewhat voyeuristic column here, where New Yorkers write in and tattle on one another. Sort of like personal ads, but with a twist. It's called 'I Saw You.' You'd be going through the mail entries and the online submissions forms, choosing the most exciting and readying them for publication. Is that something you think you're up for?"

I can't wait to tell Jack. I grin. "Something tells me I'd be perfect for it."

················

As soon as I told him about the job, Jack laughed at how suited I was for it—and offered himself as a slush reader if I need an assistant. We both still read Missed Connections; only now, we read them together while snuggling. Now, I'll basically get paid to do the same thing!

When he was done teasing me, Jack kissed me, slowly and deeply, and asked what I wanted to do to celebrate.

I told him to take me to the hottest club in New York—his.

The line stretching down the block makes me disgustingly smug. I love that I was right about Frisk being the next big thing. I squeeze Jack's hand. "I'm proud of you."

He closes his eyes and presses his forehead to mine. "Thank you."

"I mean it. You worked your ass off for this." And he did. He's been telling me all the behind-the-scenes responsibilities—and seeing his phone blow up with work-related issues cements how much of his time goes into the business and how hard he works. Despite that, he's taking the night off to stay by my side.

It's only been six days, but we've been inseparable. Jack feels like home.

The cab pulls up to the curb outside the club.

"We're not going to leave until you're sick of dancing. And then?" Jack kisses the sensitive spot just below my ear. "Remember that night I bent you over my counter and—"

"Oh God, I remember."

He chuckles, hands some cash to the driver, and leads me from the cab. I feel like a movie star as we stroll past the line, heading straight for the door. Pete's meeting us inside with a few more of our friends. People look on, suspicious and envious that we get to bypass the lengthy wait.

But just outside the doors, I hold back. "Blake said he'd meet us here."

Jack nods. "The doorman's waving at me. I'll be right back." He kisses my cheek and heads to the entrance to be the boss.

I love when he does that.

It's funny. I thought I'd feel some confusion or residual attraction for Blake, but there's nothing. Jack being my Missed Connection feels like winning the lottery. There's no room for regret.

Besides, Jack's more my type than Blake. I invited Blake to Frisk tonight because him getting me an interview with Melanie is the reason we're all out celebrating.

I wave when I see him, and he heads over to me. "Hey, Blake. Thanks for coming."

He smiles. "Like I'd turn down an invitation to Frisk. Have you heard about this place?"

"Oh, one or two things." I grin. "For real, though, thank you for getting me in at H2T."

"You got yourself in. Mel's tough but fair. She wouldn't hire you just because I pointed you in her direction."

"Yeah, she definitely doesn't strike me as a pushover."

Jack's still dealing with…whatever. We could head in, but I want to wait for him. I remember the way Melanie blushed while talking about Blake. "So, feel free to tell me to mind my own business, but did you and Melanie ever go out?"

Blake shakes his head. "Mel? Nope, she's just my best friend's kid sister. We practically grew up together. It's been a while since I've seen her, not that that's a bad thing. She's a total pain in the ass, but don't tell her I said—"

"Fancy meeting you guys here." A hand snakes over my shoulder, and I reflexively shrug it off when I see who it belongs to.

"Phyllis." I spit the word out like it tastes bad.

She raises her eyebrows at me, then smiles at Blake. "Looks like the gang's all here."

My head whips around. "Ziggy and Fern are here?"

Phyllis rolls her eyes. "No, just me and some friends." She waves at the snooty women a few feet back in the line. "How have you been doing, Sarah? Find another job yet? I hear it's a jungle out there."

"I've been doing fine, thanks."

She smirks. "I'm sure. Fern and Ziggy have been telling people that you moved back in with your parents because you were having a hard time dealing with things."

So much for Fern and Ziggy being good people. The urge to brag about my new job and Jack rises, but I press my lips together. She's trying to bait me, but it's not going to work.

"Don't believe everything you hear," Blake says, flashing his dimples my way.

"Are you two here together?" Phyllis's eyes narrow.

Blake puts an arm over my shoulders. "I couldn't turn down her invitation."

"Wow." Phyllis stands taller.

"Everything all right here?" Jack steps up to my other side.

Blake leans across me, but I see his wink. "Sarah and I were talking to Phyllis."

Phyllis's gaze ping-pongs between Jack and Blake, like she can't decide who's hotter.

Jack's eyes light up.

Uh-oh.

He slides his left arm across my lower back so now I'm sandwiched between him and Blake. "Is that right?"

Phyllis licks her lips. "Sarah and I were work buddies at Inner Space."

My eye twitches, tension rolling through my body, but the boys crowd a little closer to me.

She leans in. "So, you guys are…"

Blake bites his lip. "We're going to have an amazing time."

"Damn right we are." Jack grabs my hand and kisses the back of it.

"They're *both* with you?"

I nod at the incredulity in her tone. Man, she's hard to be friendly to.

Phyllis's eyes are bugging out now. "We should totally sit together inside."

I could get her inside now, but maybe I'm enjoying this too much. She thinks I'm screwing both of these hot men—maybe at the same time.

And I love Blake just a little bit for laying it on thick.

I should be the bigger person and get her in the club. Let bygones be bygones.

But then she leans in with a wink. "We can tell the boys about the time you spelled my name wrong."

"You know what, Phyllis?" Jack says. "We won't be sitting together because there's no way in hell I'd ever let you into my club."

"*Your* club?" She makes a face like she doesn't buy it.

"Yup. I'll be sure to tell my guys at the door not to let you in. And you be sure to give my regards to your friends—who also aren't welcome." He nods at Blake, and they turn us and stride to the door where Jack does exactly what he promised. I can't resist glancing back to see the shock and regret on Phyllis's face.

I should feel worse about her not getting in.

But I don't.

If she'd treated me better, I might have invited her. If Jack hadn't heard all about the shitty things she'd done to me, maybe he'd have let her in. But I'm sort of glad Jack and Blake closed ranks around me.

Okay, I'm *ecstatic* about it.

Neither of the boys releases me until we get inside out of sight.

"Sorry, Sarah," Blake says. "I shouldn't have done that, but—"

I hold up my hand. "No apologies. Did you see her face? God, it feels like Christmas."

Blake nods at Jack. "I wasn't trying to overstep with you either."

Jack shakes Blake's hand. "You're VIP for life, man. That chick is such a—"

"Pain in the chakra?" I supply.

Our smiles last all the way to the VIP section.

Acknowledgments

For all the bosses—the good, the bad, and the hippies.

I've worked for amazing people, amazingly bad people, and everything in between. This book had slivers of my own work experience with bosses in all kinds of industries—padded with a lot of fictionalization for comedic sake. The takeaway shouldn't be that New Age modalities are bad but that staying true to yourself is the real path to happiness.

Eternal gratitude to my fabulous agent, Nicole Resciniti, for her unflagging support and infallible advice. You're more than an agent; you're my friend.

To Mary Altman and everyone at Sourcebooks, you're my people! You've been nothing short of amazing to work with, and you deserve raises and massages. Steer clear of Phyllis. ;)

Thanks to my family for being the quirky delights who keep me striving to be better—and for always loving me for who I am.

Jessa Russo, I mean, here we are again, me trying to encapsulate everything I appreciate and love about you into the back of a book and failing. My love for you can't be squished into puny, little words. Hearts aren't big enough. I love you with all my butt. <3

Cait Greer, what the hell would I do without you?! Let's *never* find out! Love you more than sateen!

People who made this book so much better—or perked me up when I needed it most: Rosey, Amanda, Brandi, Lydia, Sara, Melissa, Suzy G, Jasmine.

To Amber and Heather, for the flails and laughs and snarkiness when I needed it most.

The Naturals: Laurelin Päige, Sierra Simone, Melanie Harlow, Geneva Lee, Kayti McGee.

To Angie McLain (and Jenna Tyler of Fangirl Book Blog) who are *always* there for me without fail. I wish more people were like you. Angie, your love of books and *huge* heart are so unique and important in this life. The sheer amount of work you put into promoting authors is *so* appreciated. Thank *you*!

Full-body hugs to everyone who reads my books and leaves a review. Thank you, thank you, thank you for spreading the word and letting us authors (and other readers) know you care. <3

For my hippie-free colleagues at the library, your support means the world. Our patrons are the best.

About the Author

Tamara Mataya is a *New York Times* and *USA Today* bestselling author, a librarian, and a musician with synesthesia. Armed with a name tag and a thin veneer of credibility, she takes great delight in recommending books and shushing people. She puts the *she* in That's What She Said and the *B* in LGBTQIA+.